PRAISE FOR KAIRA ROUDA

Beneath the Surface

"Original, clever, deftly crafted, and featuring the author's distinctive and narrative-driven storytelling style."

—Midwest Book Review

"*Beneath the Surface* is a perfect summer escapist read."

—*Mystery & Suspense Magazine*

"When the wealthy patriarch of a family business invites his children on a trip from Newport Beach to Catalina Island aboard his new yacht, Rouda fans will know to buckle their seat belts . . . King Lear goes to the beach. Yes."

—*Kirkus Reviews*

"It's *Succession* on a yacht in this delicious and fast-paced thriller! *Beneath the Surface* has it all—secrets, lies, and rich family drama. Filled with characters you love to hate, this was a twisty and entertaining ride I never wanted to end. Rouda is at her best!"

—Jeneva Rose, *New York Times* bestselling author of *You Shouldn't Have Come Here*

"Devious, twisty, and completely unputdownable, Kaira Rouda's *Beneath the Surface* is *Knives Out* meets *Succession* but on a billionaire's yacht! *Beneath the Surface* is Rouda at her stupendous, binge-worthy best! I devoured this delicious thriller!"

—May Cobb, author of *A Likeable Woman* and *The Hunting Wives*

T0036083

"*Succession* meets *The White Lotus* on the open seas. With a penchant for revealing the darker side of wealth and the antics of family values deteriorating, Kaira Rouda takes us on a journey where an embattled family gathers for a high-stakes weekend, clambering to the top, and risking everything."

—Georgina Cross, bestselling author of *One Night, Nanny Needed,* and *The Stepdaughter*

"Kaira Rouda has cornered the market on scandal and intrigue among the one percent. Suspenseful and glamorous, full of scheming and twists, *Beneath the Surface* is *Succession* meets Elin Hilderbrand."

—Michele Campbell, bestselling author of *It's Always the Husband*

The Widow

"A deliciously diabolical take on marriage, politics, and the lies that bind."

—*Library Journal*

"[A] wild mix of intrigue, secrets, and corruption."

—*Publishers Weekly*

"What happens when 'the woman behind the man' has a dark secret of her own? Slick and rocket paced, *The Widow* by Kaira Rouda is a top-notch political thriller. With hairpin twists and turns, insider knowledge, glamorous settings, and a whole cast of untrustworthy characters, Rouda expertly ratchets up the tension, keeping her readers breathlessly turning the pages. And the deliciously devious Jody Asher is as cold and calculating as she is riveting. A captivating read!"

—Lisa Unger, *New York Times* bestselling author of *Secluded Cabin Sleeps Six*

"*The Widow* pulls back the curtain to reveal an insider's look at the fascinating and duplicitous world of DC politics. This stunning page-turner has a cast of characters with dangerous secrets and hidden motives. Rouda's best so far!"

—Liv Constantine, internationally bestselling author of
The Last Mrs. Parrish

"Known for her fiendishly cagey characters, Kaira Rouda introduces readers to her most diabolical cast to date in the cleverly crafted *The Widow*. Tense, sharply written, and ticking with suspense, *The Widow* is a killer edge-of-your-seat thriller with an eye-popping glimpse into DC politics and simmering grudges. Rouda is at her best with this devilishly smart novel that kept me guessing to the very end. Clear your calendar; you don't want to miss one scintillating minute with *The Widow*."

—Heather Gudenkauf, *New York Times* bestselling author of
The Overnight Guest

"Kaira Rouda is back with another delicious and darkly comedic tale, this time pulling back the curtain on the glamorous and backstabbing world of Washington politics. Rouda takes her readers into the heart of a messed-up marriage, where scandal threatens to sap a congressman's reelection campaign. Packed with juicy secrets and intrigue, *The Widow* is a propulsive, unputdownable tale of a couple's battle for power, and an incredibly fun ride."

—Kimberly Belle, internationally bestselling author of
My Darling Husband

"With her signature dark wit and clever insights, Kaira Rouda takes us deep into the fascinating world of power and politics, where ambition and manipulation reign and shameful secrets become weapons. *The Widow* is a breathless page-turner with a ruthless and conniving protagonist that you can't help rooting for. This might be Rouda's best book yet!"

—Robyn Harding, bestselling author of *The Perfect Family*

"Kaira Rouda is on top of her game with her latest thriller, *The Widow*, a suspenseful tale filled with backstabbing, page-turning goodies: Capitol Hill shenanigans, manipulative lobbyists, adulterous politicians, opportunistic interns, and dirty backroom deals. In other words, welcome to Washington, DC—a place where the secrets have secrets. Rouda's 'I'm not a bitch, you're a bitch' protagonist is an overly seasoned, 'supportive' spouse living her best life in the hallowed halls of Congress . . . until that lifestyle is threatened. Then look out: Rouda will come at you with zingers and power plays, giving the coldhearted widow her veil of opportunity, proving repeatedly that it is the political spouse who wields the *real* power on the Hill, and she has no intention of letting go."

—Lisa Barr, *New York Times* bestselling author of *Woman on Fire*

"Gripping and brimming with insider intrigue, *The Widow* delivers with each scandalous, suspenseful page! With a main character I loved to hate, this story has all the twists and turns readers have come to expect from Kaira Rouda. Grab your copy and get ready to tear through *The Widow* faster than a pile of unmarked bills."

—Elle Marr, Amazon Charts bestselling author of *Strangers We Know*

"I tore through this book in two breathless sittings. With *The Widow*, Kaira Rouda has given us a political thriller that's ingeniously structured and packed full of razor-sharp observations about the machinations of Washington power couples. It's smart, timely, and wickedly fun. You won't be able to put it down."

—Grant Ginder, author of *Let's Not Do That Again* and *The People We Hate at the Wedding*

"In *The Widow*, Kaira Rouda perfectly captures the experience of being a congressional spouse and all the complicated intricacies of that lifestyle and then adds her signature flair to make it a riveting story that only she could tell. It is impossible to put down."

—Lacey Schwartz Delgado, filmmaker, former congressional spouse, and Second Lady of New York

Somebody's Home

Listed in "Best Thrillers Coming in 2022" by She Reads

"Whatever the opposite of family values is, Rouda seems intent on perfecting a genre that enshrines it."

—*Kirkus Reviews*

"Suspense and thriller readers will be on the edge of their seats for this novel that exposes the dark underbelly of human nature."

—*Library Journal*

"There are great characters moving the story along, that sweep away the reader in this story of families, revenge, and secrets."

—*News and Sentinel*

"A truly unputdownable novel that had me gripped—and anxious—from the first sentence! Captivating, fast paced, and unsettling, *Somebody's Home* is astonishingly good. I gulped it down."

—Sally Hepworth, *New York Times* bestselling author of *The Good Sister*

"*Somebody's Home* kept me riveted from the first page to the last. A gripping psychological thriller you don't want to miss!"
—Lucinda Berry, bestselling author of *The Perfect Child*

"*Somebody's Home* starts like a hurricane out at sea: some wind, some waves, a sense of approaching danger. But the story moves fast, gains velocity, and suddenly you are turning the pages, unable to stop, heart in your throat, knowing that something terrible is going to happen and nothing will stop it. The threats come from all sides, and it's so hard to know who to trust. The characters are wonderful and complex; the setting feels like the house next door, which makes it all the more terrifying; and the ending nearly killed me. Kaira Rouda has written a terrific, gripping thriller."
—Luanne Rice, bestselling author of *The Shadow Box*

"With an intriguing cast of characters and a killer premise, *Somebody's Home* is a thriller worth staying up all night for. Fast paced and relentless, Kaira Rouda cranks up the tension with every turn of the page. With unexpected twists and jaw-dropping revelations, Rouda knows how to draw readers close and keep them entranced."
—Heather Gudenkauf, *New York Times* bestselling author of *The Overnight Guest*

"Privilege, social disenchantment, and extreme family tensions are the threads running through this tense novel. Kaira Rouda lets us into the lives of two families and what happens when their paths cross. Gripping and fast paced with an explosive conclusion!"
—Gilly Macmillan, *New York Times* bestselling author

"Taut with foreboding from the first page, Kaira Rouda's *Somebody's Home* is an unsettling portrait of an antisocial man, a master of the universe, and the women caught between them. The rotating points of view and incisive, clear writing are sure to keep you flipping the pages until you reach the shocking conclusion!"

—Katherine St. John, author of *The Siren*

"Trust your instincts and grab a copy of Kaira Rouda's *Somebody's Home*. In Rouda's latest thriller, a mother trusts her instincts when she knows the person on her property is threatening her family. But what if the threat is coming at her from all sides and more than one person is hiding a dark secret? A compulsive, fast read, *Somebody's Home* reveals what people will do to protect not only their homes but the families within those four walls. A captivating read."

—Georgina Cross, bestselling author of *The Stepdaughter*

The Next Wife

"Rouda hits the ground running and never stops . . . [*The Next Wife*] is so much fun that you'll be sorry to see it end with a final pair of zingers. The guiltiest of guilty pleasures."

—*Kirkus Reviews*

"This gripping psychological thriller from Rouda (*The Favorite Daughter*) offers a refreshing setup . . . Rouda keeps the reader guessing as the plot takes plenty of twists and turns. Suspense fans will get their money's worth."

—*Publishers Weekly*

"In *The Next Wife*, two women go ruthlessly head-to-head. Kaira Rouda knows how to create the perfect diabolical characters that we love to hate. Equally smart and savage, this is a lightning-fast read."
——Mary Kubica, *New York Times* bestselling author of *The Other Mrs.*

"Rouda's talent for making readers question everything and everyone shines through on every page of her propulsive new thriller, *The Next Wife*. Her narrators are sharp and unpredictable, each one with a tangle of secrets to unravel. *The Next Wife* will leave you tense and gasping, with a chilling twist you won't see coming."
——Julie Clark, *New York Times* bestselling author of *The Last Flight*

"One of the most insidious, compulsive books I've read recently. Kaira Rouda has a way of drawing you in with great characters, fast-paced writing, and a story that won't let you go. Brilliant, dark, and dazzling."
——Samantha Downing, *USA Today* bestselling author of *My Lovely Wife* and *He Started It*

"One man. Two wives. Kaira Rouda has masterfully created cunning twists and sharp narration that take you on an unexpected and delicious journey and will leave you with a gasp. Devious and fun, *The Next Wife* should be the next book you read!"
——Wendy Walker, bestselling author of *Don't Look for Me*

"I absolutely inhaled *The Next Wife*. Nail-biting suspense, dark humor, and family intrigue. I savored every page and now have the worst book hangover. Loved it!"
——Michele Campbell, internationally bestselling author of *The Wife Who Knew Too Much*

"No one writes deliciously devious narcissists like Kaira Rouda. *The Next Wife* showcases her remarkable talent for making unlikable characters alluring. With twisted egos, lavish wealth, and three women vying for power, this compelling, compulsive thriller is sharp, fun, and shocking. I was riveted by every word."

—Samantha M. Bailey, *USA Today* and #1 national bestselling author of *Woman on the Edge*

"Kaira Rouda has a gift for writing characters we love . . . to hate. Dark and devious, *The Next Wife* is a fast-paced, twisty thriller that will have you laughing, shaking your head, and gasping out loud right until the end. A perfect one-sitting read."

—Hannah Mary McKinnon, bestselling author of *Sister Dear* and *You Will Remember Me*

Best Day Ever

"Chilling, satisfying suspense."

—*Good Housekeeping*

"Destined to fly off the shelves."

—*Library Journal* (starred review)

"Darkly funny, scandalous, and utterly satisfying."

—*Kirkus Reviews*

"One of the 25 Books You're Going to Want to Read This Fall."

—POPSUGAR

The Favorite Daughter

"An exceptional psychological thriller from Rouda . . . Suspense fans will be amply rewarded."

—*Publishers Weekly* (starred review)

UNDER
THE
PALMS

OTHER TITLES BY KAIRA ROUDA

Suspense

All the Difference

Best Day Ever

The Favorite Daughter

The Next Wife

Somebody's Home

The Widow

Beneath the Surface

Women's Fiction

Here, Home, Hope

A Mother's Day: A Short Story

In the Mirror

The Goodbye Year

Romance

The Indigo Island Series

Weekend with the Tycoon

Her Forbidden Love

The Trouble with Christmas

The Billionaire's Bid

Nonfiction

Real You Incorporated: 8 Essentials for Women Entrepreneurs

UNDER THE PALMS

A Novel

KAIRA ROUDA

Text copyright © 2024 by Kaira Sturdivant Rouda
All rights reserved.

Published by Thomas & Mercer, Seattle

www.apub.com

Amazon, the Amazon logo, and Thomas & Mercer are trademarks of Amazon.com, Inc., or its affiliates.

ISBN-13: 9781662511936 (paperback)
ISBN-13: 9781662511943 (digital)

Cover design by Kimberly Glyder
Cover image: © marchello74 / Getty Images

Printed in the United States of America

For my mom,
Patricia Robinson Sturdivant,
who taught me to love books, the beach,
art, and the magic of children's laughter.
Thank you for being a fantastic grandmother, Mop.
All ten grandkids love you to the moon and back.

I suddenly realized I was in California.

Warm, palmy air—air you can kiss—and palms.

—Jack Kerouac

The Kingsley Family

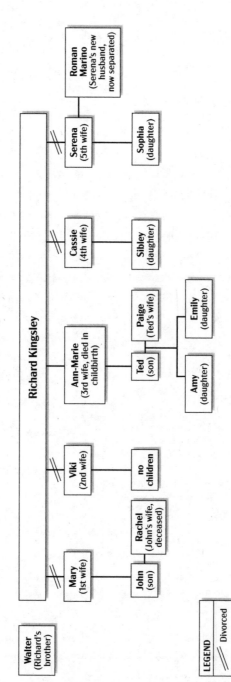

OC SCOOP

Attention, Kingsley fans: your favorite family is back in the limelight! That's right—hot off the presses in this month's issue of *Vanity Fair* is a four-page spread featuring the fabulous new president of Kingsley Global Enterprises, the OC's very own Paige Kingsley. We all remember how Richard Kingsley shocked the world when he named his daughter-in-law of twenty years as his successor, bypassing his sons and heirs to hand Paige the keys to their billion-dollar kingdom. Admit it, dear readers, we all raised a brow (as much as Botox permitted, of course) at the notion of the tennis-playing stay-at-home mom better known as Mrs. Ted Kingsley suddenly holding the reins of a Fortune 100 company . . . But could it be that Perfect Paige is something of a dark horse? In a few short months, she's made good on her promise to usher the company into a new era of philanthropy—guess all that time volunteering as CEO of the Orange County food bank taught her a thing or two about giving to those less fortunate. (And let's face it, who *isn't* less fortunate than the Kingsleys?)

This charitable spirit is certainly a new look for Kingsley Global, and those of us who worshipped at the altar of King Richard can hardly be blamed for wondering what the die-hard capitalist thinks of this bold new direction. Is he proud of his protégée, or does he privately wish he could turn the page on Paige? And what about Ted, the golden child of the Kingsley clan, who was rumored to be Richard's first choice to helm the company before Paige got the gig? He plays the part of the doting husband in public, but one can't help but wonder how Ted feels about his wife sitting in the office he thought would be his.

Then again, maybe Ted's just happy that Paige is still alive, unlike his sister-in-law. Older brother John's wife, Rachel, as you'll recall, died tragically during a weekend mega-yacht trip to Catalina Island, à la Natalie Wood. They say she fell overboard during the storm, poor thing. A chilling death, really. And a good reminder to always wear one's life preserver while aboard one's yacht.

Of course, John's marriage wasn't the only one to end abruptly that fateful weekend. It's no secret that Richard's fifth wife, Serena, absconded to Italy with her Italian lover and baby daddy shortly after their return to shore. Nubile young bachelorettes around the world are no doubt bidding her a *buon vioggio* as they daydream about becoming the sixth Mrs. Kingsley. We hope for Richard's sake that he finds a more faithful *signorina* this time around!

Speaking of *signorinas*, we hear Richard's wayward daughter, Sibley, also ditched her boyfriend after that weekend on the yacht. And good riddance. Colson was hardly appropriate marriage material for the Kingsleys' only princess, in this reporter's humble opinion. Then again, perhaps that's why Sibley dated him in the first place. The rebellious youngest Kingsley does seem to have a knack for making choices Daddy Dearest disapproves of. Which might explain why she's currently hanging out in Florida with her uncle Walter, Richard's estranged brother. Nobody seems to know quite what the two black sheep of the Kingsley clan are up to in the Sunshine State—but we do know that where Sibley goes, drama follows. We await her next scandal with bated breath.

Oh, who are we kidding—we await news of *all* the Kingsleys with bated breath. They are, after all, the family we love to hate and hate to love. Let's hope they never change.

Richard Kingsley, CEO, and
Paige Kingsley, President,
cordially invite you to

The First Annual
Kingsley Global Enterprises
Executive Retreat

Plus-ones are invited for dinner each night.
Business casual daytime dress.
Formal evening attire.

February 24–26
Twin Palms Resort, Laguna Beach

Kindly RSVP to Justin by February 14.

The future is bright when we all work together.
Remember, teamwork makes the dream work.

FRIDAY, FEBRUARY 24

1

PAIGE

They say it's always the husband—and in my case, that's the truth. To be clear, it's always my estranged husband, Ted. I remind myself I've found a good divorce attorney and take a deep, cleansing breath.

Through the floor-to-ceiling glass walls of my office, I see him, pacing back and forth, today's ridiculous gift in hand, trying to get my attention. It's childish, this behavior. Unoriginal. This is an *every*-morning performance: sometimes he brings doughnuts; other times, flowers, or a single sparkling water tied with a pink silk bow. He keeps making these offerings, I suppose expecting a different response from me. Or maybe it's all for show, for his family, for his ego.

I pick up my phone, pretend to be on a call, and wave him away with the flick of my hand. I shouldn't be surprised he has betrayed me again. Fool me once, and all that. But this time it's business. I'm not sad. No—this time, finally, I'm angry. For so many years, I looked at his handsome face and couldn't believe he was mine. The first word that came to my mind those days was *love*. Now the only word I have for him is *betrayal*. Oh, and the phrase *I'm filing for divorce*.

I know I need to talk to Richard, my father-in-law and boss, and tell him what I discovered and why I'm ending it with Ted. I spent the morning reading and rereading the letter from the city; the attached legal notices all amount to a big stop sign for the largest project Kingsley Global Enterprises has ever greenlit. The first big land deal I approved as president. All based on Ted's insistence it was a clean deal that would mean everything for Kingsley's future. Because of this deal, Ted has driven a huge wedge of doubt into Richard's opinion of me, after I've worked so hard to turn things around at the company.

I know the employees have begun to see me as an effective leader. While I've been winning them over slowly, Richard's admiration has been slipping away quickly. It's the look in his piercing blue eyes, the downturn of his lip. He's disappointed in me, and I have no idea why. Could it be he's jealous of me? Of the fact the staff seems to like me? My seven months on the job have been marked by Kingsley Global Enterprises' reemergence into the community as a philanthropic force. A community-spirited company gains a certain type of protection from enemies, especially if ugly secrets are unearthed. And besides, I enjoy doing good in the community, and this company can certainly afford it. I could attend a fancy charity event every weekend evening if I choose to, and we have been equally well received by the media, too, touting fresh female leadership at one of Orange County's most powerful companies.

There's a knock on my door, and before I can say anything, Justin pops his head in.

"Hey, here's today's offering," he says with a crooked grin. Justin is my assistant—a dashing, too-good-looking, dimple-sporting man who is ten years younger than me. When Richard hired him a couple months ago, I was wary; he was too good to be true. Maybe he still is, but I'm embarrassed to say I enjoy every moment in his presence.

I stand up and walk over to his side. "What is it today?" I hold out my hand, and he drops a red silk bag into it.

"I'm guessing jewelry. He hasn't done that lately." Justin grins again, pushing a hand through his dark, thick hair. He's distractingly cute.

I open the pouch, and sure enough, it's a heart encrusted with pavé diamonds on a gold necklace. I drop it back into the pouch, trying to decide which of my twin daughters will get this latest gift. I roll my eyes.

Justin smiles at my reaction. "Are you all set for the retreat? Need anything else from me? If not, I'm going to head on over to the resort, get you checked in, and walk the space once more."

"I think I'm set. I just feel like I need to speak to Richard before I head over. Is he here? Can you try to get me a meeting?" I ask.

"Sure, let me go find out," Justin says. He touches my shoulder, and a tingle zips down my spine. "You know, he'll be at the retreat. He promised to attend. You could speak to him there."

"I know. I just want to get ahead of this land deal story. The reporter is running it tomorrow."

"It's not your deal, Paige. It was Ted's. Everyone knows that," Justin assures me. "I'll go find out if Richard has time to talk."

"Thank you," I say, closing the door behind him. Yes, it was Ted's land deal. Yes, his brother, John, agreed it was a great deal. But Richard said I had to make the final decision.

I believed Ted. Again. After everything he's done. After all his lies, his cheating, his gambling, his dalliance—or whatever it was—with his own stepmother. John assured me he'd looked at the numbers, and Ted promised he'd looked at all the land-use issues. Even Richard said the deal looked doable, but he left the ultimate decision up to me. I knew in my heart Ted was a liar. I never should have approved the deal. If I'm not careful, this will give Richard the ammunition he needs to get rid of me, replace me with someone else.

Sometimes, I think he wants to push me aside—I do. But other days, he seems . . . like the old grumpy Richard who is fond of me and likes having me around as president. You just never know where you stand with the Kingsley men. That's why, from now on, I will stand on my own two feet. I'm stronger now. A role model for my daughters, who are working here this summer. Hear me roar. And I'm not going to allow any of them to walk all over me again.

Particularly—and especially—not Ted.

Justin's back. "He's already left for the resort. I'll head over, tell him you would like a meeting before the retreat starts. Don't look so worried. Everything's fine."

I shake my head. "I'm well aware this weekend will be a lot like herding cats, but I must make my mark. I have a lot to prove here. You know that."

"You do, and you are. Remember, when I first started here—working with you—I honestly didn't think you would make it."

He's told me this before, but it stings every time. "I know. I seemed too nice." I take a deep breath and walk over to my desk.

"Yep. And maybe easy to manipulate, for some people," he says. "But the truth is, you're tough and smart. So pack up your things, and I'll see you over there. It's a gorgeous day. Santa Ana winds are predicted tomorrow and Sunday, unfortunately."

"I didn't know that," I tell him, filling my briefcase with my computer, extra phone, and all the charging cables life requires these days. "I hope they aren't too strong." Those winds put everyone on edge. The air changes, people's moods shift. It's dry—and itchy. Really unsettling.

Justin sighs. "It is what it is. At least it's warm and sunny, even with the winds."

I don't make eye contact. I remember the wind-driven fires in Laguna Beach, the roaring red flames of destruction above us on the hill, the ash swirling, choking the air. Our frantic evacuation. I shake my head, try to force the memories away.

The winds are not what we need this weekend. The winds remind you of how tentative everything is and how fast it can all be lost.

2

JOHN

I can't help but smile as I head out of the office, double-checking the lock on my office door. I realize—despite the fact I think this corporate retreat is a waste of time and money, and I was against it from the start—I'm excited now that it's here. Not to spend more quality time in Paige's or Richard's presence. No, not for that reason at all. Every time my father looks at me, I feel his disappointment. I see the disgust for me in his eyes.

And Paige . . . I still cannot believe Richard picked her to be president of this company over me, his oldest and most loyal son—or even Ted, the golden boy and his *favorite* son. Instead, he picked Paige, a daughter-in-law without any business sense. I walk down the hall and stare into her office. The office that should have been mine as soon as Uncle Walter was forced out. By me. On my dad's behalf.

That office sat alluringly empty for years. I dreamed of the day I'd move into it. I still do.

"Is there something I can help you with?" Justin asks.

I realize I've stopped walking, just in front of Paige's office door. This should be *my* office door. Infuriating.

"What are you, some sort of guard dog?" I snap. Ted and I talked Richard into hiring this guy, promising he'd be good eyes and ears on

Paige, helping to keep her in line—and for Ted and me, helping to bring her down as quickly as possible. But Justin's insights have been few and far between. "You haven't called for a meeting with Ted and me for a while. Why is that?"

Justin shrugs. "Nothing to report."

I glare at him until he finds something interesting on the ground to stare at. I drop my voice so that only he can hear me, although most everyone in the office seems to have left for the day. "I don't believe you. You know why you were hired, and you're not performing."

He meets my eye again, this time with a stupid smirk on his symmetrical face. "I've been doing a great job, John. I'll tell you anything you need to know, but for now, I need to get going. See you at the retreat."

What? "You're not an executive. You shouldn't be there."

"Paige insisted. She needs me," Justin says. "Teamwork makes the dream work, as they say."

What an idiotic phrase. He sounds like a brochure for a corporate retreat. He doesn't know anything. He's just some pretty face lurking around. I'm starting to think there might be more going on between him and Paige than meets the eye. Something about his tone, the way he says her name. I need to talk to Ted. Poor guy is going to be crushed if he loses his estranged wife to some lowly assistant.

"Does Paige know you're a spy for Dad and me? And for Ted? Do you think we should tell her what you're really doing here?" I ask. My voice may be a tad threatening. Who knows.

To his credit, the kid flushes and throws up his hands. "No need to try to intimidate me, man. I know who's really in charge here. And I know my place. OK?"

Whatever. I walk away without answering him. I find that throws people off. Are we OK, or are we not? That's for me to know and him to find out. I reach the lobby with the enormous gold statue of a lion— Richard's favorite—and remind myself of the reason I'm excited about this weekend away.

Krystle. My sweet, beautiful raison d'être. Without her in my life—well, let's just say I would be in a much darker place. The place I found myself in after the horrific family yacht trip to Catalina Island. Clawing my way out of that darkness was no easy feat. First, I rejoined the church, and then I met her there before a service. I'll never forget when she walked in, all smiles and sparkly eyes, all grace and light and love. Unlike me, Krystle doesn't have an ounce of negativity or anger in her. I couldn't believe it when she sat down in my pew, scooted over next to me, and smiled.

"I'm Krystle Carrington," she said, extending her hand.

As I clasped her hand, I could've sworn I saw sparks fly in the air between us. "John. John Kingsley. Nice to meet you. I've never seen you here at church before."

"Oh, really? That's odd. I've been coming for a while now. Anyhoo, nice to meet you, too," she said. "Kingsley? That name sounds familiar somehow. Are you famous?"

"Me? No. Never," I said. I looked down at my ample waist and thought about my receding hairline for the first time since Rachel died. "My father, Richard Kingsley, is well known in Orange County and beyond."

"Oh yes, that's it! Of course I know of him," she said, clapping her hands together. "But forget about him. It's you I'm talking to now."

I could feel my cheeks flush with color. She was flirting with me. Me. *Her.* "Well, I'm certainly glad you *are* talking to me."

"Me too," she said with a big smile. "No wedding ring, I see? Are you one of those guys who doesn't wear one, or are you actually single? Sorry for being so forward; it's just that, life is too short to fall for a cute married man."

My heart skipped a beat. It did. She thought I was cute? "No, I'm not married. My wife died tragically."

"Oh, I'm sorry," Krystle said. The sunbeams streaming in through the stained glass windows tossed a halo of light around her, reflecting off her blonde hair. Like an angel. *She must be* my *angel,* I thought. "How long ago did she die? Do you miss her every day? It must be awful."

"I do miss her every day," I admitted. "I think about her death—well, too often."

"That's terrible. You should focus on her life, her legacy. All the fun you had together," she said. She touched my shoulder.

"I know. I try to focus on what we had, but sometimes, all I see is when I lost her," I said, shaking my head to erase the memory.

"Maybe you need a change of pace," Krystle said. "Have you been on any dates since you lost her?"

I shook my head.

"If you're interested, I'd like you to take me out on a date. Dinner, maybe? Tonight?" she said, reaching for my hand. Her skin was so soft, so warm. "I can tell you and I would have fun together, John. It's so lonely being single—don't you think?"

I looked into her sparkly blue eyes, her sweet round face, and I couldn't believe this was happening to me. She reminded me of Rachel when we'd met all those years ago—but with more spunk, less gravitas. Could I trust myself with another woman? Did I even deserve to feel love again? I'd decided no, up until this moment.

"Yes, it's lonely," I said.

"It's settled, then. I'll meet you at The Dock restaurant. It's cozy and quiet and romantic," she said. "I'm being so forward. Excuse me. I'm usually not like this. But you're too cute to pass up. Hope to see you, say seven tonight?"

Despite being convinced it was all too good to be true, I let myself believe it was. "I'll see you there," I said. I left church that day feeling all the hope in the world, my spirits buoyed by an attractive woman who had told me I was cute.

I chuckle at the memory as I push through the lobby doors and step outside into the bright Southern California sunshine. Not a cloud in the sky. It is going to be a fabulous weekend for Krystle and me. A staycation, she says. It's her first time visiting the Twin Palms Resort *and* meeting the family. I hope she still loves me on Sunday.

"Hey, handsome," Krystle says, surprising me from behind. I expected her to wait for me in her car. She's full of surprises, this one. Not like Rachel. Not at all.

"Hey! Where did you come from?" I say, wrapping her in my arms.

"You know God sent me to save you from a lonely, sad life," she says. "Besides, I was bored sitting in my car, waiting for you. Thought I'd roam around the outside of the Kingsley headquarters until you arrived. Impressive."

"That it is," I say.

"How do I look?" She pulls off her black sunglasses and performs a little twirl in front of me. She's wearing a navy business suit—something I've never seen her in—with tight-fitting pants, high heels, and some sort of sexy top. Her blonde hair is tucked up in a low ponytail.

"You look great . . . But you do know you're not invited to the business meetings, right?" I say.

"Oh, I know. What would a simple, dumb girl like me have to say in a room full of Kingsleys?" she says, and I notice an edge to her voice I've never heard before.

"No, sweet one, you aren't simple or dumb. It's just that you aren't an executive at the company, OK?" I watch her closely.

The sunshine is back on her face. "You think I'm smart, Johnny?"

I'm not sure about smart, but I think she's gorgeous and so much fun to be with—in bed and out. "I think you're perfect in every way and that I'm lucky to be going on a staycation with you."

"But you do know I'm smart, right?" she asks, walking toward my car, rolling her suitcase behind her.

I hurry to keep up with her, reminding myself again that I need to lose weight, start working out, do all the things middle-aged guys like me should do to be able to keep a younger girlfriend happy. She told me she's forty, but I'm not convinced she is much older than midthirties. Meanwhile, I'm in my midfifties and look like I'm in my sixties.

She makes it to my car before me and turns around, hands on her hips. "Right?"

"Yes, of course. Of course you're smart; you're with me," I say, grabbing her suitcase and sliding it into my trunk. I suddenly wonder if maybe this is a mistake, bringing Krystle to the executive retreat. What will my father think of her? My brother? It's too late for all that. Maybe I can convince her to stay out of sight, just hang out inside the suite? Not likely. I open the passenger-side door and help her inside.

"This is going to be so fun! Can't wait to meet the whole Kingsley family! I'm going to work hard to charm them all," she says, and I slam the door closed.

Yep, this is a mistake. My family members are not the type to be charmed; they're people to be wary of. And, at heart—truth be told—so am I.

FIRE-WEATHER WARNING ISSUED
FOR LA AND ORANGE COUNTIES

Strong Santa Ana winds are expected to blow through Southern California this weekend, bringing an increased risk of fire danger Saturday and Sunday. The most powerful winds are forecast to arrive Saturday night, when damaging gusts between 40 and 60 mph will be possible across the coast and valley locations, with mountains and foothills experiencing gusts between 55 and 75 mph. The offshore winds will bring critical fire conditions on Saturday and Sunday as humidity lowers to between 8 and 15 percent. These dangerous conditions come with the possibility of rapid fire growth and extreme fire behavior should a blaze erupt this weekend. Residents are urged to remember the *Ready! Set! Go!* Program in case evacuations are ordered.

3

RICHARD

I approve of this place. Five stars. *Just the sort of luxury I'm accustomed to*, I think, looking around the spacious suite I'll be enjoying this weekend. The place has three bedrooms, a large kitchen area, and a living and dining room. It's decorated tastefully with expensive art—mostly seascapes, of course, in the plein air style: a nod to Laguna Beach's history. The area rugs are thick, off white, soothing. And the view—well, it's almost as spectacular as the one from my own home. I suppose Paige is right about one thing: a change of scenery will do us all some good, even if it's just down the coast from our corporate headquarters.

The minute I walked into the lobby and saw the sparkling pool, the namesake twin palm trees, and the ocean beyond, I felt a little better. It helps that there is a bevy of bikini-clad beauties lounging around the pool. And my suite has a glorious view of all of them. I step out onto the balcony and notice a few of the women looking my way. I give a small wave and a smile.

I'm Richard Kingsley, my smile says, *king of the world*. Well, at least for as long as I'm allowed to live in it. I touch my chest, thinking of my traitorous failing heart, slowly draining the life out of me. Such a shame, really, because I have so much more to do.

That's why I've made an important decision, and I will implement it this weekend, no matter what anyone has to say about it. You just really can't please any of them—not for long, it turns out. And the feeling is mutual.

A gorgeous woman in a tiny, shiny yellow bikini is walking my way. She's a floor below me on the pool deck. She stops beneath my balcony. "Hello, Richard. Is that you? Oh, wow, what a small world. Do you remember me?"

No, I have no idea who you are. "Have we met?"

"Yes, a long time ago. I'm Julia, a friend of Serena's," she says. "Why don't you come down to the pool? We can catch up."

"I think not, Julia. And . . . Well, you do know Serena and I are divorced? It didn't end on a 'positive note,' shall we say." I think of my fifth ex-wife and her Italian lover, who impregnated her while I was still married to her. Charming. I hope the small town in Italy where she lives now suffers a horrible natural disaster. I really do.

"She wasn't a nice person—at least not to you," Julia says. "But I am." Julia removes her sunglasses, revealing stunning blue eyes the color of the pool behind her. She is gorgeous. But I am here for business, not pleasure.

Oh, who am I kidding. I'm always about pleasure. Ha.

"Julia, dear, thank you for the invitation to join you. But I am here on a business retreat with my company," I tell her. "It wouldn't be my best look to be spotted lounging by the pool."

Julia pouts. "I could join you in your suite?"

"Tempting, but I have some business to attend to this afternoon. If you're free this evening, perhaps we could arrange something," I suggest, although I know I shouldn't. Exertion isn't recommended at my phase of congestive heart failure. But so what?

"I'm just here for the afternoon, visiting an out-of-town friend who's staying on property. But I can come back. I live in Laguna." She bends over and rummages through an oversize beach bag, then stands back up. "Text me?" She tosses a business card in my direction, and it lands on my balcony.

"Nice throw," I say, picking up the card. She's a massage therapist. "How did you meet Serena?"

Julia shrugs. "I gave her massages. And then prenatal massages."

She knows about that, too, it seems. "So you weren't friends, just acquaintances, right?" I ask. That's much easier to deal with.

"Sure. Right," she says.

"Uh-huh. Well, I'll text you later, maybe." I walk back inside my suite. I need to focus on my family, on my company.

Someone knocks on my door. *Let the games begin.* I open the door to find Justin.

"Let me guess," I say. "Paige wants to talk, explain why the biggest deal in our company's history has become the laughingstock of the commercial real estate industry—hell, the entire *business* community. I do not enjoy being laughed at." Justin is a handsome young man, a solid employee, and—it turns out—a terrible spy. Unfortunate, the last quality.

"Yes, sir, she does. But you know it wasn't her deal. It was Ted's, with John's full support," he says. He's wearing khakis and a blue polo. He could work at the resort—by the pool, even. Maybe that's what I'll suggest when I fire him. Which will be soon.

"Paige is president of this company. She greenlit the deal. It's her deal now," I say.

"Can you meet with her? Please? She's very unsettled about it."

"Sure. Wouldn't want Paige 'unsettled' by the prospect of us losing millions of dollars because of her decisions." I smile and watch him squirm. He cares about Paige more than he should; that much is clear. I mean, Paige is a nice woman—a good mother to my granddaughters, a good wife to my wayward son, Ted—but she's no president. She doesn't have the respect from the employees that I do. Nobody is afraid of her. Fear is an important part of leadership. I hate to admit I've made a mistake with her, but I have.

"When can you speak with her?" he asks. Pushy.

"Send her over in an hour or so, son. Oh, and could you find Ted and have him come to my suite? I don't know where Gina ran off to," I say, although the truth is, I didn't want my assistant around for the retreat weekend. It's best I handle things one on one, without any extra ears. It's the first time I've traveled alone, anywhere. No body man, no assistant, no wife. Just me. At my age, I'm enough, I've decided.

"Sure, I'll see if he's checked in. Do you want John, too?"

John's presence disgusts me more every day. He's impulsive, hot-headed. An embarrassment. I swallow the bad taste in my mouth. "No, not now. Thanks."

Justin backs away, but before he can leave, I say, "Do you know anything I should know—about Paige, about the company, about anything she's planning as a surprise this weekend? Anything at all? I hate surprises, and you seem to be very close to your boss these days. Remember, you were hired to be *my* eyes and ears."

Justin smiles with the goddamn dimple. "You know everything there is to know, sir."

It takes everything in me not to fire him on the spot. "Go find Ted. Now." I slam the door in his smug face.

The younger generation just doesn't understand who to show respect for these days. Like my granddaughters, Emily and Amy—Paige and Ted's kids. As much as I love them, they just don't show me the deference I deserve in the office. I warned them not to call me "Gramps," not in front of the employees, but sure enough, all during the Christmas break while they worked as interns in the marketing department, all I heard from them was Gramps this, Gramps that. I blame their upbringing. Ted was busy being a playboy and, well, I guess that means it's mostly Paige's fault.

Everything is Paige's fault these days. But I know how to fix that—and I will. Remove the problem creator, and the problems go away. I walk back out onto the balcony. Julia spots me from the lounge chair she's reclining on by the pool and blows me a kiss.

I chuckle. That's the kind of sucking up I deserve from everybody.

4

SERENA

As I walk into the lobby of the Twin Palms, the view takes my breath away. I'm drawn to the open balcony across the lobby; to the sight of the California coastline, the palm trees, the sparkling Pacific Ocean. This place is gorgeous. Why did I ever leave?

Oh, right. I thought I had found the love of my life. Roman Marino ended up being a fraud. Everything he told me was a lie. I scan the lobby for Kingsleys, and I'm relieved when I don't see any of them. They likely arrived earlier and are all tucked into massive suites.

I would like to make sure to surprise them all with my return.

"Ma'am, the baby is fussy. Can we go to our room now?" Tata asks, appearing exhausted from the international flight. I guess it's because while I slept, she looked after little Sophia. I glance at my tiny, beautiful girl and smile. She has my lips; my eyes; and her miserable, lying father's thick, dark hair.

"Hi, baby. Isn't it pretty here? Just like momma promised." I reach for her little chubby hand as she squirms in the stroller, each of her baby knuckles like little dimples. She's so beautiful. Her baby hand swats mine, and she bursts into tears. Tata picks her up quickly, trying to calm her. Who knew a baby could be so exhausting?

"Let's go to your room, right now," I say, grabbing the stroller and ushering them toward the elevators. "The man said it was just down the hall this way. Hurry. People are staring."

"Yes, ma'am," Tata says over the wailing infant. *My* wailing infant. "When does Mr. Marino come here?"

Never, I don't say. "Within the week, I'm certain. But you'll be flying home before then." We step into the elevator. *That reminds me . . . I need to find a replacement nanny.* "You'll get some rest and then fly back to Italy. Sound good?"

The poor woman nods. She looks like she's going to start crying, too.

"Hand me the baby," I say. She does so reluctantly. For some reason, I haven't won the Mother of the Year Award from my husband's family or the townspeople in Amalfi, Italy. They don't like me there. Not anymore. But the feeling is mutual. As soon as I arrived, Roman and his family began to ask me for money: Money to fix up the family villa, which had been handed down for generations until *this* generation— these losers—who couldn't afford it. Money for homes for his parents and sister. Money for a home for us, when all the time we were dating, he pretended to be rich—royalty, almost. I was such a fool.

I'm lucky I was able to escape; I really am. And now I'm here, safely back in the States. I likely haven't heard the last of Roman and his family, unfortunately. For me, and for my baby, I need protection, security all the money in the world can buy. And I realize now, after I tossed it all away, I liked my life with Richard. I loved Richard, and I still do. Convincing him of that, though—after everything I've done to him—will be tough. But I'm determined to try. I know he misses me. And I know he hasn't moved on, or else it would be in all the tabloids. I'm here now, and I hope it's not too late. I take a deep breath and remind myself I'm tough and I'm part of a team.

The baby calms down in my arms as the elevator doors open. "Your room is right down here," I say to the nanny. And sure, I got her the cheapest room—but this is a five-star resort. It's nice. I hand her the key, and she pushes the door open.

"Bellissimo," she says without much enthusiasm.

"Yes, so why don't you take a shower, get refreshed, new clothes on, and I'll take care of Sophia. Will an hour be enough?" I ask. I'm a generous employer.

"Si," she says, covering a yawn. She really needs a nap, but I need her awake more.

"OK. Get going. I'll be in my suite with the little one." I write my room number on the hotel notepad. "See you in fifty-eight minutes!"

With the little darling passed out on one shoulder, the diaper bag slung over the other, I make my way to my suite. It would be wonderful not to see Richard until after I've cleaned up, changed into my evening attire, ready for the opening night's festivities. My phone pings with a text, but my hands are full. It will have to wait.

The elevator doors open, and I step inside, nodding to an older couple, who smile and coo over my sleeping little girl. I tell them to hush and give them the stink eye. Never wake a sleeping baby, people. Don't you know that?

I get off on the next floor. My suite is lovely. Not the biggest. Richard—and I'm assuming Paige, too—got the best rooms. Ah, Richard. What will he think of my dramatic appearance tonight? Will he welcome me back with open arms? I doubt it. Will he send me away, out of his sight, still too angry to have a civil conversation? I guess we'll find out. Ted will be there, too, unfortunately. I had hoped by now Paige would have kicked him out of the company, out of the pool house behind her home, and out of our lives.

But she hasn't. I'll just ignore Ted. He will be the easiest one to handle.

I think back to the little dalliance I had with him. It was stupid and wrong. I know it; he knows it. I was bored and restless, and I wrongly assumed Richard was leaving me for his next wife. I mean, he does have a pattern of doing just that. But he was hiding a bigger secret, flying all over the world to try to find a cure for his heart condition. I thought he was wooing a new lover, but in reality, he was fighting for his life.

Poor Richard. Meanwhile, there was Roman, who crept into my life like a sneaky, creepy spider. I wonder now how I didn't see through him. He was a con artist, plain and simple. A handsome Italian con man with impeccable manners, amazing taste, and no heart or shame. Once I became his wife—in a small, rather tacky ceremony in his parents' backyard—everything changed. His charm evaporated, and all that remained was a constant demand for cash.

I watch Sophia sleep peacefully on the king-size bed. So tiny, so innocent. She is my only reminder of the biggest mistake I've ever made, but it's a constant one. Her father was the opposite of everything he said he was. A fraud. A pretender. I fell into the arms of a handsome playboy, who was only ever after my money—Richard's money—and continued to sleep around with his Italian lovers even after we married. I felt so alone, so used. And something else, too. Watched. Roman's "friends," as he called them, were everywhere, watching me with cold, dark eyes. I shudder at the memories.

I walk across the room to the glass door, slide it open, and step out onto my balcony. I remind myself I'm safe now, and so is Sophia. I take a deep breath and admire the scene: a direct, sparkling view of the Pacific and the coastline south to Dana Point. It's gorgeous. I take a deep breath, enjoying the ocean breeze and the sunshine on my face.

I am free and starting over. My attorney secured an immediate divorce, and Roman waived any rights to our baby. I've legally changed my name back to my former last name: Kingsley. It suits me; it really does. I'm ready to be a Kingsley, to reunite with the king and rule over all the Kingsleys again.

For some reason, John's face pops into my head. He never liked me, but I'm not sure he likes anybody except his daddy, who, ironically, doesn't like him. Sad, really. If John says one derogatory thing to me—if *any* of the Kingsley men do, they'll be sorry.

Turns out, it's the Kingsley women's time to shine.

OC SCOOP

Attention, Kingsley family stalkers, I mean, lovers! We just received a tip that the entire Kingsley clan will be camped out at the fabulous Twin Palms Resort in Laguna Beach this weekend. If any place is fit for a Kingsley, it's this one. Picture a sprawling resort tucked away on a private bluff overlooking the Pacific. Guests enjoy thirty acres of privacy; two outdoor pool decks; a twenty-thousand-square-foot spa, where one can spend the day being pampered from head to toe; and three signature restaurants whose dishes are designed to delight the palate—and lighten the wallet.

Oh, and get this: the Catalina Suite, where we hear Richard Kingsley will stay, will set you back a cool ten thousand dollars a night. Don't worry; there are less pricey options, too. But by "less pricey," we mean four figures rather than five. Regular rooms—and we're talking the cheapest—start at more than one thousand bucks a night. Yes, you read that correctly.

Who would go anywhere else, especially if you're loaded? And guess what? The resort itself, Twin Palms Laguna Beach, is owned by another fabulous billionaire, but we'll focus on the Kingsleys for now. So what, you ask, will they be doing on the property? We hear it's being billed as an executive retreat, so supposedly they'll be doing business. But if I were a betting reporter, I would bet there's more than a little pleasure on the agenda, too. Don't be surprised if you spot the Kingsleys swimming in the spectacular mosaic pool, the centerpiece of the resort, and then retreating to one of the private cabanas to sip something cold and refreshing. I bet they'll also hit that glorious spa, maybe do some yoga, and treat themselves to a little shopping.

Please tell us, dear readers, what the Kingsleys are up to. I know at least a few of you who can sneak into that tony resort and fill us in. Remember, no detail is too trivial to share. Those of us who will be living vicariously are hoping this will be a weekend to die for.

5
RICHARD

There's a knock on my door. I presume it's Ted as I go to answer it. I'm wrong.

"Hey, Dad," John says.

I start to close the door. "I'm busy, son."

He puts his hand on the doorframe, stopping me. He is so annoying these days—he really is. I remind myself to try to be calm. The man does everything I ask and more. A loyal fool.

"Dad, please. This will only take a moment. I want to introduce you to someone special." He pushes the door all the way open, revealing a rather attractive bleached blonde wearing a very revealing top as part of a sexy business look. They step inside my suite, despite me trying to block their entrance.

"Hello. Are you a hooker?" I ask. That was mean, I know. Both John and the young woman startle. *I guess not.*

"Dad, no . . . This is my girlfriend, Krystle. We're in love," John says, wrapping a protective arm around her.

"Uh-huh." I'm surprised John has a girlfriend, and especially surprised she looks like Krystle. Although, I suppose his bank account makes him attractive to a certain type of woman, like this one.

Judgmental? Yes. But I'm usually right. "Well, nice to meet you, Krystle. Where did you meet each other, if I may ask?"

"At church," Krystle says.

"Really? How unexpected. I thought perhaps a strip club." I squint at John, then turn to the young, supposedly churchgoing woman by his side. I sniffle. I'm finished here.

"Mr. Kingsley, look—I've heard you are tough, mean, and controlling, but that was just plain rude what you said about me. I'm not a hooker. I'm a Christian," she says. Krystle crosses her arms and glares at me, defiant, before walking past me into my living room. "Wow, nice view. All of this is just for you? Seems like it might be a waste."

"Krystle," John says.

"I mean, a waste because he's all alone, aren't you? That's too bad." Krystle turns her back to the view, facing me again. "Maybe you need to come to church with us. Change your ways."

"Ha!" I say, watching her. She's got some fire; I'll give her that. I do like the spunk. Compared to John's former wife, Rachel—who was a brilliant but dour attorney whom I didn't care for much—I think I could appreciate this choice in a mate for John. Nice to look at, amusing sense of humor. Doubt she'd try to double-cross me like Rachel did. Although, from what I can see at this moment as she chews on a fingernail, she could use some refinement.

Also, she needs some education. It's about decorum. No one talks back to me. No one.

"Well, Krystle, yes, I am single at the moment. My choice, I assure you. Women fling themselves at me, as you may suspect. And as for my comment about you, I call things like I see them," I say. "If it's any consolation, my ex-wife, Serena, looked very much like a hooker most of the time, but I liked it. Maybe it's a compliment."

"Dad, stop," John says. "Look, we just wanted you to be the first to know about our relationship so you can give us your blessing."

"Come now, John, shouldn't you have outgrown the need for your father's blessing by now? And speaking of grown men, have you seen

Ted? I really need to speak with him. And you two should be on your way."

"Why do you want to speak to Ted?" John asks, stopping just outside my door. Krystle pulls up short behind him, hands on her hips.

I start to close the door. "Because I do, son. That's why."

"Ted and I are a package deal now," he says. "As you know, recent events only strengthened our brotherly bond. I don't see why you can't talk to us both, together."

"A bond cemented over jealousy is a bond with cracks in its foundation, son," I tell him. I know the two of them think they are close now, scheming and dreaming up ways to bring Paige down from their respective corner offices. I have watched them. "Besides, with this deal going south, well . . . perhaps you should be giving Paige your sympathy rather than your envy."

John's face brightens with a grin. "You're getting rid of her. I knew you would."

"Now, son, I'm not saying that." I *am* thinking it, but he doesn't need to know that. I miss being the center of attention in Orange County business circles, in the media and otherwise. All this woman-power stuff is getting old. #MeToo is over, if it ever was a thing. #MenRule is more my speed.

"I'll go find Ted and be right back with him," John says, his desperation mounting.

It's very unattractive.

"You said we could go to the outdoor restaurant overlooking the ocean, have a welcome drink," Krystle says with a large pouting lip.

"Do that. Take Krystle to the pool, son. You're at a resort. Relaxation is the name of the game tonight. There will be plenty of time for business tomorrow. Go. Enjoy." I make a shooing motion with my left hand while pushing the door closed with my right.

"Nice to meet you, Mr. Kingsley. You're going to find you like me; I just betcha will," Krystle yells as the door slams.

There's something off about her, I realize, but I can't put my finger on it. Sure, she's nice enough, and she's attractive. Too attractive for John, for sure. They are mismatched, although John wouldn't believe it. He looks at her like he's won the lottery—finding her at church, of all places. I wonder if he's introduced her to his mom, my first wife. Now *there's* a truly religious woman, one who dumped me as soon as I stepped out on her. It was against her religion. *I* was against her religion. Ha. But she's a good woman.

John is using religion to hide, to convince himself he is a good person despite all he's done. I wonder what Krystle has found at church—or rather, I guess I know *who* she's found. I make a note to get one of my guys to do a background check. You just can't trust that anyone is who they say they are these days. Sad fact of American life. Everybody wants something from you, whether they say it or not, and everybody lies on social media. Yes, I'm aware of all the ways we're creating a generation of narcissists.

I come by my narcissism naturally, no need for a selfie. I smile at my reflection in the oversize mirror in the suite.

My phone rings. It's Paige. I bet she wants to see me.

"Hello, Madam President," I say. "What can I do for you?"

"I'm heading over to your suite. I need to talk to you," Paige says.

"If it's about the land deal, Paige, dear, I'm really not sure what there is to say. I just can't believe what a disaster our biggest project has become, all under your leadership. We put everything on the line to get the deal through, but it's going south. Tell me what you would do in my situation." I walk over to the sliding door and push it open, then step out onto the balcony. There's Julia now, sitting by the side of the pool, dipping her toe in it. She waves at me, and I wave back. Why not?

"You can't pin this on me. It's Ted's deal," Paige whines.

There's a knock on my door. It better be Ted.

"I have to go," I tell her. I hang up the phone.

I go back inside and open the door to my suite. It's Paige. She doesn't look good. She has dark circles under her eyes like she's been staying up late and worrying about everything. She's thinner, too. This is too much for her; the responsibility of running Kingsley Global Enterprises is just too heavy a burden for her slight shoulders to bear. I'll be doing her a favor—that much is clear.

"Richard," she says. "May I come in?"

I let out a puff of air. I hope Ted doesn't show up while she's here. That would be awkward.

"Sure, come in. I hope your accommodations are as lovely as this," I say.

"They are. I have the next-best suite. It's wonderful," she says. "Look, Richard, I know the land deal Ted advocated for didn't exactly turn out the way we planned. But there are bigger problems afoot. I'm getting anonymous threats."

"What? Since when?" I ask. I am so rarely surprised—I see too much and know too much to be caught off guard often—but these threats are news to me.

"For the past three months or so. Somebody claiming I'm covering up what really happened to Rachel that night on the *Splendid Seas*."

Oh, brother. I guess keeping Paige in the dark about that stormy night on my yacht may not have been the wisest course of action, but it is what we all agreed to at the time—or rather, what I decided. And now it has become the truth and will forever be.

"You know what happened: she fell overboard. It was a tragic accident. Whoever is claiming otherwise is crazy. You need to talk to my security team immediately. Why did you wait so long to tell me about this? We'll find the person and take care of them. Problem solved," I say.

"The notes say that Rachel was murdered and that I'm covering it up, that I should be removed from being president and that I had something to do with her death," she says, shaking her head. "Richard, tell me—is there something I need to know? I didn't want to bother you with this, and maybe I didn't really take the threats seriously. I thought they'd stop. But they haven't. Is there something I should know? It seems like there is. This was waiting for me when I checked in."

Paige hands me a white piece of paper with black handwriting—all capital letters, mismatched, like you'd get from a kid. I read the note: *I'M HERE. I'M WATCHING YOU. I WILL GET THE TRUTH THIS WEEKEND OR ELSE.* I fold the note in half.

"How charming," I say. I seem calm but inside, I'm seething. Who would do this? What do they know? And why are they targeting Paige, not me? Well, I know why. They wouldn't dare.

"And you have no idea who is threatening you?" I ask.

"No, but it's getting more edgy—the threats are. Is there anything I should know?" she asks.

This line of questioning is certainly inconvenient. Fortunately, I'm a man who knows how to turn any situation to my advantage. "Poor thing. You're under too much stress, and it's messing with your brain. Stress causes all kinds of bad things to happen," I say. "You know what? I think I'll promote someone else to be president; then you can rest. You've been a great placeholder, but everyone is expendable. Besides, you look terrible."

"What? No. I will not step down. I have the full support of the board, and the employees love me," she says. "Don't try to play games here, Richard. I am doing a damn good job leading your company. You and I both know it." And with that, she marches out of the suite, slamming the door behind her.

Hmm. Seems I've created a bit of a power monster. Interesting. But she really should know better than to tell me no.

OC SCOOP

Thanks to one of our helpful tipsters, we can confirm that Richard Kingsley is staying in the largest suite at the Twin Palms Laguna Beach and that he was seen flirting from his balcony with a gorgeous young woman lounging at the pool. Richard has still got it, it seems. Is he on a business retreat or on the hunt for wife number six? Who says it can't be both? In the meantime, he might want to keep his eyes peeled for wife number five. That's right, you heard it here first, dear readers—we can exclusively report that Serena Kingsley has been spotted at the Twin Palms, and her Italian Stallion is nowhere in sight! Does Richard know his beautiful ex and her equally beautiful baby girl are on the premises rather than an ocean away? Only time—and our eagle-eyed spies—will tell.

6

KRYSTLE

This resort is the most gorgeous place I've ever visited. I feel like I'm in Disneyland for rich people. Everywhere I turn, there are tall, skinny women carrying designer bags, wearing the most fashionable clothes, flashing huge diamond rings, and smiling with the whitest of white teeth. I mean, it's crazy. We're sitting at the outdoor restaurant, people-watching and drinking margaritas. The ocean twinkles in the sunshine. I could sit here all day.

"Sweet one, could you finish your cocktail, please?" John says, interrupting my enjoyment as usual. I should have let him go find his brother an hour ago.

I pretended to be upset over his dad's comments so he'd take me around; that way I wouldn't feel so self-conscious walking around this place by myself. But now, with my liquid courage, I'll be fine sitting right here until he does whatever he needs to do. I just don't like how stressed he is already. This family weekend isn't good for him—not at all. Me either, likely, but I did want to get up close and personal with the Kingsleys. Careful what you wish for, I guess. All these years I've dreamed of walking among the rich and famous, and . . . well, so far, it's not all it's cracked up to be. But my margi is good.

"Why don't you go find your brother, and I'll sit right here, get another drink, and wait for you?" I ask.

"Really? You'll be OK on your own for a bit?" John stands before I can answer, eager to get away from me.

Maybe I came on too strong with his father. I'd better sweeten up. "Sure, of course. I'll be just fine. Do come back soon, though, honey. I'll miss you. Absence makes the heart grow fonder, they say."

He smiles and kisses my cheek. You do catch more flies with honey than vinegar; it's true.

"I'll be right back," he says, and then he's gone, faster than I've ever seen him move.

I wave to the cute waiter, who zooms over to my table.

"Could I have another margarita, please? It was so good," I ask.

"Of course, ma'am. Coming right away. Does the gentleman need another?"

"No, he's gone to a meeting. Say, do you know—are there any shopping opportunities on the property?" I know I stick out like a sore thumb in this stupid business suit. I asked my mom what I should wear for this big important weekend, and she said, *Can't go wrong with business.* She *was* wrong. As usual.

"Yes, the spa has an amazing boutique. And up on the main floor, right where you came into the lobby, if you turned left, you would bump into our main boutique. And outside, in the circular drive, there's another store with even more offerings. You don't have to leave the resort. You could get an all-new look, everything you need, right here— for a price, of course."

"Of course. You are making my dreams come true," I tell him. Although, in reality, John is.

"I'll just go get your margarita," he offers.

"Actually, wait. You know what? I'm going to skip the second drink and go shopping now that you told me there's so much available. And my boyfriend is working. While the cat's away, the mouse will play, don't ya know?"

"An admirable philosophy. In that case, here's the tab. You can just sign it to your room," he says.

"Are you sure this is ours? We only had two margaritas and guacamole and chips," I ask, staring at the bill. This amount should cover a full meal, not cocktails.

"It's yours, I'm afraid," he replies with a shrug. "Have fun shopping!"

I quickly sign the tab and put a big tip on top. Why am I acting like I care how much it costs? It's the Kingsleys who are paying—*will* pay. Not me. Old habits, I suppose. I take one more look around at all the fabulous people dining on the terrace. I'm watching what they're wearing and how they sit, what color lipstick they have on. I'm a fast learner; my mom always told me that. And today I'm going to learn how to fit in with the beautiful people at the Twin Palms. It's California cool, I'd say, mixed with extraordinary wealth, made to look effortless. Sweatshirts are fine, as long as they are the right brand; tennis shoes are everywhere, but they are white, as if they haven't been worn before. I see a lot of cashmere, too. Oh, and expensive jeans.

I'm ready to become one of these beautiful people. I stand up and realize people are looking me over. They've decided I don't fit in. I can tell by the downturn of their mouths, the quick look-aways when I try to make eye contact. Oh, and sunglasses. I need dark sunglasses so I can hide the hurt in my eyes. *Well, soon, I won't be the one being judged,* I remind myself.

I find the spa first. I smell it, really, from the walkway. It smells like freshness, lavender, money, and peace. I step inside and the two women behind the counter both welcome me with big smiles.

"Are you here for a treatment?" one of them asks.

No, but I could do that tomorrow, I realize. "I'd love to book some treatments, and I also need to pick up a few more resort-like clothes. I want to look California cool like all the people at the restaurant out there. Can you help me?"

She smiles a white-toothed grin. "You've come to the right place. And you're not going to believe all the things we have here—all the best athleisure brands and the softest cashmere sweaters, the thickest sweatshirts. Where do you want to start: booking treatments or trying on new clothes?"

"New clothes will help you relax," the other woman says. "Why don't you shop, try some things on. Carrie can assist you. I'll look at the calendar tomorrow, see what treatments I can put together for you. Sound good?"

"Would you like a glass of champagne while you shop?" Carrie asks.

I'm trying to act nonchalant. I really am. But oh my gosh. Pinch me.

"Champagne would be lovely," I say. "And I'm assuming I can bill this all to our suite?"

"Of course," not-Carrie says.

This time, when I pay—or sign the bill to make John pay—I will not look at the total. I deserve this. I really do. And champagne . . . Always champagne, because that's what rich people drink. I need to get into these habits, all of them. Well, first, I need him to put a ring on it. But this weekend, I'll practice, and I'll be sweet, and charming, and cool. I have a plan, and I am following it. Well, actually, my momma has a plan, and I'm following it. I think of my brother and wonder if he'd be proud of me, of where I am and what I'm doing for the family. I think he would be. I really do. I push the prick of tears from my eyes; I miss him. I turn to Carrie.

"I'll need at least four outfits, and I'm kind of tight on time," I say. I have at least two more stores to hit before John remembers I am here again. Something tells me when he gets to talking with his brother, about the company and taking it back from Ted's wife, they'll be scheming for hours. At least, I hope so.

I have much more fun with John when he's distracted, focused on his dad's empire. Although why he's so loyal to that man, I couldn't tell you. From my first encounter with Richard Kingsley—the jerk I've always heard he was—I can tell John is not the favorite. Ted is. Poor John. I wonder what he did to fall out of favor.

As long as he isn't cut out of the will or the company, I guess it doesn't really matter. This family has so much money it will take generations of mistakes to lose it all.

"Thank you," I say when Carrie hands me a glass of champagne. It's a crystal flute that's so delicate I'm in awe of its beauty and simplicity. I take a sip, the bubbles tickling my nose. This is the good life I'm tasting, and once you've tasted it, you can never let it go. I know I won't.

7

JOHN

I'm sweating bullets even though it's a pleasant day at a five-star resort. I've been racing around, searching every corner of this hotel. Where the hell is Ted?

I dial his phone. Straight to voice mail again. "Ted, it's an emergency. Call me immediately. Dad's trying to divide us again. Don't let that happen. Remember our pact, brother."

I've looked everywhere for Ted, without luck. He's not at the pool or any of the bars. He's not in his room—or if he is, he isn't answering the door for me. What is he up to? Where is he hiding? He only has about an hour before our first meeting begins. I need to talk to him before Richard does.

I realize my only option at the moment is to rejoin my date. This is our first overnight trip together, and so far, I'm regretting every moment of it. I shouldn't have introduced her to Richard. When I see her now, through his eyes, I see what he sees, not whom I fell in love with that morning in church. Richard sees Krystle as beneath him; he as much as said it himself. Ironic, since he also said Krystle reminded him of Serena, his former wife. Dad doesn't think my Krystle is worthy of dating a Kingsley, and now I'm starting to doubt my attraction to her myself. Then I imagine Krystle's touch, her warmth, her smile. But I don't feel anything tingling inside. Damn it. I don't know how to get back to that feeling.

I am terrible at getting Richard out of my head.

Sometimes I wish he'd just die already. I mean, he's sick, he's lonely. He's been an even bigger jerk since Serena left him for that Italian stud. I don't blame him for being sad that his last marriage didn't end well, but I think he's taking it out on me. Blaming me for everything that is wrong.

Truth is, he made his bed. He picked Paige to head Kingsley when we all knew she'd fail, be too weak to helm such a huge ship. Now she's hiding behind her assistant, Justin, sending him around to do her dirty work. And he was supposed to be on our side, not hers.

I call Ted again, expecting voice mail.

"Hey, what's up, brother?" Ted asks.

His voice sounds funny, like he's been drinking. "Where are you?"

"I'm at the beach. It's great here, just like I expected. They bring you anything you want, before you even know you need it," Ted slurs. "Met a cute girl, too."

"You are unbelievable," I say, but I note with relief that if he's been on the beach, Richard hasn't been able to speak with him, either. Not yet. "You know we kick off the retreat in an hour. Business attire. The whole board will be there. You can't show up wasted, Ted."

"I know," he says. "Problem is, I am. So I'll skip it. You can handle it. Tell them I really did think the deal was good. I did."

"They aren't blaming you for the deal. They're blaming Paige. You're good," I assure him. Although, if I was playing my usual game, I'd throw Ted and Paige under the bus for the deal and become the only succession option. Maybe I should go back to that game plan.

"I'm not good, brother. You and I both know it. I'm a fuckup. All I have are my looks, and those will be gone soon. Got to maximize my chances for happiness while I can. This girl is great," Ted says.

"Ted, you are not on spring break. And remember, you're supposed to be trying to woo your wife back. You are on a corporate retreat that begins in less than an hour now. Get yourself together, and I'll see you at the meeting." I hang up.

Interesting development. I know a good brother would go down to the beach, drag Ted's drunk ass to his suite, tell him to get ready.

I also know I need to shower and change before the meeting. I should check on Krystle, too; hopefully, she is not in the same state as Ted by now. But she's a grown woman. A Christian and, from what I've experienced, not much of a drinker. I'm sure she's fine.

I think about Ted on the beach and shake my head. You know the old saying *Put on your mask before helping others*? I'm going to the suite and will get ready for the meeting. As I wait for the elevator to arrive, I stare in the direction of the lobby. I do a double take; I swear Serena's doppelgänger just walked by.

It can't be her. She's in Italy, with a husband and a baby. She couldn't be sauntering through the lobby of this hotel. But I need to be sure. I hurry down the hallway into the breathtakingly beautiful open lobby. I scan the bar on the right side of the grand room but don't see anyone matching Serena's curves. I hurry to the entrance of the hotel, search the seating area by the fireplace, and then walk over to the opening that overlooks the pool and the Pacific Ocean. Serena isn't here; she can't be.

My mind is playing tricks on me. I hurry back to the elevators just as the doors open, and I step inside. I remind myself to breathe. Rachel would tell me to calm down; she would tell me to remember who knows all the company secrets, and she would say I'm the one Richard turns to when push comes to shove.

Oh, gosh, that was a horrible metaphor, given everything that happened.

Sorry, Rachel. Sometimes I still cannot believe I pushed her overboard on Dad's yacht. But it's true. Another buried secret.

I'm terrible, a flawed human.

And a murderer. I hear her scream in my mind despite trying to force it out. Poor Rachel. May God rest her soul.

But still, I'm the best of the Kingsleys. So what does that say about us all?

8

PAIGE

I don't like the look on Justin's face when he enters my suite.

"What is it?" I say, dropping into the cozy white sofa. Despite the beautiful day outside and the luxury of the setting, I can't find anything to be happy about. And now things are going to get worse.

"I think you're right. I think Richard's going to try to remove you as president of the company. I'm so sorry. You've done such a great job. Maybe too good for his ego," Justin says. "What do you think we should do?"

"We go to the five o'clock meeting, and I run it as planned," I tell him. "I will keep the agenda moving quickly. If the board has questions over Ted's deal that I approved, they can ask Ted. I will make him responsible, as we discussed. And if John tries anything, well . . ."

"He won't. Not without Richard's blessing—and he doesn't have that."

I can only hope he's right.

"Have you heard from Serena? Is she here? Checked in?" I ask. Serena's presence is a key component to me surviving this board retreat as president; I'm certain of that now. She's the key to many things Richard-related, it turns out, despite the divorce.

"No answer on her phone, but the plane landed on time. She should've arrived a couple hours ago," he says. "I'm sure she's lying low until we tell her when to appear. It should be fun."

"I'm not sure 'fun' is the way to think about it," I say. "But we need her—we do."

"Um, so Richard asked me to find Ted, which I didn't do . . . But he also asked me for dirt on you. What should we give him?" Justin walks over to the window and stares out at the view.

"I don't know. He probably wouldn't like the news that I've been named Orange County's Businesswoman of the Year."

He turns around. The dimple appears. "That's fantastic. Wow! Well deserved. Richard will have another reason to be jealous."

"He said I was expendable. A placeholder," I say. "It's clear he wants to force me out."

"He's an idiot." Justin crosses the room and joins me on the couch. "Look, we're going to figure this out. I'm going to help."

I give him a fake smile. I appreciate the optimism, but he doesn't know these people like I do. The doorbell to my suite rings. Justin touches my shoulder. Tingles roll down my spine, despite everything.

"I'll get it," he says, and returns with Serena in tow. She looks fabulous. Tanned, relaxed, sexy as always.

"Hello, Perfect Paige," she says, but this time it's said with warmth. A friendship of sorts has developed between us.

I smile and hurry to give her a hug. "Welcome back, Serena. I'm so happy you're here."

"It's nice to be needed," Serena says. "Now, who is this guy, and how long have you been together?"

Justin flushes. "I'm her assistant. That's all."

"Right." Serena winks.

"I'll leave you two to talk. Call me if you need anything, Paige," Justin tells us, then leaves the room.

Serena watches him leave and says, "He's hot. I know you two are flirting; I can feel it. Nice room, Madam President." She takes in the view, drawn to the beauty beyond the windows, like everyone who steps into this suite. Finally, she turns and looks at me. "How long do you think you have before Richard pulls something?"

"Hours," I say. "I really need your help."

"I know. That's why I told you the truth—so you'd have leverage. John pushed Rachel off the yacht, and then Richard covered everything up." She wraps her arms around herself. "You're lucky you didn't see it. I still have nightmares."

"Someone else knows what happened, or suspects something. I'm still getting those threatening notes." I remember calling and threatening Serena. I thought she was behind the intimidation. After what had happened with her and Ted—whatever it was—I thought the worst of her, truth be told. I thought it was either Serena or Sibley. When Serena denied any involvement in the threats, I believed her. We have forged a bond ever since. "I'm glad it isn't you."

"No, it's not me. I'd like Richard back, as you know. He's terrible, but I still love him, and I made a terrible mistake with Roman," Serena says. "I don't want to bring him down. But if you must use it, you must. And you will keep your end of the bargain?"

We've forged an agreement of sorts, the Kingsley women have. I reached out to Sibley to find out if she knew the truth about what had happened to Rachel, but she reminded me she had left the yacht before it happened. I asked if she'd be willing to fly to Italy, to talk to Serena and find out the truth. Sibley agreed as long as I paid for the trip—first class, of course. Sibley's vacation on the Amalfi Coast was worth it and then some. Knowing that John murdered Rachel but having the rest of the Kingsleys still think I believe their story that she fell . . . well, it's a good position to be in.

"I will only use it if I must, as we agreed. He's been miserable without you. He needs to step down as CEO and spend the rest of his life enjoying the finest the world has to offer, with you and Sophia by his side. How is she? I can't wait to meet her."

"She's tired and cranky but adorable. I'll bring her tonight." She smiles. "A double whammy. Richard does like babies—at least, that's what he said."

Our eyes meet. We both know Richard liked the idea of the baby a lot more when he'd thought he was the father.

"Turns out, you can't trust what Richard says," I remind her. "Not ever."

"How's Ted? I can't wait to see his reaction when I walk in the room, escorted by you," Serena says.

"Ted's the same—maybe worse. I've decided to divorce him, despite my promise to Richard. I can't keep up this charade any longer. And I shouldn't have to." I think about Richard's request, his one condition of me being appointed president: that I stay married to Ted, even if he sleeps in the pool house for the rest of our lives. It's a facade. It's ridiculous. I cannot do it any longer. "Don't try to change my mind."

"Oh, don't worry. I won't. But you do know that's going to be tough on Richard," Serena says. "The golden boy's final failure. A failed marriage reflects on Richard personally."

I shake my head. If I know Ted, it won't be his last failure. Just his latest one. Richard will simply have to get over it. I decide to change the subject.

"The girls are excited to see you. I told them you were coming but swore them to secrecy. They will be at the conference tomorrow, helping out."

"Good," Serena says with a smile. "The more Kingsley women around, the better. Oh, I should go check on the baby and the nanny. She's exhausted. She was up the whole flight with Sophia. It's hard when they're babies, yes?"

Unless you have a full-time nanny, I don't say. "It is. OK, I'll text you when the time is right to appear. Likely when we are breaking for dinner, around seven."

"I'll be there with bells on."

"You'll steal the show, bells or no bells."

"Let's hope this works," Serena says.

"It will," I say, but I really don't know what will happen next. I walk her to the door of the suite and give her another hug. "Thank you for coming."

"Thank you for the check; it really helped. And the divorce attorney. She was good," Serena says. "You should use her."

I know I need to pull the trigger. Fear of Richard's retaliation has stopped me so far. But even if I do everything he says—and I have—I disappoint him. No, more than that . . . I *annoy* him. I see the way he looks at me now, a mix of dismissal and disgust. He's not happy with me, and very few people can turn his opinion around.

Serena used to be able to sway him, to soften him, to change his mind. Maybe she still can.

"I'll talk to the attorney—I will," I say. "Let's get through this retreat, get things calmed down, and then I'll have the mind space to deal with Ted and our ridiculous arrangement. First things first: I stay president of Kingsley Global Enterprises, or I'm promoted to CEO."

"From your lips to Richard's," Serena says with a smile. *"Ciao, bella."*

9
RICHARD

As I walk past the pool outside, I realize all the bathing beauties are gone, including Julia. That's a shame. The weather has changed this evening; my hands are dry, itchy. I feel on edge. It's the Santa Ana winds—"the devil winds," as they're called. Devil winds are quite apropos for this gathering, I suppose. I promoted an angel, and she's turned into the devil.

I find the meeting room easily and note the time. If you're fifteen minutes early for a meeting with me, you're typically late. Tonight, however, I'm the late one, by about twenty minutes. It's a test. Would they dare start the meeting without me? Teamwork makes the dream work, blah, blah, blah, but they're nothing without me.

I push open the door. Paige stands at a whiteboard, scribbling. They did start without me. She turns my way, as do the others seated around the table. John is here; Meredith and Evan, our two outside directors; and soon-to-be cabana boy Justin. One of my sons is missing.

"Where's Ted?" I ask calmly, moving inside the room and taking the seat at the head of the table. I'm in command.

"Good evening, Richard," Paige says. "So glad you could join us. I was just reviewing this weekend's agenda with the board."

"How enterprising of you. But now you can be seated," I tell her. "I have a different agenda."

"Sir, is something wrong?" Meredith asks. She's been with the company from the start. A great comptroller and a loyal employee. When she retired, I begged her to join the board, and she agreed, with a hefty quarterly compensation for her services.

"Meredith, don't worry. This isn't your concern. You've been a fabulous member of the board," I assure her. I don't want the old woman to have a heart attack or something. "I'm upset with management. Specifically, upper management."

Meredith's focus turns to Paige and then back to me. "OK, yes, I understand. We need to discuss the land deal," she says, back on sure footing now that she knows she's not the target of my fury.

"Yes. The land deal—the one Paige approved—is a bust. We will lose all our money on it," I say. "I'm afraid I've over empowered her. She's in over her head."

"That's not true," Paige fires back.

"It's a big deal, as I remember. Is it failing? Have we lost the zoning?" Meredith asks.

"We have," I answer.

"We never had it. Ted lied," Paige says.

"You approved it. You are responsible—and now you're fired," I say.

"Wait just a minute, Richard," Evan cuts in. I knew he'd be a problem. Should never have put him on the board. "There are processes we need to go through. You can't just arbitrarily fire her. You can't."

"You can't," Paige says. "He's right. And besides, your son Ted is the one who brought the deal to us. He's the one who said the zoning was free and clear, that the city welcomed our development. It was all a lie. My mistake was believing him. Again."

Paige and I lock eyes across the boardroom table. I feel John's desperate stare, and finally I address him. "Yes, John?"

"Dad, you know I can run this company," he says. "I am the only Kingsley you can trust, the only one with the experience we need. Meredith, Evan, I know you agree. We've talked about it."

"I do like your finance background, but Evan is right. There are procedures in place to remove a sitting president. We need to follow the corporate bylaws," Meredith says.

Interesting. John has a fan in the room, it seems. Didn't see that coming.

"So you think I should pick John to be the next president of Kingsley, Meredith?" I ask.

"I think he's a solid candidate. Yes. If you decide a change is warranted, with the proper process," she replies.

"This is ridiculous," Paige says. "I'm president. I'm doing a great job; you all know it. The entire company supports me and my leadership."

I smile at her, amused by her desperation. I *hope* it's desperation. She sounds too calm to be desperate, though. Perhaps I'm projecting.

"Where is Ted?" Evan asks.

"Drunk. At the beach," John says.

No wonder I couldn't find him. What a mess. And here I was, thinking he would be my successor, that I'd maybe even give him the CEO title. John might be lying, though.

"It's a little late for the beach, isn't it?" I ask.

John shrugs. "The last time I talked to him, that's where he was. But we don't need him, Dad."

"No, we don't." Paige stands up. "Now, can we get back to the agenda?"

"No, we cannot," I say. "I don't want you as president anymore."

"Dad, I can step in right now," John says.

"I don't want you, either," I say. It's true; I couldn't take it. Besides, he's a murderer. "I need Ted." I look at the cabana boy. "Go find my son like I asked you to hours ago. He's apparently at the beach."

"I tried to find him for you, sir, but I didn't think to look down there, and he's not answering his phone," Justin says.

"I know. Go fetch him. We'll take a twenty-minute break." I scan the table. Paige and John both stare at me, emotions hard to read. Meredith and Evan look concerned, furrowed brows and the like. "Go. Now!"

Justin looks to Paige for permission. My God, this is infuriating. I stand up and slam my fist on the conference table.

Paige nods at Justin, who hurries out of the room like a scared mouse.

"Dad," John says, "you don't look well. You should calm down. Everything is under control."

"You're kidding, right?" I bark. "We've been hemorrhaging money since she took over. Tossing buckets of cash to charities, approving land deals that would never come to fruition. She's a disaster."

Paige smiles and turns her back on me. No one does that. It seems I have underestimated her again. Most people would crumble under my anger, my disappointment. But Paige seems to be growing stronger. Why? I'm cutting her legs off—I am. Right now. Doesn't she realize that?

"How dare you turn away from me?" I roar. And before I can stop myself, I've hurried over to her side and grabbed her arm, spinning her around to face me. "I am in charge, do you understand me? I always was and always will be."

"Really? You need to resort to violence to prove your strength? I expected better of you. I really did." Paige shakes her head at me, like I'm a child who drew on the wall with permanent marker.

I release my grip on her arm. "Well, you shouldn't have."

"Don't ever touch me again." She walks over to the door, and I follow her.

I lower my voice so only she can hear me. "You will step down as president, resign, or however you want to handle it, or I will cut the twins off for life. They won't have any money for college or anything else. Ever. Is that what you want?" I say, even though it would make me sad not to be in touch with Emily and Amy.

Paige has pushed me too far.

"Congratulations, Richard. You've just become an even shittier grandfather than you are a father, and I didn't think that was possible," she says. "And you know what? If I've learned anything in my months on the job, it's that you don't give a damn what I want. You never have."

With that, she turns and walks out of the room.

10
SERENA

I see Paige's text and can't help but feel a flutter of excitement. I'm dressed in a tight green silk dress, emerald earrings, and I've doused myself in Richard's favorite perfume. I'm ready to wow him, or at least try.

The winds have started blowing, hard, and I grab my long hair in my hand to keep it from becoming a mess, lean into the wind, and hurry inside the main building. When I reach the conference and meeting area, I look for Paige. *There she is.* Waiting for me as promised.

"You look perfect," she says before kissing both cheeks. "Thanks for being here."

"Are you kidding? I'm so happy to be back home with family. But I'm nervous," I say. "What if he won't even talk to me?"

"He won't be able to help it," Paige says. "He's in there, with John and the outside directors."

"Ted?" I ask.

"He didn't show up, the loser," she says. "Let's go!"

Paige pulls open the door, and I walk inside.

"Hello, Richard. I hope I'm not interrupting anything important," I say, speaking only to him. Richard is the only one I care about in this entire room.

Richard sees me and blinks. Blinks again. "Sisi? Is that you?"

"It's me. In the flesh. You're looking well, Richard." I walk closer to him.

"But what are you doing here?" he asks.

I twist my fingers together in front of me like I'm nervous. "I've come because I couldn't stay away. I've missed you terribly, Richard."

"Hmm. Well, I would have thought your husband and baby would have kept you too busy to think about me at all." He folds his arms across his chest.

Uh-oh. I rush to his side, drop to my knees. "The truth is, I've come to beg you to forgive me, to let me come back home. I miss you, Richard, so much, and I never stopped loving you," I say. That I ever believed in Roman and a future with him is such an embarrassment. I need Richard and the security he can provide, physically and financially, for me and Sophia. But the truth is, I also love him and the power I feel when I'm by his side. "Please, let's talk?"

"Clear the room!" Richard barks. "All of you. Out!"

I watch as everyone hustles out of the room. I take a deep breath, tighten my grip on his hands even as I wonder if he means I should leave, too. My heart has dropped. This voice, this anger . . . It reminds me of the last time I saw him on the yacht. He's furious because of me.

"Serena, get off your knees. Sit, please," Richard says. "Sisi, I can't believe you're here. Why?"

The tone of his voice has changed and softened. I hear something new: kindness. And I feel something bubble up in my heart; it feels like hope. I pull out the chair next to him, move it close to his chair so our legs touch. "I missed you."

"You married another guy," he says.

"We're divorced now. He wasn't what he seemed," I say. "But you always were true to yourself, Richard. And to me."

"Yes, I was, Sisi. You had his baby."

"She won't ever know him. I have sole custody of little Sophia. You will be her father, if you'll have us back." I know I'm laying it on thick, and fast. But I also know that's Richard's style. I touch his knee with my hand, and he covers it with his own.

"This is quite a surprise. So you've just moved back here to Southern California? Where are you living?" he asks.

"I'm staying here, at the Twin Palms. I was going to call you, try to set up a proper date, but then I discovered you were staying here, too." This is the script Paige and I have practiced.

From the twinkle in his eye, I believe the plan might be working.

"Well, well, well. Life works in mysterious ways," he says. "Have you seen Ted?"

"No, and I don't want to. That was stupid. I thought you were leaving me. I made such a mess of things. All of it was a mistake. Richard, I want us to start over. I want to be with you, take care of you, travel together. I want you to be Sophia's father. She's a beautiful baby."

Richard sighs and stands up. "You make it sound so appealing, Sisi. Like we could just pick up where we left off, as if you didn't cheat on me. As if nothing happened. But it did."

"I know. I'm sorry. I can make it up to you," I say, standing. I put my hands on his shoulders and lean in for a kiss. He kisses me back. That's the hope springing to life again. He's still mine, deep down inside, beneath the surface of his hard shell. I know how to crack through that shell. I've done it before; I can do it again.

"See? You still love me, too. I can feel it. We still have each other's hearts. Let me back into your life. Please, Richard." I keep my tone loving, not too needy. He hates weakness.

"Tempting. You are very tempting, my dear," he says. "I need to think about it. It's such a surprise."

I can't let him waffle. I won't. This is my only chance to salvage what we had, what I ruined. And I know he still needs me. It's in his eyes, I'm in his heart. "Let's have dinner tonight. Just the two of us. And then tomorrow, you can meet Sophia. Please." I know Sophia will help melt his heart, too.

"We have a stupid board-retreat dinner tonight," he says.

"You don't want to go to that. I know you don't." I wrap my arms around his waist, push against him. "You want me; that's what you want."

"You are convincing, dear. I guess you always were. You know just how to wrap me around your little finger, don't you?" he says. I'm relieved to see he's smiling.

"I know you miss us, too. I know you did. I'm so sorry I hurt you. I'll never leave you again. I'll be by your side forever," I promise. I hope he can tell I mean it.

"You're still gorgeous, Sisi. Especially when you're begging me to forgive you. You know I shouldn't even be talking to you. After what you did," he says.

"Please, Richard. Dinner, for old times' sake," I plead, then bow my head.

"I suppose a dinner wouldn't hurt anything. And it would get me away from all this mess."

"Yes, that's the spirit. Let Paige handle the boring business stuff. She is the president, after all. And we can have some fun. You need to laugh, and smile, and love," I say.

"Yes, well, there are issues—leadership issues—but I can deal with it tomorrow, I suppose."

"You are always dealing with so much," I say. "What issues now?"

He looks at me the way he used to look at me, when he loved me, before I betrayed him. He's softer for a moment, more human. I touch his shoulder.

"It's always about succession, Sisi. It always is," he says.

"Paige has everything under control," I assure him. I need Paige to hold her position as much as I need to regain mine in this family. It's a win-win when we help each other; she helped me see that. "She's a great president. Your company is in good hands. It's you who needs some attention." I wink. I hope I'm not pushing too hard.

He smiles. "Uh-huh. I guess one more night won't matter. Sure, why not. I can fire Paige tomorrow."

"Why would you do that? You love Paige," I say. "I love Paige. Everyone loves her."

He pulls away from me. "She's messed everything up."

I can tell he's becoming agitated, so I change topics. "I hear they have a gourmet restaurant down by the ocean that they only open for special occasions. I took the liberty of scheduling a special evening there for the two of us." Actually, Paige had her assistant, Justin, handle all the details, but it sounds fabulous.

Richard smiles. "One dinner, Sisi. That's all I'm promising you. You broke my heart, and my heart already had enough problems."

"I know. I'm sorry," I say. "I'll make it up to you. I will."

There's a knock on the door.

"Sir, I couldn't find Ted," Justin says. "I'm not sure where he could be."

"It's fine. We're adjourned until tomorrow. Let everyone know," Richard says.

"But the meeting wasn't over," Justin insists. "And what about the group dinner?"

"It's over. I won't be at any group dinner. I'm sure all of you and the board will be happy to dine tonight on Kingsley Global's dime, with or without my presence. Now scram," Richard says.

The door closes, and we're alone again. "You didn't have to end the meeting for me. I can wait for you to finish."

"Yes, I did. You've walked back into my life when I needed you the most. That's more important than business," he says. "I just hope you aren't lying to me again, Sisi. You know I hate liars."

I swallow and smile. I'm not really lying about that much—not really. I can love him and help Paige, too. "I'm not lying, Richard. We belong together, forever."

"Would have been a lot easier if you'd figured that out before you ran off with that guy," he says.

I nod and kiss his cheek. "All I can do is ask for your forgiveness."

"Let's take this one step at a time. Dinner tonight is a good start," he says.

I smile, and as I walk away, I can feel him watching me. I add a little swing to my step. I know he appreciates the effort when I hear a chuckle. I don't turn around. I need to keep moving forward and leading Richard back to me every step of the way.

11
PAIGE

I can't believe he cleared the room for Serena, but I'm relieved. Maybe she will be able to get back in his good graces, and help me get back there, too. As I stand outside the boardroom—across the hallway from Meredith and Evan, who are busy on their phones—I wonder where John went.

He was furious when he left, possibly angrier than I am. I'm waiting for Justin to get back, to hopefully fail in his mission to retrieve Ted. The last thing we need is my soon-to-be-ex drunk in the board meeting. What if he hits on Serena? I push that thought out of my head. It's too gross, too messed up.

I knew Richard would try to fire me. It's utterly unfair. We all agreed to the deal, even if I was the one who ultimately gave it the green light. To add insult to injury, he is murmuring about Ted taking my place. And threatening the girls, too.

It's unacceptable, truly. I'm so glad I've set the Serena plot in motion. She literally saved me this evening.

My phone rings.

"I found him. He's in the lobby bar, with a couple women," Justin says. "What should I do?"

"Leave him there," I say. "Richard is in the boardroom with Serena. Come back here, tell Richard you can't find him."

"Will do," he says. "Have you talked to Meredith or Evan? Seems like you need to get them on your side a bit. The Serena distraction can't keep him preoccupied all weekend."

"I know. I will. It's just so frustrating."

"I bet. But hang in there. I might have some ideas how we can move past the land deal, get you a win."

"Really?"

"Really," he says, appearing in the hallway and flashing me a big smile. "OK, let's get rid of these people."

"Sounds like a great idea," I say.

I watch as he knocks on the meeting-room door and walks inside. I stand in the hallway, nerves rattling my spine, but I will not show any emotion. He nods at me. I take a deep breath.

I say, "Meeting is adjourned. Richard will not be at the dinner tonight and suggests everyone eat on their own. Which, given the tension around here, might be a good idea."

Across from me, Meredith and Evan do look relieved.

"We'll do our own thing, then, Paige. See you tomorrow," Meredith says. "And we will need to review your performance metrics. I am concerned about the financial fallout from the deal you approved. And I'm not discounting Richard's perspective, just that we need a process."

"Fine with me," I say. "I'm happy to prove to you I'm the best fit for the job."

"We'll see," Evan says. "We'll look forward to hearing from you. Good evening."

I fume with rage as they walk away. They are both Richard's puppets; we all know that. But I didn't expect this sort of betrayal, not after everything I've done right for this company. This is all John's fault for stirring the pot, and Ted's fault for not showing up and therefore dodging Richard's rage and his increasingly erratic behavior. Maybe it's because he's feeling bad, with his failing heart. Or maybe it's because he is heartless.

Whatever the cause, Richard is blowing things out of proportion. I will not step down. I won't be forced out.

"Hey, take a deep breath," Justin says. "Let's go walk outside, get some fresh air."

"Good idea." I follow him down the hallway and outside to the pool area. That's when I feel it: the hot, dry winds, blowing strong. Fire winds. "Shoot, the Santa Anas are here already."

"They'll be around the rest of the weekend, I'm afraid," he says.

We watch as the palm trees bend and sway with the hot blasts.

"I hate these winds. I feel so unsettled, like anything can happen, and all bad," I say. My mind flashes back to the fires on the ridge of our hill, two streets above our home. I remember like yesterday the sound of the roaring wind, the wall of flames. I wonder what else these winds carry our way in addition to the risk of fires and bad air quality. "What is the purpose of the winds, for nature? I never understood."

"Funny . . . I have," Justin says as we reach the park with a walking path that snakes along the edge of the coast, the waves crashing below. "I did a paper on them in college."

"Really? Why?"

"I thought I wanted to be a weatherman for a bit," Justin says. "I know, don't laugh—but I did."

"I love weathermen," I say, and then catch myself. I'm flirting. *Stop it, Paige.* "So why aren't you a meteorologist?"

"My dad nixed it. 'My son will not be on TV talking about rain showers, blah, blah, blah,'" he says. "Anyway, here's the thing about the winds: they do affect people's moods and behavior."

"It's not the winds I worry about; it's the fires I'm afraid of," I admit, right before a big gust pushes me into him.

"Sorry," I say.

"No problem," he says with a smile, putting his hand on my arm to steady me.

"Thanks for the weather lesson," I say. "We should get back. I need to find Serena. I hope Richard's falling for her again."

"It looked like things were going really well between her and Mr. Kingsley. They were hugging when I popped in."

"Good. Great. Keep your fingers crossed for a reunion."

"I will. It's nice of you to facilitate that," he says.

"It's not nice—not really. It's business," I tell him. "I think I'm becoming more of a Kingsley every day." Ironic, really, that I'm becoming more like this family just as I plan to end my marriage and give up the last name.

"In what way?" he asks. We've reached the pool area. The palm trees are shaking in the wind; crazy rustling sounds fill the air, like a caged animal scratching to get free.

"Not a good way," I say.

"You aren't like them. I've been watching, learning, the whole time I've worked for you. These guys are all jerks, self-centered and entitled. You aren't. You're trying to help the company, the employees."

"But I like the power, maybe too much," I say. And I realize I do. I like the challenge of negotiating deals, the thrill of leading a big organization, and the respect that comes along with it all. Respect from everyone but Richard, that is.

"It looks good on you." He pulls the door to the resort's interior hallway open for me. I step inside, relieved to be out of the winds but sad to end our talk.

"Thanks," I say. "And I want to hear your idea for the future."

"Let's make sure you keep the president position—and then, yes, I'll tell you everything," he says. "It could be great, for both of us."

When he talks like that, it's all I can do to maintain my professionalism. It's so wrong to be drawn to your assistant. But I am. I'm becoming an office cliché. Technically, I guess I already was since I'm a nepotism hire of sorts. I smile at Justin.

Oh well. I'm a double cliché, and I don't care.

12

KRYSTLE

John walks into our suite with a dark cloud over his head. I swear I can see it.

I hope it doesn't have anything to do with my little shopping spree. I'm wearing my new California-cool jeans; a T-shirt; a cozy, thick cotton sweatshirt that says CALIFORNIA in pastel colors; and some fabulous tennis shoes that I've never heard of but everybody who is anybody is wearing them, according to the helpful saleswoman. She even brought out a glossy magazine and showed me somebody famous wearing them. This one little outfit cost more than I make in half a year working at my mom's store.

I think of all the Twin Palms shopping bags I stashed in the closet, along with armfuls of new clothes. I cannot imagine what all this must have cost when you add it all up, but I'm sure it's a pile of money bigger than I've ever seen in my entire life. As I promised myself after my jolt of concern over the price of margaritas, I didn't look at the total on the receipt; I just signed it. So fun. So fabulous. All three boutiques treated me like royalty. I loved it. *Princess of the day,* one of the shop ladies called me. I really hope John doesn't make me take everything back. That would make me angry.

"Hi, honey. How was your meeting?" I ask and bop over to him, new tennis shoes springy and fun. "I did a little retail therapy. Hope you don't mind. I bought something extra special to wear for both dinners. Need to make a great impression on all your relatives."

"What? No. I don't care," he says. He's distracted, tense.

He doesn't care what I spent. Yippee. I force a frown of concern. "Is there anything I can do to help?"

"No, you can't help. I need a plan. You need to give me space. The dinner tonight is canceled."

Getting away from him and this mood sounds good to me. I've never seen him like this. "Sure. Great. I'll just go have some dinner on my own, then. Do you want me to bring you back anything, sweetie?"

"I just want you to leave. Please."

He sounds desperate and angry. And, well . . . rude. Guess he is just like his dad at heart. I'm surprised, but I know I shouldn't be. But if he wants me out, I'm out. Whatever he wants, as long as he still loves me after he gets over this little episode. "Fine, honey. I'll get out of your hair. I love you. I'll do anything for you," I say, but he doesn't seem to hear me. I should go. "See ya!"

I hurry out the door and make my way through the long corridor that I know leads to the lobby. I just want to sit at one of the tables there and people-watch. I want to see and be seen, for once in my life.

My little brother, Joey, and I used to pretend we were rich. We'd talk to each other with fake British accents and chatter about all our houses and boats, about our lavish vacations to exotic destinations. We'd overhear the rich kids at school bragging about ski weeks and spring breaks, and about European vacations with their families. Joey got closer to getting rich than I ever did. He had a good job, was working for a rich family. And then he died. My little brother didn't deserve to die. My mom and I are certain he was murdered. But we couldn't even find an attorney to take our case. They all just said my brother slipped and fell on the jobsite, a terrible accident, that it was his fault alone. My poor momma didn't even get a dime. Just his body and a lifetime of sadness. My dad died of a heart attack right after the accident. A broken heart, for sure. I shake my head and push Joey out of my mind for now. I will focus on the resort around me, how lucky I am to be here, and all there is to do.

The lobby is hopping tonight. There's a guy playing the piano and gorgeous rich people seated everywhere, drinking and eating and laughing. Like nothing could ever be wrong in their lives, like no one could ever touch them. Like they own the place—and maybe one of them does. Who knows? All I know is, for as much as they think they have it all, we all end up in the same place. And sometimes, the rich fall. Sometimes they're revealed. Sometimes karma gets them, too.

As I make my way to the bar, I spot John's brother, Ted. I've never met him, but I've seen his photos in the news and at John's house. He's a good-looking guy, that's for sure. The opposite of John. I'm into John for his personality, of course. This one—*this* Kingsley—I could be into for much more. Too bad he's unhappily married. But I digress. I walk up behind Ted, who is busy flirting, sitting at the bar between two women too young for him. I tap him on the shoulder.

The bookend girls both give me the stink eye.

Ted turns around and gives me a questioning look. "Can I help you?" He is slurring his speech. He's drunk.

"Hi, Ted. I'm Krystle, John's girlfriend. I've heard so much about you I just had to say hi when I saw you sitting here with these lovely ladies," I say with a big grin. I stick my hand out for a shake, but instead, Ted stands up and gives me a big hug.

"Nice to meet you! Yes, John has told me all about you. He's in love. He really needed you to come along," he says. "Lucky guy."

"Why, thank you."

"Where is the grump?" Ted asks, looking behind me.

"Oh, he's back in the room, pouting. I guess the meeting tonight didn't go so great or something." I shrug. "Was it bad? For John?"

Ted shrugs, too. "I skipped it. They are all driving me crazy. Who needs them?"

"I suppose you do; they're your family," I say.

"Not really. They're all out for themselves. Well, except John and me. We look out for each other these days," he says. "Want a drink?"

"I'd love one. Champagne, please?"

Ted turns back to the bar to order my drink, and one of the two bookends glares at me, like she can make me leave, like she's stronger than me. She's not. I stink eye her right back, and she turns her attention elsewhere.

Ted hands me a glass of champagne and says, "Let's find a table. I need to eat something. I've been drinking all day. Hungry?"

"Starving," I say and follow him through the crowd. This is like one of those stories my brother and I would have invented—me, holding a glass of champagne, walking through the lobby of the most gorgeous resort I've ever seen, following a billionaire's son to a table for two. *Krystle, you're doing something right,* I tell myself.

As we get settled at our table—candlelit and everything—Ted asks, "Did John tell you anything about the meeting?"

"No, he literally just told me to go away. So here I am." It makes me sad, admitting that, even though I was relieved to get away from his dark cloud of a mood. I wish he would open up to me, turn to me for guidance. He won't. Not yet.

"I'm sorry. He can be a big jerk when he's angry. I'll talk to him, tell him to be nice," he says. "Maybe he'll come join us."

He picks up his phone and calls John. I can't hear what John says, but it sounds like he's yelling at Ted from the minute he picks up the phone. Ted doesn't say anything, just hangs up.

"We'll just leave him alone for now," he says with a grin. "Ready to order?"

"I am." What a nice Kingsley I've found. How refreshing. There must be something wrong with him, but for the life of me, I don't know what it is. Time will tell, my mom would say.

It's while we're eating our cheeseburgers—we both ordered the same thing—that everything changes.

Ted's phone pings with a message. And his face falls. "Shit."

"What's wrong?" I ask.

"My dad is furious with me, but he also wants to talk to me. And his ex-wife is back. Here at this hotel. He wants to know what to do about that," Ted says.

"Why would he want your help?"

"Because I had a fling with her; that's probably why," he says.

My eyeballs almost pop out of my face, but I shove a french fry into my mouth and try to act like what he said is no big deal. I keep chewing. How gross. His dad's wife? And he's married? *Ick.*

"I can't believe she's back," he says. "I have to go talk to my dad. I've been avoiding him all day. Time to man up, as he'd say. He wants to give me a promotion."

"OK," I say. Wow. "Good talking to you."

"Do you mind handling the check? I'm in a rush," he says. And before I know it, he's gone.

I take back my former opinion of handsome Ted. He's worse than John—way worse. And he left me holding the bill? Horrible. I'll stick with John; that's what I'll do. Hopefully, he'll stick with me, too.

13

RICHARD

There's a knock on my door, per usual, and this time I know it's Ted. He finally responded to me. Ungrateful bastard.

"Ted," I say, opening the door. "How very nice of you to finally answer your father. You missed the board meeting."

"I know. I was, um, under the weather," he says, bright-blue eyes flashing with a lie.

"Is that so? If 'under the weather' means 'on the beach, under a palm tree,' I suppose you were. Come in," I say. "I don't have much time."

"I heard dinner was canceled." Ted walks into the suite. "Nice room."

"It *was* canceled, by me. No need for team bonding and all that stuff Paige proposed. We all know who we are, what we are," I say.

"Yes, that's true," he says and drops onto the thick white couch. "So what did you need to see me about?"

I can't tell if he's drunk or just tipsy. He's off, glassy-eyed. And pompous. But isn't he always?

"Earlier today, it was about a promotion. Now, it was just to look into your face and tell you, don't ever ignore me again. If we're on a business retreat, and I'm paying for it all, and I ask to see you, you come running. If there is a meeting scheduled, you will be there, or you won't be with the company any longer. Am I clear?"

"Dad, don't be so dramatic," he says. "You and I both know Paige's stupid bonding retreat was a bad idea. You said so yourself." He covers a yawn. "Look, fine, I'll be there tomorrow. Satisfied?"

What a disappointment. I've never been this angry at both my sons at the same time. "Did you know Serena is here, at this resort? Have you seen her?"

"What? No way. I haven't seen her since that night on the *Splendid Seas*. Why is she here?" Ted asks.

Sure, he looks stunned—mouth dropped open and all—but you never can tell when this kid is lying. Well, actually, he usually is. Why is she here, indeed. "You tell me."

"I have no idea. I'm not in contact with her. Dad, that was a stupid thing. It meant nothing," he says.

"It meant something to me," I say. I stare at his face, trying to decide if I can believe him. If I should trust him. I don't. Not at all. He's a liar and a cheat, a phony and a fraud. I am not over his betrayal. I realize I may never be. "Get out. I have plans."

"You're the one who summoned me. But sure, OK," Ted says, standing and heading for the door. "I'll see you later. And I'm open to that promotion whenever you're ready to talk about it. I knew Paige wouldn't last as president. Just say the word, and I'll step up."

He has some kind of nerve.

I'm fuming. "After how you behaved today? You must be kidding."

"You're going to need me, Dad; you always do." He sounds confident, but I know I've rattled him, the jerk.

He doesn't make eye contact with me, seeming to find something fascinating to stare at on the ground. He's weak, despite the bravado of his words. He's all talk and devious action.

"I don't need you, Teddy. I've never needed you. You need me. Without me, you'd just be another washed-up, aging pretty boy. In fact, you're doing a really good job playing that role so far this weekend.

Bravo, spoiled loser. Maybe I should just cut you off, see how you'd fare in the real world," I suggest. I'm shaking with fury. I am finished with him, once and for all. I have reached my limit.

"You'd never do that—cut me off. Family is everything, remember?" he says, but he doesn't sound so sure.

I ignore him as he walks out the door. No apologies. No remorse. Only entitlement.

I check my watch. I'm going to be late for dinner with Sisi. What an end to an exhausting day, reuniting with the woman who left me for another man, only to reappear, baby in tow. A baby she now says can be mine.

She wants a fresh start. And despite everything that has happened, I realize I want that, too. I missed her so much it hurt at times, although I wouldn't admit that to anyone. I longed for Serena over more than just her companionship in my final days. No, it was our easy banter, her way of managing our life so I didn't need to worry about the details, the way she dressed for my eyes only. The way she made me feel loved, and respected. Until she didn't. In my dreams, she returned, apologetic, missing us. This is my dream, and it's become reality. She's back. Maybe someone like God answered my prayers?

I don't really believe in prayers being answered, but Serena came back. So I guess it's possible. I look in the mirror, check my tie. I look as good as I can, I suppose.

I make my way outside to the private restaurant perched on the bluff and cannot believe how strong the wind is. These Santa Anas are such a strange force of nature. Uncontrollable, unpredictable. And unsettling. Like someone has aimed a huge fan at us on the coastline to blow dust, sand, dirt, and all the inland-empire grime down here to the beach. I cough as some of that grime blows into my face. The palm trees whip around like mad. I hope one of those fronds doesn't snap off and kill me. I reach for the door of the place, called the Perch, and step inside, relieved to be out of the wind.

"You're here! I was getting worried you wouldn't show up," Serena says, gliding across the room, joining me in front of a fireplace, handing me a glass of champagne. "Cheers, darling. I'm so glad we're reconnecting. I've missed you more than you can imagine." She touches my shoulder and smiles.

I'm trying to decide what I want. I know what my heart desires, but my brain is rationalizing. Do I want her, again, when she's disgraced me? Could I ever trust her—really trust her—again? I take her hand in mine. She's gorgeous, as always. She leans in for a kiss and I accept.

"That was nice," I say about the kiss. It was. "I see you salvaged the earrings I gave you when we were first dating. The emeralds. Sibley didn't swipe them. Good." I remember my daughter, Sibley, and her no-good boyfriend as they left the yacht, a bagful of Serena's jewelry over her shoulder, Serena's diamond necklace around Colson's neck. I thought it was amusing, and rather industrious of her. Serena was furious. But, as Sibley pointed out, she has plenty. *Had* plenty. Good to see she hasn't pawned the emeralds. Yet.

She touches the stones at her ears. "I'm sorry I hurt you, Richard," she says. "Remember, these were one of the first gifts you gave me?"

"I do remember," I say. And then I consider her words. It was more than hurt; it was a deep betrayal. On the other hand, I'm an old, dying man. Maybe I should take this, take *her* back. Having a loving wife for my final days would be the easy way out for the end of my life. I do believe she loves me. I do. It just became complicated.

"I'm starving. What have you got planned?" I ask.

"That's my Richard. Always thinking with his stomach," she says. "Come this way."

Serena leads me to a candlelit table set for two tucked in next to a window with a spectacular view of the crashing waves below. Ours is the only table in the place. She must be forking out a lot of cash to entertain me like this. It's an investment to her, I suppose.

I pull out the chair for her and sit down myself. As much as I'd like to settle in for a long, romantic dinner, I'm finding myself stressed and anxious instead of happy and loving. I realize, just now, I'm still completely furious with her behavior. She had an affair while I was fighting for my life, she flirted and more with my own son, and then she left me for her baby's daddy. For someone like me, all this should be a deal-breaker. What am I doing here?

I start tapping my foot, hoping to dissipate these emotions. My heart races in response. Too many thoughts, too much for me to deal with here and now. It's not working.

"Richard, what's wrong?" she asks.

"Can you maybe invite someone else to join you for dinner?" I say, thinking of Ted. My rage intensifies. "I'm sorry, but I must go." I toss the napkin on the table and stand up. "I was happy to see you, Sisi. But I realize I cannot go backward. I cannot. Too much harm was done. Have a good life."

"Richard, wait!" Serena yells. Is she desperate? Does she need money? Probably. She runs after me and grabs my arm. She looks panicky, her eyes wide and shining with fear; there's sweat on her beautiful brow. "Please. I love you. I need you. I'm not safe. Baby Sophia isn't safe. I told him she's yours."

I slide her hand off my arm and take a couple of steps back.

"As you know, that's impossible," I say, although I had dreamed that somehow the vasectomy hadn't worked and the baby was mine. I was a fool, though. I won't be a fool again.

"Nobody knows that except for us. She's yours, Richard. I am yours." She takes a step toward me. "Please, for Sophia, let's try again. We need you. I'm afraid of what Roman is capable of doing."

Well, he's capable of stealing my wife, impregnating her, and swooping her away to Italy. I doubt he's capable of more, since he's broke and, from what my team dug up, a minor thug with a criminal record. Of course I had my team look into the guy. I mean, he did steal my wife away from me, and I had to try to understand why. I couldn't. The more information I dug up, the more disgust I felt. Serena chose very badly indeed. She got what she deserved when the truth about his situation became obvious. She'd never been used for her money before, I suppose. I do feel bad for the baby; she could have had me for her dad—although maybe it's for the best, considering how Sibley turned out. Ha.

"I'm glad you came to your senses and left that loser. In the long run, it will be for the best for both of you. But I'm sorry—I can't get past the betrayal, no matter how hard I try. Not now. Not ever," I tell her.

"Don't you want to help me? I know you still care, Richard. I need you, please," she says, tears streaming down her face. "We aren't safe. Think of the baby."

"I have, my dear, for far too long," I say and walk out of the room, across the lobby with the glowing fireplace, and back out into the windstorm. The baby has been in my thoughts since I learned my wife was pregnant, before she even knew it herself. I fantasized about being the baby's father, even though I knew it was highly unlikely, given my vasectomy. Still, I had hope for a while. In fact, I've thought about the baby too much, for far too long. At one point, when the truth was revealed about Ted and Serena and whatever dalliance they were having, I thought the baby was Ted's. A horrible development that thankfully proved false. Serena wants me to think about the baby. I have, my dear. The baby belongs to your Italian lover. I'm finished thinking about that baby. She was not meant to be mine.

As for my former wife, I loved Serena from the moment I saw her—well, yes, of course that was lust. But over time, I grew to respect her humor; her way of helping me manage my life, my kids. My kids. I think of Ted and Serena, the betrayal that shook me to the core. I see again the video of them, kissing, on my fucking yacht. No, I cannot go back to her. I will never be able to forgive her for Ted; for the Italian man she had an affair with, had a baby with, married. No. I love her—I do—but I must let her go. Forever. *Goodbye, Sisi.*

I walk quickly back to my suite, and as I do, I wonder if Julia still plans to come by tonight. That might be just what the doctor ordered.

Who am I kidding? I just need to order a big room service meal and go to bed. Heads will roll tomorrow, and this hellish weather is the perfect backdrop.

14

JOHN

I cannot just sit here and do nothing. I need to walk. I need to talk some sense into Richard. And I should find Krystle, too, I suppose. I was mean to her; I know it. And why did Ted suddenly call when I've been trying him all day? And why didn't he stick to the plan?

We are a team now. A united front with a common enemy in Paige.

I needed him at that board meeting, and he decided on a drunken beach day instead.

He's proven once again that I can't trust him.

I walk into the closet to find a change of clothes, and I stop in my tracks. Krystle's side is filled with new clothing, price tags poking out everywhere. Shoes and hats and all sorts of accessories, too. What the hell? She can't afford this kind of spending, and she better not think I'm paying for it all.

Now my blood is boiling again. I change quickly and hurry to find Richard. He must be dining somewhere in the resort. The man doesn't miss a meal. I'll start there. Krystle will be easy to deal with compared to my father.

I've decided what I'm going to do, once and for all. I will leave him no choice. He will give me the company—at least the president's title—or else. I have a plan to recoup the lost investment from Ted's land deal. Sure, it's going to take years, but I'll get the company back on solid financial footing. It's my expertise. I'm a fixer. And this situation needs to be fixed.

Teamwork doesn't make anything work. Ruthless leadership will save us—save Kingsley—and I am that leader. I'll just force Richard to trust me again.

He really doesn't have another choice, and he knows what I'm capable of. I guess we all do.

15
PAIGE

I can't believe I thought I could enjoy a massage right now. Justin insisted I keep the appointment, that it would help me calm down. So here I am, lying on this soft, warm table; soothing music playing; the smell of lavender and other oils filling the room. I'm too jittery, too on edge to be here. I begin to sit up when there is a knock on the door, and then a voice says from the other side, "Mrs. Kingsley, are you ready?"

It's the masseuse. His name is Donald, and he has kind, dark eyes.

I slip back into my robe. "No, not quite," I say. I should be relaxing on the table by now instead of being lost in thought. Richard's unacceptable anger and outbursts have drained my energy and thrown me off balance. I'm sure that's part of his plan.

"Take your time, Mrs. Kingsley. I'll just go get a glass of water for you and be right back. I'll knock first, of course," Donald says through the door.

"Thank you." I drop my bathrobe and begin to slide my underwear off, and that's when a white envelope slips in under the door. I start to shake all over. It's another one of the threatening notes. I pick it up and open it.

This weekend I will know the truth. I'm watching you, every minute. Enjoy your spa treatment, if you can. We will meet soon.

A chill rolls down my spine as I pull on the bathrobe and yank open the door. I look both ways down the hallway, but there is nobody there. I duck back into the room, trying to decide what to do. Hands shaking, I shove the note into the pocket of my bathrobe. I am, at this moment, completely on edge.

"Mrs. Kingsley, are you ready now?" Donald asks.

I don't know what to do. I need advice. I need to get on the massage table and think. So I do. "I'm ready," I reply, although I'm the opposite of relaxed despite the comfortable massage table I'm lying on.

Donald sweeps into the room. "How is the temperature of the room? The table? Is there anything else I can get for you? Anything you need, you ask."

And with those kind words, before I can stop myself, I burst into tears.

"Oh, Mrs. Kingsley, I'm sorry. Have I upset you?"

Now I'm sobbing, face down in the head cradle. This is all too much. The threats, the truth I now know, the lies this family continues to perpetrate. The way I am undermined at every turn. It's too much.

Back when my parents were developing my perfection streak, my wires were crossed. That's the only explanation I can come up with. When I'm furious, as mad as mad can get, I burst into tears. And right now, I'm furious: with Richard; with the entire situation; with Ted and, yes, John; and all the lies. I've been a great leader, an applauded president who has steered Kingsley Global Enterprises into a respected position as a community leader and a good global citizen. All my hard work seems to be a threat to these men and their egos. Instead of praising my accomplishments, they try to undermine me and belittle me at every turn. It's infuriating, to say the least. And now there is someone stalking me, threatening me, so close they were on the other side of the door just a few moments ago.

But what adds fuel to the fire? Kindness.

I need to get myself together. "I am so sorry. I don't think I can handle a massage tonight," I say. I manage to get myself into a sitting position on the table while also wrapping the sheet and blanket around myself. "It's not your fault."

And then the lights go out in the room.

"Oh my gosh. What's happening?" I ask, tears giving way to fear. "Did you do that?"

"No, Mrs. Kingsley. It's the Santa Ana winds. Sometimes the power goes out. Sometimes, worse," he assures me. "We have a generator. Be calm, and all will be fine."

I reach my hand out in front of my face, but all I see is blackness. I won't let myself get more worked up—I won't. I need to call my girls. I need to tell them not to come to the resort. Not this weekend. Not with all this happening.

I still don't want to accept that Richard has turned on me, even though I've watched him play power games with his kids for years. I know Ted and John have been in cahoots since I was appointed president. But Richard? I thought I was different. Special. He told me as much. But I'm the same as the rest of the people he plays with. I know I shouldn't be surprised, but I am. A tear works its way to the surface. No. I refuse to be sad anymore.

I will not let this happen to me. I will never forgive him for humiliating me during the board meeting tonight. It was one of the worst days of my new career. It won't happen again.

The lights flicker to life and then remain on.

"Oh, thank goodness," I say.

"Maybe, Mrs. Kingsley, we try some calm, loving breaths? Breathe in some lavender?" he suggests. The kind, dark eyes think I've lost it. I can tell.

Maybe he's right.

"No, thank you, Donald. I'm going to have to leave—but I'll pay for our session, don't worry," I say. "If you could excuse me?"

"Oh yes, of course. Apologies again for the lights." He backs out of the room.

I slip on the comfy bathrobe and slippers and rush out the door. He's waiting for me in the hall, concern and worry marring his face.

"It's not you; it's me," I tell him. "Thank you." I dismiss him at the ladies' locker room and hurry to my locker. The minutes spent in absolute darkness with a caring stranger made my decision clearer, in fact. I dress quickly and make my way to the spa lobby, where two concerned staff members await.

"Oh, Mrs. Kingsley, we apologize for the power outage. Please, let us make it up to you with a massage service tomorrow," one says. "Donald says you were quite upset."

"I'm fine. Please add a twenty percent gratuity to my tab for Donald," I say. "Have a good evening."

I move quickly along the pathway beside the pool. Dressed in black leggings, a black T-shirt, and a black zip-up hoodie, I look as if I'm a burglar. The wind howls, and the unsettled air dries my eyes and skin as I make my way. My fingertips are dry, as if I touched sandpaper, when in fact, all I've done so far is step outside in this wind event. The lights flicker—off, on again, then off—as I open the door to the hallway. I'm inside, which is a relief, and an emergency light illuminates the space where I stand in front of the elevator. I feel the threatening note that is shoved inside my jeans pocket now. I look around, wondering who could be leaving them for me. Anyone, that's who. I need to keep moving. I need to stay safe.

I decide I should take the stairs instead of waiting for the elevator, so I do. Sometimes, life leaves you with no choice but to make your own path and steadfastly pursue your choices. I intend to remain president. It's a choice I've made, and I will fight to remain in the position, no matter what it takes. And as for the person threatening me, I will stay one step ahead of them, literally and figuratively, until I decide what to do about it.

16

RICHARD

My stomach growls with hunger as I wait for room service. My text to lovely Julia of the yellow bikini resulted in a long diatribe about my ex-wife being in town and that she was hurt I was leading her on when all the while I was reuniting with Serena. Per Serena. They must have seen each other here. And while I must admit I like being fought over, I'd rather have had the attention. I swiped and deleted Julia from my phone. *Goodbye, Julia.*

I decided to order a feast for one. That's fine. We all enter this world alone, and most of the time, this is our fate—loneliness. It would be hard to imagine a different outcome for a jackass like me.

The lights flicker and go out. I freeze, waiting for the darkness to be replaced by the resort's generator-driven light. I'm sure a place like this has redundant power. It seems like it takes forever, but it's only a matter of a minute or so. And there it is—the lights are back on. It's easy to realize all you have taken for granted, all the simple things in life, when you're plunged into darkness, suddenly helpless as a baby. That's why I'm so tough on my family. They need to be on guard, ready for anything. You never know what life will throw your way. And until one of them proves to be ready to take over the company, it's much better with me at the helm. I know how to stay in front of everyone and everything. It's why I'm where I am today. I look in the mirror. I'm old, alone, and possibly hated by my children; their spouses; and my only brother, Walter. Oh, and my ex-wife likely isn't pleased at the moment, either.

Enough reflection for now. I remind myself to plug in my phone; it's low on battery, and who knows how long the generator will keep this place alight. I hope long enough to cook my meal, at least. I carry my phone into the large master bedroom of my suite, plug it in next to my bed. I'm heading back to the living room when there's a knock on my door.

"Room service!" a man's voice calls out.

"It's about time," I say and make my way to the door. I yank it open.

"Good evening," the waiter says and smiles. "Where would you like this set up? I'd suggest over there, by the windows, but it's up to you."

"Sure, fine, wherever works. I'm starving." My stomach growls again when he lifts the silver cover off my steak: filet mignon; medium rare, on the rare side. I watch as he places a crystal vase with a single white rose in the center of the table. *Hurry up, already.*

"Would you like me to uncork the wine?" he asks.

"Yes, of course," I say. He proceeds to do so with a flourish. I sit down, forcing myself to wait before taking a bite, as he pours me a taste of the cabernet franc. "It's perfect. Please pour, and then I'm digging in."

"Absolutely," he says, pouring. "Can I get you anything else, Mr. Kingsley?"

"No," I say, dismissing him with the wave of a hand, and he's gone. I slice the steak easily using my butter knife instead of the steak knife provided and pop the first bite into my mouth. Savory; juicy; perfectly cooked; tender, with peppery seasonings. I take a bite of scalloped potatoes. Cheesy, tasty. I'm so happy. Life is good. I'm Richard Kingsley, and I don't need anyone but myself.

I'm so busy eating I didn't notice company had arrived.

"What do you want?" I ask with a sigh. I don't really care. Not anymore. All of them and their desires are starting to blend together in my mind. They're so selfish, so needy. So interchangeable. Like sheep.

"Your respect. Your support. I know it's too much to ask for your love, but that would be nice, too," the sheep says. *Bahhhh* is all I hear. I don't care anymore.

"Don't be needy. Needy people are so annoying." I pop another bite of steak into my mouth. "How did you get in here?"

"The door was propped open."

"Stupid waiter."

The sheep takes a seat across from me. "You've tried to ruin me. My reputation. My life. Why?"

"What the fuck do you want me to say? I made you who you are, so I can take it away if I want to—all of it," I say. I'm more than tired of these games. I take another bite of my perfectly cooked steak, blood oozing onto my plate, and look out the window to the blackness beyond.

"I want you to apologize. I want you to fix everything. I'm serious. It's my time to shine and lead this company."

I turn back to the table. "What do you want?"

"To be president. Oh, and I want an apology. Say you're sorry."

I will ignore the sheep, I decide, and slowly slice another bite of steak with the butter knife. It's that tender. I feel the stare, but rather than looking up and making eye contact, I say, "Rule number one of business: never say you're sorry. And that's one of the many reasons I cannot ever trust my company to you."

I stab the steak with my fork and put it in my mouth. I am so tired of this incessant *bahh*ing. *Bahh, bahh.*

"How dare you? It's always only ever about you, isn't it? You never think of anyone else. Do the right thing, for once in your life!"

"Enough!" I roar. Then I can't speak. I've inhaled my bite. The steak is lodged in my breathing tube. I stand, put my hands around my throat—the universal sign for choking. My enemy smiles. I need to find something to do the Heimlich maneuver on myself. I try the chair but flip it over with my weight. I search for something else to ram into, keeping my fists clenched together just below my ribs. I can't find anything the right height.

I'm pleading with my eyes, *Help me.* More staring.

I need to breathe. I don't have much time left. I make prayer hands, an unfamiliar posture. Surely, they don't want me to die. Not like this—not now. I'm begging for help now.

My nemesis steps forward, I'm sure, to finally help dislodge the piece of steak. The sheep caused this. All of this. But I still have time to be saved. I reach for the hotel phone, dial zero for the operator.

But before my call is answered, the sheep yanks the phone out of the wall.

With my last ounce of strength, I lunge forward to force some sense into the sheep if I have to. I grab the traitor's shoulder, intending to demonstrate my dominance even now. Instead, I see a glint of steel and feel the blade of a steak knife enter my neck. The sheep must have taken it from the table.

The pain forces me to double over. I try to pull the knife out, but I'm losing strength through lack of oxygen. Blood spurts everywhere. I drop to my knees. I hear myself gagging. I don't want to die, but I know I'm going to—I'm sure of it. I've underestimated my opponent. I suppose there is honor in losing to a worthy foe, but I wasn't ready. Not yet. I stare once more at the wolf in sheep's clothing before my legs give out from under me.

What will the newspaper headlines say about my death? About my life? I should have had a press release written months ago, when I found out my heart was failing me. *Control the story,* I always say. But foolishly, I didn't. Will my children remember all my accomplishments? Of course not. But I will be remembered as a lion in the industry, a great man. I can't believe this is happening to me.

It's not supposed to be this way.

And finally, everything—mercifully—goes dark.

17

KRYSTLE

When the power goes out, I find myself all alone and a little scared. Maybe I'm in over my head with this whole Kingsley clan. They seem restless, and mean, and desperate, despite the fact they have so much. I wish John would come find me, would act worried that I'm out and about without any lights or anybody with me. If my momma didn't need this so much, I think, I might just run away. That's the fear talking, I know. My heart is thunking in my chest, and I'm breathing shallow, like in my throat. I can't have a panic attack. Not here, not now.

"Remain calm, everyone. The generator will kick in shortly," someone yells.

The waiter wasn't as friendly to me once Ted left, probably assuming—correctly—that I wasn't going to leave a big tip. Well, I'm not paying for Ted's meal on John's room; I know better than that. The lights turn on, thank goodness. I take a deep breath and push the panic away. I wave my hand.

"Say, my friend had to leave suddenly. He's staying at the resort, too, so can you divide the check in half, please?" I ask.

"Sure. Our systems were down with the power outage but should be back up and running," the waiter says. "Be right back."

I watch him walk away, and that's when I see John scurrying across the lobby.

"Hey! John!" I call to him from my table but then jump up to catch him. "You sure are in a hurry. Slow down, would ya?"

"Oh, hey, Krystle," he says, finally stopping. He's a bit out of breath, it appears. "How's your evening? Sorry for being so short earlier."

"My evening has been terrible. First, you yell at me; then your brother leaves me in the middle of dinner; then the power goes out, and then you try to sneak past me in the lobby. I'm about to have a panic attack. Yeah, not a great night," I say. I feel my hands on my hips. I'm being a bit of a brat. I drop my arms and smile. "I miss you."

"Uh, yes, I miss you, too, sweetie. Um, so you ate dinner?" He isn't making eye contact with me, though; he's scanning the lobby.

"Yes, with your jerk brother," I say. "Who are you looking for? Have you eaten? I have a table for two, just over there."

He takes a deep breath and seems to calm down. "Sure, I'd love to have dinner. I haven't eaten yet. I just need to go back to the room for a minute. I'll be right back. Could you order me something?" He says the last bit with a smile, so at least he's trying to be fun and nice.

"Sure, what do you want?"

"I'm in the mood for steak, actually."

"OK, I'll get you one. Medium rare, right?" I ask. I've been paying attention.

"Yes, thank you," he says, distracted again.

"Hey, when you go back to the room, you might want to fix your hair. It's sort of a mess," I note.

"The wind is hectic out there." He pats the top of his comb-over. "Tumultuous night. I'll be back."

And then, much like his brother, he leaves me all alone in the lobby. I shrug. At least he hasn't brought up my little shopping spree, so there's that. I walk back to my table for two and flag the waiter.

I see he's dropped the check already.

"I need to order another meal, for my date this time," I say. "A fillet, medium rare, and whatever else comes with it. Oh, and a glass of cabernet—your finest. And I'll have another, too. Thanks so much!"

He nods, picks up the old check, and hurries away. I watch the lobby. I wonder which other Kingsleys are out and about tonight. I have memorized their faces from news accounts online, and my mom is a huge fan of the OC Scoop gossip site that seems to track them wherever they go. She makes me study it like homework. I know my mom may have even given a couple of tips—harmless ones, of course—during my time with John. She says it's good to up my profile. Truth be told, I don't mind. I've always wanted to be famous and rich, just like my brother, Joey, and I dreamed of. And being with these people makes me feel like I am. I'm rich-adjacent and almost famous. Just you wait.

Oh, look, there's Paige. President Paige. She's also in a hurry, headed in the same direction John was going before I stopped him. Wonder what she's doing, roaming around the resort this late at night. I pegged her for an early-to-bed, early-to-rise kind of gal. But you never really know, do you? Oh, and there's Ted. He and Paige practically collide in the center of the lobby.

They exchange a few words, but both look angry, leaning forward, mouths closed, arms crossed. Hard to believe the two of them were once considered the golden couple, according to John. He said that even when his wife was alive, Richard never liked them as much as he did Ted and Paige. Like I said, it was easy to fall for Ted—I did, myself, earlier tonight. It's just that he puts on a good front, but underneath, he's trouble. I guess Paige knows that now.

I wonder why she hasn't divorced him.

I wonder, too, if there are any happy Kingsleys. It seems like, just maybe, all this money and the family business combine to ruin people. Turns them rotten and makes them forget how lucky they really are.

Makes them treat others as disposable, interchangeable, not worth taking care of in the long run, no matter how loyal they were.

I see Paige is walking away from Ted, and Ted is heading back to the lobby bar where I found him hours ago. The bookends are still there, happy to welcome him back between them. Oh, there's John. Hair combed. He's changed into jeans and a blue cashmere sweater. It makes him appear relaxed and happy. He's not.

"Your wine, ma'am," the waiter says, pouring my refill just as John reaches the table. "Welcome, sir. Your meal should be ready shortly." He pulls John's chair out for him.

"Go ahead and pour my wine," John says, without so much as a *please* or *thank you.*

"Yes, sir," the waiter says with an edge.

I almost want to apologize for bringing him another Kingsley man. But I can't, so I smile at the waiter. *I get it,* my smile says. *I want to smack him in his pompous face, too.*

"Penny for your thoughts, John," I say when the waiter leaves. "Did you get a chance to sort things out with your family?"

"I don't want to talk about them right now." He takes a big gulp of wine.

Something has happened. I don't know what.

"Do you like my new outfit, sweetie?" I ask, trying to lighten his mood. "These tennis shoes are what everybody who's anybody is wearing, the girls at the shop told me." I hold up my foot to get his attention.

"You need to return all that stuff in the closet. You're out of control," he says. "I didn't tell you to buy everything at the resort."

The waiter arrives and places John's meal in front of him. John dismisses him with a wave of his hand.

"I didn't buy everything, just what I need to fit in this weekend, to not be embarrassed around your family." My eyes mist over with tears. "I wanted to make you proud to be with me."

He slices a piece of steak and then looks at me. That seemed to have worked. I see his eyes soften.

"Those are great tennis shoes," he says. "I'm glad you're along this weekend. Things have gotten frenetic."

I reach for his hand on the table. A soft touch is what he needs. A calmed-down, nice-as-possible John is what I need. Seems we're on solid ground again. For now.

NEWS ALERT: High-wind, red flag, and high-surf warnings issued for Orange County through Sunday as roaring Santa Ana winds return.

Winds reached speeds of up to 45 mph on Friday night as the Southland witnessed one of the windiest days of the year. Parts of Los Angeles and Orange County are under a high-fire-danger Red Flag Warning, meaning critical fire-weather conditions are either occurring now or will shortly. The Red Flag Warning will remain in effect through 7:00 p.m. Sunday, as the strong winds kick up during the overnight hours on Friday. These fast, hot winds cause vegetation to dry out, increasing the danger of wildfire. Once the fires start, the winds fan the flames and hasten their spread. Be prepared and review your evacuation plans.

SATURDAY, FEBRUARY 25

18

SIBLEY

Nice place Paige picked to host this little family get-together, I think as I walk into the lobby. Had I known how swanky it is, I would have arrived yesterday. But I like to throw them all off by appearing suddenly, as if by magic or by premeditation—you decide. I look around the joint. Parquet floors, smiling concierge people, a huge lobby with a fireplace on one end and a bar on the other, and a sparkling view of the ocean straight ahead. It's almost too perfect.

Just what the doctor ordered after my long flight. Sure, Paige told me to come, that I'd be welcomed by everyone. She thanked me so profusely for talking to Serena and finding out the truth about what happened to Rachel—um, *murder* much, John? Of course at first, it was the trip to the Amalfi Coast, but when I heard the story . . . wowza. I called Paige immediately and gave her the scoop. I mean, my brothers are horrible people, sure, but I didn't know they were capable of murder, too. I'm an opportunist—and spoiled, I'll admit it. Still, they're so much worse than even I knew. But now I know everything, about both of them. Serena confessed to a little fling with Ted. So gross.

Obviously, I'm not here to see my brothers. But I must admit, I sort of bonded with Serena in Italy, and I'm actually loving the fact Paige wants me here with the family. And then there's my dad. It's time for a reconciliation between the two of us, I've decided. I mean, he's sick and old. He's not going to live forever, and I'm his only daughter. So I'm here to see Dad and screw over my brothers. Sounds fun to me. I know Paige really wants me here this weekend to help keep the brothers in line, but I know no one else does. And if you ask me to tell you the absolute truth, I'd admit that maybe—just maybe—I want to feel like part of the family again. So here I am.

"Would you like to check in?" a helpful staffer asks, and I smile. I mean, he may work valet, but he's super cute and could come in handy. You never know what's going to happen when the Kingsleys gather. Just ask anyone.

"Yes, thank you," I say with a wink.

He flushes and points to the registration desk. "Right over there, miss."

I walk away, strutting my stuff, knowing he's watching me. I'm wearing my favorite jeans, high heels, a tight white T-shirt, and a pair of earrings that I swiped from Serena. I hope the hooker doesn't ask for them back; I don't think she will. We've reached a sort of understanding, one could call it. All because of Paige.

Paige needed my help—go figure. It was a few months ago now, and I was back in Florida, doing what I do: playing golf and yachting with Uncle Walter, scheming about my next trip to some exotic destination, and dodging guys who wanted to date me. What can I say? I've got it going on . . . Well, I do if you like a certain type. Tattoos turn some guys off, and that's fine. Anyway, here I am, because Paige and I are buddies now. I never saw that coming.

"Can I have the name on the reservation, please?" the front desk person asks.

"Sibley Kingsley," I say.

Her eyes widen. "Oh, Miss Kingsley, welcome. We've been expecting you. Your suite is ready."

Thanks, Perfect Paige, I think. She really does want me here after all. "Great."

"I'll just need a credit card for incidentals," she says.

"Oh, put it on Paige's bill, please. She said to." I give her a smile. "Which way to my suite?"

"You can follow me." Handsome Guy has reappeared, and he's got a cart with my luggage piled on it. I don't believe in traveling light—not if you don't need to.

"I will follow you anywhere, cutie," I say, and we make our way through the gorgeous lobby. I think about Paige again. She called me out of the blue when I was on Uncle Walter's yacht. I had to sneak away to take the call, because he hates all the Kingsleys but me and would have done something rude.

"Sibley, look—I want a truce between us. I need your help," she said.

"Tell me more. What's in it for me?" I asked, of course, still shocked she'd even called me.

"Money. And travel. Look, I need to know what really happened to John's wife. I think there's more to the story," she said.

Interesting, I thought at the time. "I left before it happened, remember? I bet there is something fishy, though; there always is with my brothers. They are quite literally the worst."

"I know you left. But Serena was there. She must have seen what happened, must know what really took place that night," Paige said. "I need you to go talk to her, ask for her help."

"The hooker? That's funny. Last time I saw her, I stole all her jewelry. We're not what you'd call 'on good terms,'" I say. "Besides, you were still on board. Don't you know anything?"

"No, I was down below," Paige explained. "But look, I've hired a private detective to find Serena, to see if her help would even be a possibility. And I know it is. I haven't talked to her, but I happen to know for a fact that she's unhappy in her marriage. She needs money, too, and a good divorce attorney. I have enough for both of you, all of us. I just need to know what happened. I need leverage at the company. The president's position—well, it feels tenuous right now. And I bet

Serena wants to get back with Richard; they truly were in love before she messed it all up with the Italian guy. We can help her reunite with Richard."

"Well, that's a pretty ambitious plan, Perfect Paige," I said at the time. But then I figured, why not? A free trip to Italy, a chance to spy on the hooker and see if she really was miserable . . . "OK, I'm in."

The cute guy stops in front of an elevator. "You're on the bottom floor."

"Is that good?" I ask. I look at his name tag. Ty. I like it.

"It's the best. You'll see," Ty says. I follow him into the elevator, still remembering the call from Paige that brought me here today and put so much more into motion.

"OK, so you need leverage on Dad and John and Ted for covering up whatever happened to Rachel. Right?" I asked.

"Yes," Perfect Paige said. "And in return, you get money. Lots of it."

"I like money," I said.

"And, Sibley, I also need your help with Uncle Walter," she said. I don't know if she knew I was with him or not.

"What kind of help?" I asked, making sure he was still fishing on the back deck and out of earshot.

"I know he's considering another hostile takeover."

I don't know how she'd figured it out, but he had been talking about it. "I don't know if there's much I can do about that," I said. "He's as pigheaded as my dad."

"He called and threatened me. He wants me to reinstate him at the company, or else," Paige said.

That didn't sound good—or stoppable. Not really. "I can talk to him. Tell him he has a great life down here in Florida. Why would he want to ruin it to move back to commie California? I mean, y'all are about to fall into the ocean anyway, right? Everybody's moving out and coming here. You should see all the license plates. And the crime and people on the streets. I'll tell him all of that."

"Thanks. But it's going to take more than that to make him stand down, I bet. And just . . . well, give me a heads-up if you notice him getting serious about a run for the company," Paige asked. "I have to go. Please plan on flying to Italy as soon as possible. Serena isn't expecting you, but if the private detective is right, she'll welcome you—and the money—with open arms. She needs us."

Cute guy Ty looks quite excited by my room's layout. He pushes the door open. "Oceanfront suite. Isn't it grand?"

"Yes," I say. "Everything is grand."

As I step inside the suite—and it is gorgeous—I wonder if I'm worthy of everything Paige is expecting of me. I typically let people down. Big-time.

"So, Ty, do you know where the rooms are for the other members of my family?" I ask, checking out the space. I could move in here. Maybe I will.

"Well, I know your dad, Mr. Richard Kingsley, has the unit just above yours, overlooking the pool. You can see his balcony if you look right there."

"Looks like I could surprise him by popping up on his balcony, right?"

"You could, for sure," he says. "It's not too much of a climb. I've done it, but don't tell anybody." I watch as he carries all my luggage back to the bedroom. "Come see the view from in here."

He's totally into me. I join him in the huge bedroom and stand beside him, looking out to the sparkling Pacific Ocean.

"Amazing," I say. "It's like paradise here."

"It is special. Even though I live in Laguna Beach, every time I come to work, I feel like it's Laguna, just elevated. Everything sparkles more; even the people are prettier," he says with a smile.

"I agree. There are some cute people here," I say with a wink. "Well, I better get unpacked and go find the rest of my crazy family. Do you have a card? How can I get in touch with you?"

"How about my number?" Ty asks, and I hand him my phone.

"That works." After he inputs his info—his last name is Spencer—I remember to give him the tip I dug out of my purse. "Here you go. Thank you for all your help. I'll text you later."

"I'll look forward to it. Anything at all you need, I'm here."

I remind myself I'm here on business, not pleasure. Perfect Paige would not appreciate me flirting with the staff. But, I dare say, she wouldn't be surprised. Either way, she's going to be so happy when I give her the file Uncle Walter and I stole from John's computer. All John's illegal firings and other dirty deeds. This, plus what he did to Rachel, means she has everything she needs to keep him in line.

But I don't have anything on Ted—not more than Paige already knows about him and Serena. Disgusting. He's going to be the real problem, if you ask me. Maybe I can help take him down, too? We'll see.

19
PAIGE

I wake up—or rather, finally decide to get up—after a fitful night's sleep. There is so much tension in this family; it's enough to push anyone over the edge. I walk to the bathroom and look at my reflection. Dark circles, new wrinkles. This job really takes it out of you.

I remember late last night, after one, when Ted loudly banged on my door, begging to come inside. He was drunk—as usual, for this trip—and slurring his words, but his message was clear. He wants me back . . . in his bed, his life. He wants back in the house, too, of course. And more than anything, I know he wants my job.

"Paige, you're in too deep. This is all too much for you," Ted slurred through the door. "Let me take over for you. You can rest, spend time with the girls."

I warned him I'd call security if he didn't leave me alone.

"I miss us. I really do," he said.

I knew he was lying. It's all about the company, the president title. The only *us* there is anymore is me and my girls. He's so out of my heart that this pathetic late visit doesn't make me sad. Just angrier.

And then I remember I need to tell the girls not to come, despite how much they love the Twin Palms. There's too much going on, too much at stake. I text them in our group chat.

Girls. Please do not come to the Twin Palms today. The retreat isn't going as planned, although I will get it back on track today, I hope. Grandpa is being, well, difficult; your father and his brother are, too. I know you understand. You've seen it. So stay at school, enjoy your weekend, and I'll call you both on Sunday. Xo Mom

Better to keep them safely tucked away at their respective colleges than add to the drama going on here. I need a shower. Which helps but doesn't calm the anxiety coursing through my veins. I need to talk to Serena, find out how her time with Richard went, and Sibley should be checking in anytime now. I hope she didn't change her mind about coming here this weekend. It's funny to think that we're an alliance. A year ago, I never would have imagined trusting either of these women with anything. And now I'm trusting them with my future.

Emily texts first, of course: Mom, no problem. I have a date so I was going to cancel. Love you!

I can't help but smile, and I send her a kiss emoji. Hopefully, Amy takes the news with the same joy.

She texts next: I have a lot of reading to do for the test on Monday. No worries. Don't let them stress you out, Mom. xo

I text: Love you both. Don't worry about me. Oh, and stay safe. The winds are strong through Sunday night. Have a plan! Xo

Californians learn to plan for earthquakes and out-of-control wild-fires from an early age. This means having a go bag and supplies. I look out the window at the wildly blowing palm trees, the white caps on the ocean. If a fire started here, or in the hills above this resort, we'd all evac-uate to the beach, I suppose. I don't know if there would be time to get out any other way. In fact, Laguna Beach is a bad place to be trapped in a fire. I shudder at the memories again. There is one road out through the middle of town, through the canyon, and then Coast Highway. That's all.

Why am I thinking such dark thoughts? I need to get back in charge of this retreat. I need to quite literally show the Kingsley men who is boss. I dress quickly in dark jeans and a white cashmere sweater. I put on more makeup than usual to cover the dark circles, and I pinch my cheeks for color. I shrug at my reflection. As good as it's going to get.

Out in my suite's living room, I find the Nespresso and pop in a pod. There's a knock on my door.

"Coming," I say. I hope it's Justin. I want to ask him what he's been thinking about, to get us out of Ted's horrible land deal. I open the door. It's Sibley.

"Perfect Paige! It's me!" she says and flings her thin arms around my neck like we're long-lost besties. We're allies, sure, but this is over the top. "I'm so happy to see you!"

I can't help but smile. She's charming when she wants to be; she's just never wanted to be to me. "Thank you for being here. And for all of your help so far," I say. "Come in!"

"Your suite's just like mine," she observes. "But I'm on the ground floor. I can just walk out to the grass and the ocean. I can climb onto Dad's balcony, too, if I wanted."

"Don't do that!" I say, more sharply than I meant to. "I mean, we're going to make you a surprise, remember? We have a plan."

"Sure, sure. So where's the hooker? Did she hook up with Dad again last night?" Sibley asks as she makes herself a cup of coffee.

"I haven't spoken to her yet," I say. "But I don't think it went well, unfortunately. We need to give it some time. Richard is in a terrible mood. I'm not sure anyone can get through to him now."

"Want to go walk the beach? I need to have my toes in the sand at least once a day. It's grounding. Healing."

That might be just what I need. "Sure. Why not? The meeting doesn't start until noon, if it even starts. I'll go get some flip-flops."

As I head into the closet for shoes, I think about the last time I saw Sibley. She was leaving the yacht trip early, with a backpack filled with all of Serena's jewelry stolen from the safe in Richard and Serena's room. And Richard just let her leave. Crazy family. It really is.

I look over at the few pieces of jewelry I brought with me here to the resort. I take a moment and pop them into the safe, using the code Ted and I always used together: his birthday and mine. Old habits die hard. But that's all I have left of our relationship. After today, I will file for divorce. And no one is going to stop me.

Nobody will be surprised, either. Just because he has overstayed his welcome in the pool house, bent over backward to bring me embarrassing gifts each morning at the office, and otherwise pretended to suck up to me doesn't mean I have to fall for any of it. His behavior yesterday confirmed he's a small boy living in a man's body. He only cares about himself, his pleasure, his power.

If he cared about the girls and me, it was only to improve his outward perception, to make Richard believe he was the perfect family man. I believed that false picture for too long—way too long.

"What are you doing in there, Perfect Paige?" Sibley asks, appearing at the door to my closet.

"Nothing. Just thinking." Fortunately, she didn't catch me closing the safe. I do want her to believe I trust her.

And I very much need her to trust me.

A doorbell rings. I didn't know the suite had a doorbell, but I like it. It is the largest room at the resort; I made sure of it. Even though Richard believes his is.

I shrug at Sibley's questioning face, and we walk together toward the door.

It's Serena.

"Hey, hooker!" Sibley says, with genuine affection . . . I think.

"Hey, Sibs. How's your Italian coming along?" Serena asks, walking inside. I look down the hall to be sure no one saw her coming. I'd like this new alliance to remain just between us girls for now.

"I didn't work on it any more after I left you. But you left him anyway, so we can just speak good old English. That guy was something," Sibley says. "Paige, you would've hated his whole family, too."

"I never met him," I say. "But from what Serena has told me, he sounds like a nightmare. Coffee?"

"We were just about to go walk on the beach," Sibley tells Serena. "I need grounding. Want to come?"

And with that, Serena bursts into tears and drops onto the couch. "Richard hates me."

"Oh no," I say. This isn't good. "No, he loves you. He was in a terrible mood last night. You need to forget anything he said then. You were his favorite and last wife; there is power in that."

Sibley says, "Hooker, listen. My dad just needs to get over what you pulled. I mean, it was like something he'd pull, truth be told. Where's the kid?"

"With the nanny," Serena chokes out between sobs.

"Don't worry. Everything is going to work out," I console her. Although, ever since last night, I've been struggling to figure out how.

Things do seem to keep getting worse.

"We can't all three walk together on the beach," I say, trying to take control of the situation. "Remember, we are a shock-and-awe team. Sibley, you go, get grounded, and then come back here. Don't try to find Richard. We want the element of surprise."

"Yes, boss," she says. "OK, I'll text you when I'm finished."

"Good. Great. Serena, get yourself together," I command. "Richard hates weakness, remember?"

She nods and tries to smile. "Turns out, he also hates me."

"*Hate* is a strong word," I say, although I must admit, Richard does incite strong emotions in all of us.

"Maybe you should go take a walk. The walk along the water is beautiful. Birds-of-paradise, native succulents. It's gorgeous. Clear your mind. We'll figure everything out. Don't worry," I say. But I'm being a hypocrite. I'm beyond worried.

"OK, yes. I'll go for a walk," Serena agrees. "Should I plan on being at the meeting at noon?"

I wish things had gone better with her and Richard last night. I really do. "No, I don't think you should be there—not until you and Richard have an understanding," I say. "I'm sorry."

Serena stands up, checks her face in the mirror, and covers her eyes with large black sunglasses. "It's my fault. Don't be sorry. I created all this mess. Text me later and tell me what to do."

I give her a hug, and she's gone. She's wrong, though. She didn't create all the mess. There's enough blame to go around.

There's a knock on my door. "Delivery for Mrs. Kingsley!"

I glance through the peephole and note a young man in a Twin Palms uniform. I open the door and he smiles, handing me a sealed envelope on the resort's stationery.

I recognize the handwriting: all caps, written with a black Sharpie. Goose bumps cover my arms as I take the envelope from him.

"Who gave this to you? Did you see who dropped it at the front desk? How long ago was it delivered?" I ask him.

"I really don't know anything about it, ma'am. The front desk just sent me to deliver it," he says.

"Thank you," I say as dread overwhelms me. Whoever has been threatening me these past few months, they're here. I look past him, and there is no one else there. Not now—but they know my room number. They knew the treatment room I was in while waiting for my massage. They are getting closer each moment.

"Oh, and ma'am? Just so you know, the winds are blowing something fierce," he says. "They're unpredictable. So just be aware when you're out and about today."

"Yes, thank you. I know the winds. I'm from here." I close the door. Maybe it's the winds; maybe that's why I'm so on edge? Then I look down at the envelope in my hand and think about all that's happened so far on what was supposed to be a bonding retreat.

The winds are just adding to the edginess I feel. I rip open the envelope and, with shaking hands, pull out the letter inside.

20
JOHN

Krystle is still asleep in the bedroom. Must be nice to be so simple, so carefree, that sleep is assured every night.

On the other hand, I'd be bored if I was as dumb as Krystle, so I guess I should be grateful. I check my watch. Nothing with my father went as planned. I am meeting Ted at the restaurant on the second floor in ten minutes. Hopefully, no other prying family members will be around. We need to make a plan. And he better be sober by the time I see him. I will not abide any more drunken meeting-missing sloppiness. This is important for both our futures. Well, I suppose, mostly mine. Because once I secure the presidency—or maybe even the CEO position, depending on what happens with Dad and the board—then Ted can go away, mess around, get wasted, do whatever it is that makes him happy.

Because one thing is for sure, despite what I say in front of Paige: Ted should be fired over the land deal he talked us into pursuing. He lied about getting clearance from the city officials. He sold us a deal we could never develop, and he should have known it. Period. And when I'm in charge, he will be gone. Besides, he's a loser. The older he gets, the more his looks will fade, his charm will evaporate, and he'll become one of those guys you see sitting at the end of the bar, alone. A regular.

The thought makes me smile. Sure, he's been nice to me ever since Rachel died, and he *was* a witness. But he wasn't the only one. And all of them have participated in the cover-up, so none of them will come forward and expose what I've done. If they did—if *Ted* did, he'd expose his own complicity, too. I like that, that we're all in that particular boat together, so to speak.

My phone buzzes with a text. It's from Uncle Walter. Now that he stopped blackmailing me over the file I should have never kept on my computer—stupid, on my part—we have become cordial. We text. We chat. We may in fact have a few similar goals. No matter what, keep your enemies closer, as they say.

And he just landed in Orange County. I text back that I will see him after today's meeting. I've booked him a room at the Ranch, a lovely canyon hotel that has all the charm of old Laguna Beach oozing from its pores. It's conveniently located across the street from the Twin Palms. We'll see what will come of our first in-person meeting since I helped Dad drive him out of the company. Who knows.

Krystle appears in the living room, wrapped in a Twin Palms bathrobe and slippers. She looks quite at home here, with all this luxury. I thought she'd be overwhelmed, but she seems to adapt well.

"Hey, honey, how did you sleep?" I ask. "Coffee?"

"Please," she says and slippers her way over to me, then kisses me on the cheek. "I slept a lot better than I do even at home. Wow, were you restless? I didn't even notice. Did you sleep at all? What's on your mind? You can tell me. I'm your partner in crime."

Interesting choice of words. "No crime," I say, pushing the button to make her a cup of coffee. "Just business. It's always the business. It's up to me to save it, as usual." Why am I telling her anything? "Cream? Sugar?"

"No, thanks. Strong and rich, just like you," she says. "What do you have to save the company from?"

Sometimes it's almost like she is paying attention. I look at her, stare into her eyes. Nope. There's nothing there but simple curiosity, I decide.

"Oh, you know, honey, it's work stuff. Nothing you should worry about," I say. "So when you told me you did some shopping, you weren't kidding. Wow." Truth is, I've calmed down about that transgression. I mean, who can blame her? It's like I gave her a credit card with an unlimited balance the minute I gave her the key to our suite. Somebody with nothing could suddenly buy everything. We'll need to put limits on these sorts of things from now on.

Krystle places her mug on the coffee table and puts her hands on her hips. "I did do some shopping. It was necessary, I promise. I needed to be able to look like I belong here. Do you understand?"

"Sure I do," I say. I've never felt like I fit in anywhere—not my family, not in high school, not in Orange County's high society. I mean, money makes you rich, but it doesn't make you popular—not really. With that, my anger fires up again. Ted had it so easy all through life. It's my turn.

"I'm so glad you understand. Just wait until you see what I wear today, and tonight, and tomorrow. You'll be prouder than a peacock to have me on your arm," she says.

I smile at her. She is cute. And funny. Is she marriage material? I'm not so sure, but I'm not going to tell her that. Not yet, at least. I think Dad was right. First opinions matter, and he got a bad taste in his mouth with Krystle. Maybe with the new wardrobe, he'll take a second look. I know I have when I've bothered to notice.

"Well, look, I have a meeting now I have to get to. Order room service, if you'd like. And I'll check in with you later." I kiss the top of her head.

"'Check in.' Resort humor. I like it," she says. "I'm sad we can never seem to have a meal together."

"We will tonight. Paige rented that fancy restaurant out there, the one on the point. You bought something for tonight, I'm sure," I say.

"I have a couple of options."

I remind myself not to get mad. I force a smile. "Good. Well, OK. Talk to you later." I hurry out the door. I'll check the charges to my account so far. If she spent more than ten thousand, I'll force her to return some things. Otherwise, she can keep everything, as a gift for putting up with me and my moods. She doesn't know how lucky she is that I'm more in control these days. Poor Rachel.

I step outside only to be knocked back by a powerful gust of hot wind. I try again and lean forward to walk down the steps toward the pool. I always feel out of sorts when these winds hit. I put my hand on the top of my head to try to manage my hair, but I know it will be a mess by the time I get inside the main building. Every time the Santa Anas come, I want to move from Southern California. But here I am.

I pull on the door and finally make it inside the main building of the resort. These types of properties, common in SoCal, work spectacularly well when the weather is perfect—outdoor walkways, restaurants, pools, and sitting areas with sparkling views of the ocean. But add winds or some rain, and everything is miserable. Like me. I check my hair in the mirror, tamping it back into place. I remind myself it's only Ted, and he's seen the worst of me already.

This hotel is upside down. Lobby on the top, everything else spilling down the hill toward the ocean. The restaurant I'm looking for is on the second floor, one floor down from the lobby. I'm on the ground level now, the fourth floor, so I take the elevator up.

It's symbolic, this elevator ride. I am ascending to the top of the family tree. I am the oldest son. I will rise above and squash the rest of them on my way to the top.

21

TED

It's about time I had a say in this story. Sure, you might think you know all about me—from Paige, from John, from Serena, and, of course, from Richard. But no one really knows anyone, do they? I didn't get a word in on the *Splendid Seas* yacht trip; maybe you didn't notice. But this time, I insist.

You can really only know someone from what they choose to reveal. What they say, how they act, what they do when push comes to shove. Like John. I didn't think he was capable of murder, until he did that. I mean, he's a jerk and selfish, and he thinks he's God's gift to Kingsley Global Enterprises. But murder? He's an accountant, for heaven's sake.

I guess that proves my point. You don't really know anyone: not your best friend, not your lover, not your spouse. Not really. Not ever.

I walk through the lobby, searching the faces for my family members, but I don't spot anyone. Today, I'll suck it up and attend the "retreat." I'll pretend to care about bonding and team spirit. I'll remind myself that last night was the final straw. Paige wouldn't even open her suite door for me.

Is she afraid of me? No. Does she think she's too good for me now? Yes.

In actuality, I am the Kingsley, not her. This is my family, not hers. I hurry down the flight of stairs and arrive at the restaurant as John is stepping out of the elevator.

"Hey, bro," I say, just to annoy him.

"You sober now?" he asks, just to annoy me.

"Yep, all good. Dry and ready for corporate bonding," I say. The hostess smiles at me, proving I've still got it, despite what Paige thinks. "Table for four, please."

John looks startled. "No, two."

"Evan and Meredith might join us. I extended the invitation," I explain. "It would be good for all of us to get on the same page, right?"

"Yes, right," he agrees. "Table for four."

"Right this way, gentlemen," she says. "We're only seating inside because of the wind."

"Good idea," John says. "It's wild out there."

I haven't been outside yet today, so I shrug. "I always worry about those palm fronds snapping off and landing on my head. They weigh more than you think."

"Here's your table," she says. "I always worry about the fires. Those palm trees are like candles in the winds. One spark, and they're ablaze. Enjoy your breakfast."

"Well, she's freaking me out a little bit," John admits to me.

"Just ignore her. We have bigger things to worry about," I say. "Look, this stupid retreat gives us the perfect setting for our takeover bid. Agreed?"

"Yes, I agree. But the problem is, Richard doesn't," John says. A waiter appears and offers us coffee and water.

"It's time to stand up to Richard. He's dying, could be dead any moment; he's not capable of running Kingsley anymore. We are the only option," I say. I know John thinks he should be CEO, and he'd toss me the president title to keep me happy. But he's a murderer, so there's that.

"I'll be CEO, and you can be president," he offers.

Shocking. *Not.*

"I don't know, John. With your temper, that could be dangerous." I smile, suddenly quite interested in the menu.

"Knock it off, Teddy. There's no way you can use that against me. You'd be complicit in the cover-up. Nice try," he says. "The thing is, I'm the older brother. It makes sense for me to be the CEO. I've been with the company the longest; I know where all the bodies are buried. All of them. Including yours."

"Ah, our familiar standoff. The one that keeps us from ever truly joining forces. Right, John?" I wave to the waiter. I'm starving. And hungover. "That's why Meredith and Evan need to weigh in. We need their votes, for whatever pecking order we propose."

"True," John says as the waiter appears. "I'll have the eggs Benedict."

"Avocado toast," I say. "With a side of potatoes." I want to order a Bloody Mary, just to freak John out, but I don't. I need to appear to be all business today, despite the fact I'd rather just get the heck out of here.

I think back to Richard's furious words last night. I don't know if he meant he'd never promote me to president—or higher—at Kingsley, but it sure felt that way. I've never seen him so angry at me before. And I've never been so angry at him. Ever. This feeling inside me is new. I've always counted on my charm and looks to sway Dad back in my direction. The Golden Boy can do no wrong, right? I may have exhausted that particular angle, it seems. But I'm not finished fighting for what's mine. Kingsley Global Enterprises is my birthright. I don't really care about Richard—not anymore. There are other ways to get what I want, and I will use them.

It's unfortunate that I went to see Paige, like an idiot. I need to face the fact she's never going to take me back and just take everything I can from her. And I will. I've lost all good feelings for her. The way she looks at me is unacceptable. I will destroy her, with pleasure.

"There they are," John says, interrupting my revenge fantasies.

"Meredith, Evan, join us. We just ordered, but we can get the waiter back over here," I say, the consummate host.

Meredith always dresses like she's in a 1950s *Mad Men*–type work situation, which, obviously, she's not. She's retired. But she's always wearing a matching sport coat and skirt or dress, pearls. That vibe. Dad loves it. Loves having such a loyal, unsexy woman to ask for advice. Evan, on the other hand, is slick, polished, and pompous. He and I don't quite vibe, but I'm going to try.

"Thanks for joining us," I say. "We really appreciate your board service and know you both want what's best for Kingsley Global Enterprises."

"We do," Meredith says.

"And with Dad's failing health," John says.

"He looked horrible yesterday. And he was out of control," Evan says. "We can't have that in a leader."

"And Paige is in over her head," I tell them. "Trust me, I know. We've been married forever. I'd like to think she could handle things, but she can't. We're hemorrhaging money; the employees all think she's a joke; and, let's face it, she's flirting—maybe more—with her assistant. That's against the rules."

"I didn't know about that." Meredith sips her coffee.

"Just watch her and Justin," I say. I have been. It's disgusting but obvious. The way he looks at her is the same way she used to look at me. With love, with respect. But now it's the opposite. Again, another reason to loathe her. Another reason to take her down.

"So it's time for a change. We are asking for your support," John says. "I will take over as the new CEO, and Ted will become president."

"Well, or vice versa—whatever you guys think," I say.

"John seems most prepared to lead Kingsley, in my opinion," Evan says.

Meredith looks at me and then John. "Ted has his father's charisma," she says. "I worry about John having only Richard's temper."

"I'll keep it under control," John promises.

"But can you?" I ask with a shrug. Perhaps he'll give us a little display right now.

His face flushes, but he doesn't explode. "Yes, I'm quite capable of being calm, Ted. And honest. And good with our family's money. Can you say the same?"

"Yes, sure." You can say anything, can't you?

Evan clears his throat and shakes his head, emitting what appears to be deep sadness. "What about that land deal? It's a mess. And you brought it to the company, essentially backed it with your word, said it would change the future trajectory of the company."

Geesh, Evan. It's one little deal. I'll admit, I screwed up by not getting the local government's buy-in to our plans, but so what. Easy mistake. And besides, I like that Paige has to take the blame. I like it a lot. "It's only one deal in the lifetime of Kingsley Global Enterprises. We'll get past it; we always do. I'm already sourcing a partner to take half the land. We'll be fine," I say. That's not true, but it makes the three of them nod in surprise.

"So what do you two think?" John asks.

Our food arrives, and everyone stops talking until the servers depart.

"Truly, I think a nonfamily member might be the best idea," Meredith says. "Just to stabilize things. Maybe it should be me?"

And just like that, my appetite is ruined. She doesn't want to do this right now, does she? No way. I push my avocado toast away and stare at her.

"You're retired. Stay that way," I tell her.

"We need family, not outsiders. We proved that with Paige," John says. He means *not women*, but he can't say that out loud—not in this day and age. It's a shame, really.

"Ted's wife is hardly an outsider," Meredith says. "They have children, Kingsley heirs, together."

"She had no business being put in as president," Evan says. "I told Richard as much. He wouldn't listen. I don't know if he'll listen now."

He won't. He never does. Maybe it's impossible for him. Who knows.

"That's why we need to decide—the four of us—the plan for the future and make it so," John says. "I'm ready to take the reins. With your help, Ted."

I roll my eyes. He's so annoyingly pompous, and he won't even consider things from my perspective. I'm the natural-born leader; he was born to hide behind a desk in a dark corner somewhere. I wonder how Meredith thinks she could possibly be the one to run Kingsley. Does she have a thing with Dad? No, she's not his type. Serena is—*was*. What a stupid mistake that was. *Shoot.*

Come to think of it, it's Richard's fault he saw what he did, Serena and me just messing around. Nothing serious. The old man shouldn't be spying on his own family. It's not right. Sort of creepy. I wonder if he has cameras set up here, at the resort? No, he couldn't. I swallow. I realize the table has grown silent, all of us lost in our own thoughts.

Unfortunately, it turns out at least three of the four of us here at the table want the same thing. And only one of us can have it: me.

OC SCOOP

Hey, Kingsley fans. We knew one of our very own would make it to the Twin Palms to give us a glimpse of the lifestyles of the rich and famous. Thank you to Julia for sharing these great photos of the one and only Richard Kingsley holding court on the balcony of his fabulous suite. We hear his suite has four rooms, a huge balcony, and amazing views of the Pacific Ocean. A little birdie told us that Richard was flirting a bit with our tipster, but she denies it, saying only that he was a perfect gentleman. Knowing Richard Kingsley as we do, that would be a first. The Kingsleys are on retreat at the Twin Palms all weekend. Keep spying. Oh, and stay safe out there. The devil winds are brutal.

22

SIBLEY

This is not a good idea, I realize as soon as I start down the ramp to the beach. Sand is being blown around like crazy. A big gust pummels me with it; it's in my eyes, my mouth. I turn around and run back up the ramp.

So much for my grounding beach walk. I guess I'll stick to the path. As I walk, I think about my dad. I realized over these last few months that I miss my dad and want a relationship with him again. I'll do better; I'll make him proud. I want him to see me as his favorite daughter. I'm his only chance, after all. And now I'm here, but so is the hooker also trying to get his attention again. Why is it never easy? I guess there is room for both of us in his life—at least, Paige assured me that was the case. I hope she's right.

Oh, and there's Serena, speak of the devil. I decided during my trip to Italy that I like her, but I also know we're total opposites. She likes dressing up and makeup and having a man take care of her. I like to be in charge and free to change my mind, to get into trouble. Maybe I'll let go of the trouble part, just to make Dad happy.

Serena is pushing a stroller. I always forget she's a mom now, too. That's a lot to deal with, even if you have a full-time nanny, like she does, trailing along behind you. I met the little person in Italy. She's adorable but so much work. I don't think I'll ever have kids. They are exhausting when they're little, and then they grow up to hate you. Hate *is a strong word.* I hear Paige's voice in my ear. I don't hate Richard—not at all. I don't. I just want him to pay attention to me. And keep the money flowing.

And, well, sometimes I just want a dad in my life. I want his love. I dream about that picture-perfect father-daughter relationship. I do. But he could never be that, even though I know he tried. Uncle Walter says everything I did to get in trouble—stealing things, breaking and entering, hanging out with the wrong crowd, that kinda stuff—was all an attempt to get Richard's attention. Maybe it was. It didn't work. But I'm here this weekend. And I'm going to fix the love between us. I'm going to make him love me, darn it.

I duck behind a huge, thorny succulent and sit on a wooden bench, hoping Serena and the nanny stroll past me. Paige told us to act like we're not together—still not friends—and for once, I'm listening to instructions. That's because I've decided I really do like Paige. And I want her to like me, too, and let me see her girls, reconnect with them. Time will tell. Thankfully, the hooker passes by without looking my way.

I'm walking back toward the resort when I decide maybe I'll just surprise Dad before the meeting. I'm sure he's in his suite, drinking coffee, chilling before gearing up to yell at people all day.

Dad's balcony overlooks the pool, so I use my key card to get inside the gates protecting the pool area. It's a gorgeous mosaic-tiled pool that looks great in social media posts, usually. But right now, it's too windy for umbrellas, and there are very few people sitting in the lounge chairs, being clobbered by wind-driven debris. Not exactly the ultimate resort experience they were expecting. I make my way to the far side of the pool. Nobody seems to notice me, until *bam*—there he is.

"Hey, Ms. Kingsley! You getting all settled in?" Ty asks with a big smile. I thought he worked as a bellman. Now he's at the pool?

"Great. Yes, I'm fine, but I may need you for something later, so don't be a stranger," I say. I need him to go away so I can surprise my dad via the balcony.

"You're thinking about climbing up to your dad's suite, aren't you?" He smiles.

"No," I say, crossing my arms in front of my chest. Dead giveaway that I was thinking just that. "Maybe."

"I can show you a shortcut so you don't need to bother scaling the fence," he says. "Follow me."

"OK, fine, you can show me. But I'm going alone."

He leads me back across the pool deck and out the gate. We walk up a path, and sure enough, my dad's balcony is a foot away from where we stand.

"Thanks for helping me," I say as he walks away. He really is cute. But I'm here for business, not anything else. Well . . . *maybe* not anything else.

I look around to be sure no one is watching me, step into the flower garden, and hoist myself up onto Dad's balcony. The next minute, I'm standing on his very large deck. I try peeking in the first set of sliding doors, but the curtains are drawn. The next set over, same problem. I pull on the handles, but everything is locked.

The curtains are open on the final set of sliders, and I can finally see into the suite. It's impressive. Same coastal color scheme as mine, just double the size. The doors are locked again, and it looks like Dad has already left for the day. Until . . . wait.

There's something in the corner of the room. I can't tell what it is. Oh, it's a room service cart. I wonder if Dad ate alone last night, despite the elaborate dinner Serena had planned. Maybe that's why she was so upset this morning?

I walk back down the balcony the way I came, hop over the railing, and land on the pathway leading to the main building. I'll see Dad at the meeting, I guess. I'm disappointed. I wanted to have some alone time with the grumpy old guy before everyone else gets their piece of him.

I should have come on Friday, I hear him say to me. I should have told him I was coming for sure, I hear him say to me. And I should never have partnered with his brother. I think that's the one thing he won't forgive me for. Not ever.

But I'll keep trying until his dying day. Fathers and daughters—it's complicated. I stop walking, suddenly realizing something is wrong.

Why were Dad's curtains still pulled tight in his bedroom? My dad is an early riser; he loves sunlight and fresh air. A chill sweeps down my spine despite the hot wind blasting me.

I run for help.

23
KRYSTLE

Well, that little encounter with John went much better than I expected. And I get to keep all the yummy clothes I bought. That's just about the best news ever.

My phone rings, and I know who it is without looking.

"Hey, Mom," I say.

"You sound good. Everything going well?" she asks.

"So well. He just bought me a whole new wardrobe. Thousands of dollars of new clothes. Can you believe it?" She'll be jealous when I show her all the loot, and she'll try to swipe something, knowing her. I'll have to keep my eyes on everything.

"And did he propose?" she asks. This is the daily question. Annoying.

"You know we haven't been dating that long," I say, as usual. "Mom, I'm following the plan and it's working. You and I both know this is going to take some time. I mean, I can't believe how fast he fell for me after meeting at that church. Love at first sight."

It's true. Mom and I thought it would take several run-ins, many more accidental meetings, before John even noticed me. But he noticed right away, and now here I am at this glorious resort. My heart fills with excitement, until I remember my mom is still on the phone, and then I think of my brother, Joey, and my heart sinks again. I know getting a piece of the Kingsley fortune won't bring him back, but Mom is convinced it will be healing for our family—or rather, what's left of it: Mom and me. I'm not sure she's into healing, though. It's more about revenge. And money. Everything is always about money if you don't have any.

"Look, you know the woman controls the pace of the relationship. He's older, not attractive, and lonely. All ingredients for a swift proposal," she says. As usual. "According to the OC Scoop, you all are staying in one of the resort's fabulous suites, so make him propose in your suite. Those photos will be great for social media and, well, just do it."

She's obsessed with that tabloid and everything Kingsley. It's exhausting sometimes.

"I'm working on it, Mom. You need to be patient." I walk back into the bedroom and into the walk-in closet. Gorgeousness.

"I've been waiting years for this, Krystle. Don't tell me to be patient," she says. I know she's talking about her waiting on justice for Joey, not how long she's waited for me to snag a Kingsley. As I said, I was fast. My mom's singular goal in life is to be paid what she thinks she is owed for my brother's wrongful death on a jobsite, despite the fact a jury ruled it an accident and she lost, walking away empty-handed. Her big payday, as she'll remind me daily, depends on my successful marriage to a billionaire.

"I know, I know. I'm trying. For you, for Joey's memory. I'll give John another push this evening. I have a special new gown that will get his attention for sure," I say. I touch the red silk dress I'll be wearing this evening for dinner at the Point. It's exquisite.

"Make something up—like you've always dreamed of getting engaged on the beach at the Twin Palms or something," Mom says.

She's exhausting; she really is. I know she's been through a lot, what with my dad's sudden death following so closely after Joey's and all, but sometimes her focus on me is a little more than I can handle. More than any one kid should have to bear. But I do because I love her. And she deserves to be happy and taken care of after everything that happened five years ago. I'm her only hope now. At least, that's what she always tells me.

"OK, Mom. I'll try to get a ring on it by the end of the weekend. Maybe I should appeal to his Christianity. Make-me-an-honest-woman type of thing?" I suggest, thinking out loud. He does have a strong faith, which he learned from his mother and obviously not his father. To be clear, I am not religious, although he thinks I am.

"Yes, I like that. No-sex-before-marriage kind of thing would work," Mom says. "This is why you're my favorite daughter."

"Um, too late for that—the sex part," I say. "And I'm your *only* daughter."

"Oh, shoot. OK, honey. Well, maybe try this. Maybe you're upset that you had sex and now, because of your religion, you can't do it again unless you know he's committed. For life."

"I could try that angle," I say. "Sure, why not."

"Just don't make him mad," Mom says. "I hear he has a wicked temper. I hear he may have had something to do with his former wife's death."

"No, he's harmless," I say.

"It's just what I hear. You know I keep close tabs on the Kingsleys, for good reason."

Boy, do I know. It's her obsession. It's almost like she's a Kingsley stalker, albeit from afar. Well, that was until she got me roped into it all.

"Look, Mom, I really need to go. John's meeting starts at noon, and I'd like a chance to plant the seed of holy matrimony before he goes behind locked doors with his ridiculous family," I tell her.

"Good. And good luck, Krystle. I'm counting on you. Rent is due at the end of the month, and I'm flat broke." She hangs up.

We're always broke. Ever since Dad died. Without life insurance. And Mom won't get a job; she says it's beneath her station. It's all up to me.

The wind rattles the glass of the sliding doors, it's blowing so strong out there. The palm trees look like those inflatable balloon men car dealers use to lure you in. Twisting, bending, tops all messed up and crazy. I don't want to go outside, but I must if I want to find John. And I do.

I dress in one of my new California-cool outfits—this time, silky-soft sweatpants in a bright blue, a white T-shirt that fits just right, and my everyone-must-have tennis shoes. I look so cute, cool, and casually elegant I can barely stand it. A little blush and some lip gloss, and I'm out the door.

It's horrendous outside. Hot, dusty air blows at me as if I'm standing in front of a giant hair dryer. And speaking of *dry*, my hands feel like sandpaper. I decide to swing by the spa and get some expensive hand cream. As I hurry down the path, a woman jogs past me with huge bright-blue eyes, long dark hair, and a lot of tattoos. She looks familiar. Was that a Kingsley running past me? Have I missed something here?

I stop and watch the young woman run into one of the hotel wings, and then I realize who she is: John's sister, Sibley. I wonder if John knows she's here. I know there is no love lost between them. Maybe I can find him, warn him, and promise I'll always be on his side, no matter what. He's going to need me, it turns out. From what little he's told me about his sister, she seems to be one step ahead of her brothers, even though they won't admit it.

I pop into the spa, and my favorite saleswomen greet me with overwhelming joy.

"You're back! More clothes?" one asks. "Love how the new outfit looks. Very chic."

"Thank you, doll," I say. "No more clothes needed—right now, at least. Lotion?"

"Oh my gosh, yes. It's so dry out there I feel like I could turn to dust right on the spot," she says. "This is what you need. Fabulous. The best."

I agree and sign for my two-hundred-and-fifty-dollar tube of lotion and head back out into the windstorm to warn John. I hope I'm the first to tell him. He'll see value in me for this; I know he will. He told me his former wife, Rachel, always had his back, always sided with him against his family. I need to prove to him I'm the same person, just wrapped in a prettier package. I want him to see me as his teammate, not the gold digger my mom has forced me to be. Sure, it's tough trying to please two very different people. But the fact is, I need to be the next wife for a number of reasons.

I smooth my new lotion onto my hands, and it melts into my skin in an instant. Amazing. My lotion at home doesn't do that. Despite the fact that this is my mom's plan, I'm a happy player. I want this life, and if that means marrying a man who might not be my type, so be it. He'll grow on me. I already find the trappings of his life very lovable.

His money makes him look so cute—if you know what I mean— and it's helping me to look amazing, too. It's really a win-win. This isn't one of my usual relationships, where it's all about sex and passion and all that. And I'm glad. What did any of that ever get me? Not a closet full of beautiful clothes and lotion that makes my hands feel like a baby's bottom, I can tell you that much. Love comes in many different shapes and sizes.

This one will be the perfect fit if I can stick the landing.

24

PAIGE

I drop the threatening letter on the floor and cover my ears with my hands. The wind is making me feel crazy. It howls, and the building moans.

I look down at the letter. I suppose I always knew it would come down to a meeting—me and this anonymous person who is convinced there was more to Rachel's death, that there has been a cover-up. And that I'm leading the cover-up. The person is wrong about that, of course. Until I began receiving these anonymous threats, I believed the Kingsley men about what had really happened that night on the yacht. I was so naive. I trusted Richard back then, like a fool.

Trusting any of them jeopardizes my role as president; that much is obvious. That's why I had to get to the truth about what happened on the yacht, to stay ahead. It's complicated, all of this. Sure, I loathe people who hang on to power and wield it like a hammer, ignorant of anyone else's needs and feelings. I'm proving you can be a leader who cares, and I know the employees feel it even if the board and leadership team don't, and I don't care. Yes, I enjoy being president, but it's a different type of power than Ted's or John's or Richard's power. Theirs is selfish, self-serving, ego-driven.

I look at my face in the mirror. OK, sure, I enjoy the acclaim I've received. I like knowing I can take care of myself and my girls and that I have the respect of the community. But I'd never treat people the way the Kingsley men do, and that's why I need to keep the president title. I'm a buffer between them and the employees, them and the community. I think about the humiliating meeting yesterday, when Richard announced his intention to replace me. I know what he is like—who he is—but still, it hurt my heart. I guess I'm human.

I take a deep breath. I won't let him win. Not this time. I will stay one step ahead of them all, despite their attempts to shame me into submission. They will not force me out. The company needs me—and I need the company, it turns out. Besides, I have all the dirt on them I need to solidify my position at this company. And I have a plan. I'm not going to feel threatened by anyone. Not anymore. I remember the letter in my hand and read it again.

As you know, I am here, at the hotel. I am watching you every minute. I demand a meeting, face to face. Come alone. Text this number and tell me when and where. Do it today.

A knock on the door startles me. I check the peephole. It's Justin, thank goodness.

"Hey, come on in," I say, relieved beyond measure at seeing his smiling face. I'm going to need his help today, on a couple of different matters.

"What's that?" he asks, pointing to the letter.

"Oh, it's from the person who has been threatening me." I walk into the living room.

"What? You never told me about this," he says. "What the heck? Should we call the police?"

"No, we shouldn't. It's about John's wife, Rachel," I tell him. "They are convinced she was murdered."

"Wow. Could that be true?" Justin asks, eyes wide with surprise.

"It could be," I say, breaking eye contact.

"Oh my God. How many letters like this have you received?"

"This is the second one since we arrived. The fact is, I wasn't there when it happened, but I know now that John pushed her overboard in a fit of rage. Richard and everyone covered it up." A chill sweeps over me. "I'm going to meet this person today, after the meeting. We'll talk in the lobby. Plenty of people around."

"Including me," he says. "I'm going to be right there with you. I'm not letting anything happen to you."

"Thanks," I say, blushing.

There's a loud bang on the door. And then another.

"Wait here," Justin says, hurrying to the door. He checks the peep-hole. "It's Sibley."

He opens the door, and Sibley rushes in. "Paige, something's wrong with Dad!"

"What? What's wrong?" I ask, taking each of her hands in mine. "Calm down. Breathe."

"I went to his room to say hi, to surprise him. But the curtains are all pulled except for in the main room. There's a room service cart—but I don't know, something's not right; I can sense it. Something's off," she says. "I should have run inside the hotel, knocked on his door. But I was too afraid."

"Do you want me to go to his room? Check on him?" Justin asks. "I'm sure everything is OK."

"Yes, could you?" Sibley says, and I nod in agreement. "I happen to know that you can hop onto his balcony from the pathway by his room."

"Sibley, no," I say. But I do find that interesting.

"There's a staff guy named Ty who would give us the key to his room, if you need it," she says.

"It's OK," Justin says. "You guys stay here. I'll be right back."

I look at Sibley and smile. "It's going to be fine. Richard is inde-structible." *Unfortunately.*

"You're right. I'm sure I'm overreacting. This wind is messing with me. I wish I could just stay inside and hibernate," she says. "Maybe I should go back to Florida?"

"No, I need you here. We'll be inside a meeting room this afternoon," I remind her. "No wind."

"Just a bunch of hot air," she says with a smile. "Do you really need me here, Perfect Paige?"

"I do. I told you that. I'd like you to stay—maybe take a job with the company?" I offer. "I could use some support."

"My brothers are terrible," Sibley says.

"They are," I agree. And her dad isn't the greatest, either, to put it mildly.

"I just kinda want to be taken seriously, you know? By my dad," she admits. "And you." Her voice is quiet, like a small child's. That's when I remember how hard she had it growing up. Everything that money could buy was given to her, but there was no one around to love her.

"He will, Sibs. I'll help position you. Promise," I say. With or without her dad, it's time for me to help her get a real job—a real life—started. No more stealing, or cheating, or scheming.

"Thanks," she says with a sad smile. "It would be nice to be respected."

My phone rings. It's Justin. I answer.

"We have a problem. A big one," he tells me.

I walk away from Sibley and into the bedroom. "What is it?"

"Richard's dead. His lips and skin are blue, like he was choking, and he's been stabbed near the throat," he says. "Maybe he was trying to save himself, or maybe someone did it? I don't know, and I don't know what to do."

Justin's words echo in my head. *Richard's dead.* Oh my gosh. I try to take hold of my whirling thoughts, try to focus on what Justin is saying. But he is silent on the other end of the line, needing direction. I push through the shock. I'm the president. I need time to figure out what to do. And I need to solidify my position as president before his death is announced. What would his murder mean to the company?

"We can't let anyone into the room," I say. "You haven't touched anything, have you?"

"No . . . Well, just the sliding door. It was unlocked, and I think that's it," he says. "I'll cover him with a sheet or something."

"Yes, great," I say. "I bet Ted or John did this."

"Seriously?"

"Yes. Quite. John's killed before—and, well, Ted is capable of everything evil," I explain. "Even patricide."

"OK, I covered the body with a blanket. The Do Not Disturb sign is on the front door. I'm coming back over to your room," he says. "We will eventually need to tell someone. My dad has a guy. I'm going to call him."

"What do you mean?" I don't want anyone else involved. I need a plan.

"He's a fixer. I'll explain," he says. "I trust him. He knows this kind of stuff."

"Dead-body stuff?" I whisper. Who knows dead-body stuff? I tell myself to take a deep breath and calm down. I'm president. I'm in control.

"Did you ever watch the TV show *Ray Donovan?*" he asks.

"No," I say, barely listening to his words. "I've got to go. Sibley's here."

"Don't worry, OK? I've got this handled. Don't tell anyone what has happened." He hangs up.

I look out into the living room of the suite. Sibley is watching me.

"What is it?" she asks. "What's wrong?"

I wonder if I can trust her to keep this quiet for now and realize I don't have a choice. I come out of the bedroom and sit down beside Sibley. I reach for her hand. "I need to tell you something. You're right: something was wrong with Richard. I'm afraid he's dead," I tell her.

"Oh my gosh, no. That can't be!" she cries. "I didn't get to see him."

"I know, and I'm sorry about that." I wrap her in a hug. Despite her grief and shock, I need her on my side. I need time. "Look, I need your help. We must keep this quiet for now. The boys cannot find out, the media can't find out, and neither can the board. I'm in the process of sorting things out to protect the company and my position. Do you understand?"

She looks at me with tears in her eyes—and something else. Resolve.

"My brothers will use his death to try to take over, to kick you out of the company," she says. "They're bastards."

"They are," I agree.

"I won't tell anyone what's happened," she says. "Did he die peacefully? In his sleep, I hope? I read that's what happens when you have heart failure, if you're lucky."

Well, not exactly like that.

"Yes, I think so," I say. Sometimes a little white lie is an act of kindness.

25

JOHN

We've finished our breakfast meeting, and I'm the only one still at the table. I need to think. It seems Meredith now believes she should be president or CEO. Unacceptable, really. But I'll outmaneuver her, just like I will Paige and Ted. It's all part of the game—a game I plan to win.

"John! Yoo-hoo!" Krystle calls out, appearing behind me. "I'm so happy to catch you before the meeting! Can I join you?"

I really want to tell her no, to tell her to go away, go back home, whatever. I think she may be a big mistake. I remind myself I didn't have any doubts about her until Richard got into my head. I should not let him ruin this relationship, too. It's his fault Rachel is no longer by my side. It is.

"Sure, have a seat," I say, standing and then pulling a chair out for her. "Want something to eat?"

"Sure," she says. She looks happy about my warm reception. I should try to be nicer.

"Nice outfit," I say, although I would never be caught dead wearing sweatpants to a restaurant at a five-star hotel—but that's me being old-fashioned, I'm sure. Krystle bought it all here at the resort, so it must be appropriate.

"Thanks. I really appreciate you letting me get a few things. I know it's only clothes, but they help me feel like I belong here."

She's sweet. "You *do* belong here. Don't let anybody tell you otherwise."

"With my new outfits, and you on my arm, nobody would dare," she coos.

"I'm glad you're happy," I tell her. I'm distracted, of course, but I'm trying to focus on my date. I did ask her here, after all.

"You know what, John? You're so wonderful, and we're perfect together." She places her hand over mine on the table. "I'd love to take us to the next step. Actually, I'm going to *need* to take it to the next step. I'm wrestling a bit, with sex out of wedlock being a sin and all."

Oh, shit. Really? "It's not a sin. I know it," I say. I think of my devout mother and hear her voice in my head: *It is a sin. Respect your girlfriend, and yourself.* Crap.

"Jesus doesn't agree," Krystle says.

"I know. You're right," I say, dropping my head. I feel my cheeks flush. The deep shame religion and my mother can make me feel is unlike any other.

"There's an easy remedy." She pulls her hand away from mine and holds it up, pointing to her ring finger. "They have some beautiful selections at the jewelry store on the property, in case you're wondering."

"So you're telling me no more fooling around unless I put a ring on it?" I ask. I must admit, I'm amused by this conversation.

"Yes, I'm afraid I am. My conscience is just getting the best of me."

Yes, the conscience can be a problem, for sure; I know all about that. So why not give her a ring? I can always take it back. And I'm not getting any sex unless I put a ring on it, and I'm a little busy trying to take over the company at the moment. Why not make her happy so she'll make *me* happy?

"Sure, OK. Why don't you pick something out while I'm stuck in the meeting. Don't go too crazy, OK? I'll properly propose before dinner. Sound good?"

Krystle looks like she just went into shock. Her eyes are wide and shiny, and her mouth is half-open. "You're serious?"

"Sure am," I say. I take a deep breath and step into my power. I can do whatever I want, whenever I want. I'm John Kingsley, the oldest sibling. A younger woman wants me and loves me, and I love her. And she's a Christian, like me, so we're above all these heathens I see running around here—including my family. I'm going to take charge of them, too.

"Wow, wow, wow. Wait until I tell my momma," she says with a grin. "You really need to meet her. Oh, and now you will. Oh! And by the way, I have a scoop for you. Remember how you said Rachel always protected you? I will, too."

I doubt that. "What is it?"

"I saw your sister, Sibley. She's here at the Twin Palms."

"No way. Dad wouldn't invite her, not after what happened on the yacht," I say.

"It's Paige's meeting. Maybe she invited her," she says. "I mean, it seems like she's the one who invited Serena, too. Your dad didn't know she was coming, did he? Did you?"

"No, he looked really shocked when she appeared." Why would Paige want Sibley here? They don't even like each other, to put it mildly. What is Paige up to? "You're sure it was my wayward sister? You've never met the creature."

"I've seen her photo, though, in the tabloids and stuff," she says. "I'm sure. She ran right past me, outside the spa."

"You shouldn't read the tabloids," I admonish. "But in this case, I'm glad you did."

"What are you going to do about Sibley? And, well . . . all the company stuff?" she asks.

"I've got it all under control. Want to order?"

She closes the menu. "I'm literally too excited to eat. That never happens to me. Do you mind if I go on over to the jewelry store? I can't think of anything else." Her blue eyes flash with excitement. "I can barely sit still." She stands up.

That's cute. She's cute. And simple. And she'll be by my side, and I need someone by my side. It softens me, makes me feel human.

"Sure. Go find something pretty, sweetie," I tell her.

"Thank you, honey," she says. "Um, say . . . what's my budget?"

I'm impressed she asked in advance this time. I don't know what engagement rings cost these days—and at a place like this—but they can't be cheap. Plus, it's a reflection of how rich I am; her ring will be a sign to everyone else.

"Think you can keep it under $500,000?" I ask.

She has that look again, the deer-in-headlights look. She sways a little in my direction.

"Are you OK, sweetie?" I ask, standing up and wrapping an arm around her waist. I hope she doesn't faint.

"This is the best day of my life," she says finally.

Hopefully, I'll be able to say the same after the board meeting.

26
TED

By now, you may have realized I'm not the Golden Boy I seem to be. I'm not sure I ever really was. I got away with a lot because of my looks, because of my last name. It started early, when my mom, Anne-Marie, died during labor with me. She was the wife Richard loved the best, and so I became the motherless son he loved the best.

By middle school, I knew I was in charge—a leader. As the saying goes, guys wanted to be me, and girls wanted to be with me. I loved the attention. By high school, I loved the freedom. You can get away with anything, it seems, when you're Mr. Popular. Nobody expected anything but the best choices, and nobody reported my bad ones. Not even the girls.

By college, I'd calmed down a bit. I was relatively tame compared to the rest of the pledges in my fraternity. But I digress.

Today I find myself in a sticky situation, but I know what I must do. Clearly, the only solution is to expose John's dirty deeds, shame him in front of the board . . . oh, and bed Meredith. Yes, that's what I said. I need an ally; she needs a lay. I can tell. I'm good at this sort of thing.

I knock on her room door.

"Ted, what's up?" Meredith asks, surprised to see me. She's wearing a conservative pink dress. Her suit coat has been tossed on a chair behind her.

"May I come in?" I smile. A wolf in sheep's clothing, you might say. I'm talking about me, not her. I am my father's son.

"Sure, Teddy, anytime," she says, eyes twinkling. "Do you need a favor? A fix? What's up?"

"Actually, I need you," I say. I touch her shoulder. Our eyes lock.

"Me?" she says, but her smile softens.

"Yes." I lean in for the kiss, my hand behind her neck, my other finding her waist, pulling her in tight. I hear her moan. I move us through the room—smaller than mine, not a suite—and push her onto the bed, breaking our kiss.

She looks dazed but happy.

"We really shouldn't," she says as I lie down beside her.

"Why not?" I ask, touching the side of her face, then kissing her neck. It's not as wrinkled as I would have thought. She's taken care of herself. "You're really pretty, you know that?"

"For an old woman," she says. "Thank you; I'll take the compliment. It's been a long time since a man tried to seduce me."

"How does it feel?" I make a move to unbutton the top of her dress.

She stops me, hand covering mine. Uh-oh. I really don't have much time here. I check my watch. The meeting starts in forty-five minutes.

"The zipper is in back," she says with a grin. She rolls to her side. "And to answer your question: so far, it feels great. I hope you don't let me down."

I laugh. A challenge. I appreciate a challenge. It occurs to me that Paige and I didn't have any fun in bed, not after the girls arrived. That's why I found comfort and fun elsewhere. She turned into a mom, not a lover. It's really her fault. She should've multitasked. I'm glad she isn't taking me back. I don't want her; I only want her job. And I'll take it, with a little help. I remind myself to focus on the task at hand.

I push Meredith over onto her stomach, straddling her as I unzip her dress. I lean down, whispering in her ear, "I won't let you down."

And of course, I don't. After, as we cuddle in bed, she says, "That was nice. Really nice."

"'Nice'? How about the best you've ever had?" I ask.

She doesn't answer.

"Look, Mer, likely we shouldn't tell anybody about this," I say. "It probably wouldn't be appropriate."

"When have Kingsley men ever been appropriate?" she says. She has a point. She's staring at the ceiling. "I remember your father, when he was your age—well, wow."

What? "You and Richard?" I ask. I hop out of bed, a bit stunned by the revelation although I shouldn't be. "Seriously? I never imagined it." Guess I never imagined me and Meredith doing it, either, but desperate times and all.

I grab my clothes and head into her bathroom to shower.

"Hey, where are you going? That was years ago, decades," she says. She follows me into the bathroom, puts on a robe.

I hurry to the shower. I really don't want to talk about this.

She opens the shower door, drops the robe, and joins me. "Your dad and I . . . Well, it was ages ago. He's an old man now. Don't feel so threatened." She touches my cheek. She's trying to start up again.

I'm not in the mood. I don't feel threatened by my father—not anymore. I have everything going for me. He has nothing. No one. Not even Meredith, it seems.

"Hey, we need to get ready for the board meeting," I say. I start washing up to get away from her. "Today's a big day. Who wins the nod to be president/CEO. I think Richard should step aside, don't you agree?"

I kiss her gently to remind her there's more if she agrees.

"Yes, he's past his prime. His health is failing. He made a rash choice, picking Paige," she says.

"Exactly." I step out of the shower. I dress quickly. Still ten minutes to spare before the meeting. But Meredith better hurry. "Hey, it's ten minutes until the meeting."

"I know. I'm going to be late. Better late than never, like you yesterday," she says. She turns off the water. "It was bad form, Teddy."

I hand her a towel. "It couldn't be helped." I'm lying. Does she know it, too?

"You were drunk on the beach," she says. She walks into the closet. "Paige sent her watchdog, Justin, to find you, you know. You're giving them a lot of ammunition."

"Who?" I ask. Ammunition? I can skip a stupid bonding retreat if I want to.

"Paige and Justin," she says. She emerges from the closet in a dress just like the one I took off in the heat of passion, only this one is lime green. "I think you're right: they're a couple."

"You know, I hope not. John and I hired him to spy on Paige. He's on our team," I say, but I see the same thing she sees. Damn it. I should check in with him, maybe after the meeting today. Threaten him a bit. Tell him not to dip his pen in company ink—especially not ink beyond his pay grade. "I'll handle Justin. I'm one step ahead, as usual. Stick with me, kid. I'm a winner."

"The land deal you sourced is a big problem," she counters. "We're in trouble over it."

"I'm coming up with a solution. Don't worry. I'll save the day, be a hero, be CEO, be your lover . . ." I smile. "How does that sound?"

"Dreamy," she says with a chuckle.

What's that supposed to mean? Not quite the vote of confidence I was looking for. I decide it's time to move on, so I open the door. The howling wind stuns me for some reason; I guess I'd forgotten about it. My focus was entirely on my mission of seduction. Sex is all about power, domination. Winning.

I lean forward into the wind. I'm ready for another battle. My work here is done.

27
SERENA

My baby girl is so cute when she's asleep. I stare at the little being in her portable crib, and my heart swells with pride. And then I can't help but look out the window, scanning the lush lawn for any sign of danger. I don't know who or what I'm looking for, but I'm on edge. Roman will not just let me run away with his baby, despite what I've told Paige and Richard. Roman is vindictive, erratic, a spoiled boy with no money. He didn't believe me when I told him Richard is Sophia's father. We sat in the attorney's office—the one Paige had hired for me—across the table from each other. I remember the rage in his eyes as they turned from brown to almost black before he began to laugh.

"Nice one," he said once he stopped laughing. "You tell me you're leaving, tell me to sign these papers, and you tell me my baby doesn't belong to me? You're a joke."

"There is a paternity test, and in fact, baby Sophia does belong to Mr. Richard Kingsley," my attorney said with practiced calm. I'd provided her with the proof—the forged proof.

"I don't buy it. No way," he said. "But you know what? I hate you so very much that I don't care about the baby. That's how much I want you to go away."

"Roman," his attorney said, patting his client's hand. "We can demand another paternity test."

Roman's eyes narrowed, and he leaned across the table, as close as he could get to my face. I didn't lean back.

"No, let her go for now. I'm sick of her ugly, lying face," he said, his words hot and hurtful in the small room. We all watched as he picked up the pen and signed the document. As the attorneys turned their attention to the paperwork, Roman leaned forward once again, whispering so only I could hear him. "This isn't over."

A chill rolled down my spine as he turned and walked out of the room, acting every bit the thug I'd learned he truly was. So now, when I check the lawn outside the baby's room, I guess I expect to see him—my former husband, Roman, angry and looking for revenge.

I need to tell Richard just how threatened I feel. Maybe that will soften his heart. Maybe, if he knows he alone can save Sophia and me, that he's the only one I know who is wealthy enough and powerful enough to scare Roman away once and for all. Yes, I will try one more time to win him over and bring him back to me. I must. I touch Sophia's cheek gently.

Time to go. Paige has invited me to come to the board meeting because it's my best chance to see Richard. I check my reflection in the mirror. I'm dressed conservatively, for me, in dark jeans, a blue-and-white-striped T-shirt, and tennis shoes. I'll walk into the meeting with my head held high, hopeful Richard will pat the seat next to his, welcoming me to the room. Of course, after he ran away from me last night, I don't know what to expect. I do know he didn't hook up with Julia; I made sure of that. I couldn't believe she was lurking by the pool, just trying to lure my husband out. Unacceptable.

As for Richard, I understand his hesitation—or, shall we say, his *anger* with this situation. Of course I do. But the past is the past. All we have is now. He's all alone, I'm alone—except for the baby—and we need each other. He loves to be the one in charge, the all-powerful king. He needs us as much as Sophia and I need him. And he still loves me.

I know he does, even if he doesn't realize it yet. I walk into the adjacent room. Fortunately, Tata has gotten some sleep, and she doesn't look as if she's about to drop dead with exhaustion like she did yesterday. Her eyes are closed now, and she's resting on the couch. It's important to sleep when the baby does; I read all about that.

"Tata," I say and touch her shoulder.

"Si!" She awakens with a burst. "Is it the baby? Is she OK?"

"Si, no worries. She is asleep, the little angel. I am leaving, though. Just wanted to tell you," I say. "I'll be in meetings most of today if everything goes as planned, and then I have a big dinner tonight. So you just order room service, play with Sophia, do whatever you'd like."

"Si," she says. "When does Mr. Marino arrive?"

"I don't know."

"Baby needs her poppa."

I really do need to start working on finding a nanny replacement. Tata leaves this week. I actually don't know why she wants my ex-husband to arrive. Sure, he is better with babies than I am, but otherwise he's a loser. "You know what? He's not coming. You do know we weren't getting along, Mr. Marino and I. You heard the fights. He lured me into his life to use me for my money. His whole family did. I filed for a divorce, and it was granted to me. So it's over."

Oh no. I've shocked her. I guess divorce is frowned upon in Italy. Well, it's normal and expected in America.

"What about the baby?" she asks, blinking.

"I will take good care of Sophia. Don't worry," I say. She doesn't look convinced, to say the least. "I'll find a new nanny. An American. You can train her, understand?"

"Si. Poor baby," she says. "No poppa?"

"I'm working on that right now," I say. I fluff my hair once more, put lipstick on. Bright red, the color Richard loves. "Wish me luck!"

I step outside and into an oven. The air is hot and thick. I sniff. Do I smell smoke? I look around, but I don't see any fires. Maybe I'm imagining it. The winds make you think terrible thoughts, I've decided. I bet they are the reason Richard was so unsettled last night, vacillating between wanting to kiss me and wanting to yell at me in rage. Maybe it was the devil winds that made him that way.

I hope he is calmer when I see him in a few minutes. I hope his heart is aching with longing for me. I hope he found it in himself to forgive me for my poor choices. I look around to make sure the coast is clear. No Roman. I take a deep breath and try to relax, feel confident.

"Hey, hooker," Sibley says, startling me by coming up from behind. "How are you doing?"

"Despite you scaring me to death just now, I'm pretty good. I guess you heard it didn't go well with me and Richard last night," I say, my heart thumping.

She blinks and turns away. "I heard."

I look over at her, but she's avoiding eye contact. We reach the main building and duck inside, grateful to be out of the gusts of dust.

"What's wrong?" I ask as we approach the elevator. "There's something you aren't telling me."

"Nothing. Um, I just wish I'd arrived yesterday," she says.

"Are you crying?" I ask. The elevator doors open, and we step inside. "No, you are."

That makes no sense. Maybe the winds have gotten to her, too.

"OK, well, um . . . do you happen to know where a person starts to find a good nanny?" I ask, to change the subject and because I need one.

"No. Why would I? I'm single, hooker. But I bet my guy Ty would know who to call. He said he can help with everything and anything," she says.

"Who's Ty?"

"He's a cutie who works here, and we're flirting pretty heavy, so I bet we'll go out," she explains. "We can stop by the front desk and say hi. Ask for his help. I bet people need nannies all the time at this place. Besides, I really don't want to go to that meeting anyway. Do you?"

"No, only to see your dad," I say. "But sure. Let's go talk to Ty. My future depends on reliable childcare, if you know what I mean."

"I don't, thank goodness. But I can see how it would be limiting, having to take care of your own kid twenty-four seven. I mean, neither of my parents did that, so I wouldn't really know. But I think it does mess a person up," Sibley says. "Wouldn't want that for baby Sophia."

"No," I agree. I don't want my daughter to turn out like Sibley, no matter how close we've seemingly become. I know it's only a matter of time before our truce is over.

28
PAIGE

Justin and I have been in the boardroom, setting up, for almost an hour, and I think we've done everything the fixer told us to do when we met briefly in the privacy of the public beach parking garage next to the resort. It was like being in a spy movie, and I was nervous the whole time. But he and Justin hugged, like family, and I guess Alex has worked for Justin's dad for decades. Justin was right: we needed someone like Alex Yeatman—if that's his real name. Sure, I have a nagging thought in the back of my mind that I'm now officially aligning myself with another family of billionaires to protect me from my own. In the movies, this never ends well. But I am telling myself to trust Justin. He's been nothing but supportive from the moment he appeared as my assistant. And really, what other choice do I have?

"You ready, Madam President?" Justin asks, dimple appearing with his broad smile. "Hey, you look so worried. They can't do anything to you. You're in charge. Richard picked you. And we both know he's not in a position to change his mind—not anymore. And Alex is here."

He touches my shoulder, and I lean into him. I can't help it. Now, with the secrets we share, we must be a team, at work and otherwise. But still, a little voice inside my head reminds me I was blind to who

Ted really was for so long. Could I be that wrong again? Maybe. I look at Justin. No. He is what he seems to be, right?

"Justin, what is your dad like? Is he like Richard?" I ask. "Why does he need a fixer?"

"You'll see. He wants to meet you. He's a great guy. Successful, like Richard, but not a dick," he says. "You're going to like him."

"He didn't let you be a meteorologist," I say.

"No, but he was right. I'm where I'm supposed to be."

"Thank goodness. I'm trying to be brave, but I feel like they're going to figure it out or try to team up, like they have been doing. And then there's the meeting with whoever is blackmailing me," I say. "It's a lot."

"It is. But you're doing this for the right reasons: for your girls, to move the company out of the good-old-boy days," he says. "Heck, everybody outside of the board thinks you're doing a great job. The media loves you. Even your competitors have grown to respect you. People like my father."

"Interesting. Your father is a competitor?" A few alarm bells begin to ring.

"Not really. They've competed in the past for deals. There's only so much land available in Southern California, so developers of a similar size are bound to run into each other. The nature of business. But you know all of that," Justin says. "You're right where you should be, Paige."

"I know a bunch of Kingsley men who don't agree," I argue.

"Who cares. You're the boss now, more than they even know."

"I hope our plan works, with Alex," I say. "And you still haven't told me about your big idea. How are you going to help me salvage our money from the failed land deal?"

"Let's get through this meeting, and then we'll tackle that problem," he says. "Trust me. I have a great solution."

I stare into his handsome face and realize I don't have any choice. I have to trust him. "OK, I do. I will."

"You know I need to give your brothers-in-law something, some scoop. They hired me to spy on you, which shouldn't be a surprise."

"Of course they did. I would expect nothing less. But you haven't betrayed me, right?" I ask, heart thumping again. Am I making another huge mistake? A Ted-sized mistake?

"No. You know I'm team Paige all the way, but they don't need to know that just yet. I need something—some kind of scoop—to make them think I'm still a spy," he says. "How about the anonymous threats? I could mention that but act like I don't know anything more. I'll ask if it's one of them."

I can't help but smile. My double agent. "Sure." The lights go out. I reach for Justin, and he wraps his arms around me. I welcome the hug, his face close to mine in the dark. My heart races as I lift my face toward his. And we kiss, a warm, delicate promise of more to come. The lights pop back on.

We step apart, but electricity zips through my body. I think I'm falling in love.

The door opens, and Sibley and Serena appear.

"I'm so sick of the lights going out," Serena says. "It's awful."

It's not the worst thing—not at all. "Good thing they have generators. Hey, Sibley, can I speak to you for a moment? Serena, we have you sitting just right there. Assigned seats for this board session," I explain. I orchestrated all the details once I decided to include Serena. Her seat is next to Richard's—and I feel a little bad about that. But it had to be that way, for optics. I do like her title, though: chief of special projects.

"Thanks for the title, Paige, and the salary. Looks like I'm going to need it if Richard rejects me again. Oh my God, he cannot reject me. I love him." She slips into her seat.

I take Sibley to the far corner of the room while Justin talks with Serena.

"Did you tell anyone anything?" I ask.

"No. I didn't say a word. Promise," Sibley says, tears filling her eyes. "I'm just so sad, though."

"I know, Sibs. Remember, he died happy. He did." Another white lie. "And he loved you very much."

"I know."

"Look, I've made you a part of the marketing team for now. And as long as you'd like to stay, the job is yours. The girls will be happy when they find out."

"Thanks, but I don't know what that entails," she says. "I'm not really the corporate-job type, if you know what I mean."

I do. "Don't worry. It will all work out. For now, just take your seat. I put you between your brothers. Can you handle that?" I ask.

"Sure, the losers. Do you think they'll show up?"

"I know they will."

And just like that, my soon-to-be ex-husband waltzes in like he owns the place. I hurry over to the chair at the head of the table, opposite Richard's empty seat.

"Ted, your seat is over there, by Sibley," I tell him.

"What is she doing here?" he asks. "She's not a member of the board."

"No, but she's helping me with the retreat, she's a Kingsley, and she's staying. Sit down," I order.

"Paige, you've really gotten a big head all of a sudden," Ted says, but he takes his seat. I watch as he drinks a big gulp of water from the glass in front of him and then refills it from the pitcher. He can tell we're all watching him. "What? After some exertion, you need a little water. And it's dry and hot and dusty as hell out there."

John and Evan walk in the room next. Did they have a meeting before this one?

"John, your seat is on the other side of Sibley," I say, watching his face to see the surprise. He seems to be aware she would be here.

"A little bird told me you'd flown into town, Sibley. When are you leaving again? Soon, I hope. Taking some more jewelry or whatever on your way out? Where's that boyfriend of yours? Colson, was it?"

Sibley looks at John with pure hate. "Colson and I broke up. I'm staying around, Johnny Boy, because I accepted a job at Kingsley Global Enterprises. Surprise!"

She points to her Marketing name placard.

"Paige, you aren't authorized to hire her," John says, hands on hips.

"Yes, I am," I shoot back. "Oh, and speaking of new hires, Serena is head of special projects, reporting directly to the president."

Serena grins. "Surprise again, John."

"I can't believe this. Ted, what is this?" he says.

Ted shrugs. "A couple women ganging up, I suppose. It doesn't matter. Dad will have a fit when he gets here, kick them out—along with Paige—and we'll move on. Don't get so flustered, Johnny. That's what they want."

Meredith walks into the room. "Sorry I'm late. Something came up."

She seems to be in a good mood. I'm hopeful, but not confident, she'll support me. We'll see.

"All right, well, it appears we are all here," I say.

"Um, Dad isn't," Ted points out.

"He's not going to make it. I can't reach him—and well, I'm sure he'll turn up when he wants to," I say. "Maybe he's sick of all this infighting."

Serena says, "I was just with him last night at dinner. He did seem tired and upset. I think you all are stressing him out. Except for Paige."

I smile. "Thanks, Serena."

"We should probably wait until we can get Richard here," Evan says. "Although, officially, we do have enough board members to start the meeting. We have a quorum."

"Yes, Evan, we should begin. I have a full afternoon planned," I say. "Anyway, let's get started. I have several team-building exercises and games to help bring us all together. It'll be fun."

John stands. "No, we aren't doing that. As fun as that sounds, we have a more pressing item on the agenda. We are going to take a vote, a no-confidence vote, to oust you as president. Evan and I reviewed the board bylaws, and we are well within the parameters. If Dad was here, he'd agree. He was ready to make this move yesterday, after all. You were a big mistake, Paige."

I knew this day would come. How did I think I would keep the power in the room? By being one step ahead, that's how. They will not force me out. Neither of them is capable of doing the job; two of them together don't add up to one of me. I stare at John with a tight smile.

Ted says, "I agree with John. Let's take a vote. May the best man win."

He is so annoying. I cannot believe I'm still married to him. Not for long. I give Ted the same steely smile. It's time to execute my contingency plan. I glance over at Justin. He mouths, *End it.* I nod.

"I guess we will not call this meeting to order, then. I'll see you all at tonight's dinner," I say, and then I rise from my chair, turn, and walk out the door.

I hear angry voices fill the room, but I don't care. Without me, they don't have a quorum. And they know it.

As I stand in the hallway, the door bursts open and John hurries out. "Nice try, Paige. We will oust you, one way or another."

"You should watch yourself, John. You have a lot of secrets that would be trouble for you if they came to light," I warn.

"You don't know anything about me," he says, leaning forward, face flushed. I feel like he wants to punch me. "You're so clueless it's ridiculous."

I remember what he did to Rachel. He thinks I don't know the truth. I'll save that surprise for later.

"Oh, but I do," I say. "I know about you. All your dirty little secrets."

"John, come on, back down," Evan says. "Sorry about that, Paige. He's frustrated. I think we all are. Things are going to need to change. You know it." He takes John by the arm and walks him away, down the hall.

Ted comes out next. This should be interesting. Will he try the fake lovey-dovey let's-get-back-together approach? I certainly hope not, since it has made him look so pathetic for the past few months.

"You think you're so clever, Paige. But you aren't. You're just a housewife on a power trip. I should never have married you. It's an embarrassment."

Well, no more Mr. Fake Nice Guy. It's a relief, actually. I feel my hands clench into fists and keep the smile on my face. "You're the embarrassment."

"Me? You are. Somehow you tricked Dad into naming you president. You fooled him for a while, but he's seen the light now. And since he's sick today, I guess it's up to me. I will bring you down. Not just take your position, but I'll ruin your reputation, too. You're a bitch, Paige, and it's time you got what you deserve."

Before I can stop myself, I slap him. Hard. On the cheek. I've never believed in violence. I've never hit anyone before. These Kingsley men are pushing me over the edge. I'm shaking with anger. Especially for Ted. After all he did to me during our marriage: his cheating; his gambling addiction; his perpetual, persistent lies. He's horrible.

Ted smiles. Puts his hand on his cheek. "See? You're out of control, over your head."

"Ted!" Meredith appears behind him in the hallway. "Come with me. Now." She touches his shoulder.

"Sure, Mer. I'll follow you anywhere," Ted says, still looking at me. "I guess we'll see you tonight at dinner."

Meredith and I consider each other for a moment, and then I see it. It's in the way she keeps her hand on his shoulder, the words Ted is using to talk to her. They're sleeping together. Oh my God. I'm sure it's part of his plan to take over the company. He has reached a new low. I want to warn Meredith, but she's a grown woman. Surely, she knows who and what Ted is.

Meredith smiles and gives a little shrug. "Come along, Teddy."

29

JOHN

I'm riding in the back of the courtesy SUV driving me a short distance to Uncle Walter's hotel, called the Ranch. Better to meet there, away from prying family. Paige is clearly up to something—that's all I can figure out. But she doesn't know anything about the things I've done. She wasn't there when Rachel fell.

But Serena was. That woman only has power through Richard. And Richard didn't exactly welcome her back with open arms. No, he didn't; I happen to know. But still, she's a problem because she was there. I need to figure out how to deal with her. And Sibley? What a joke. She's not relevant to anything or anyone, despite the fact she thinks she is. She's even managed to upset Uncle Walter, and he's been her surrogate daddy all these years. Neither of us could believe it when Sibley showed up at the Twin Palms.

Uncle Walter said Sibley told him after the trip on the *Splendid Seas* she wasn't going to have anything to do with any of us ever again. And he believed her, thought she was like a daughter. Turns out, she was playing him. Wait until I tell him that not only is she here, but she also has a job at the company, too. For now.

Well, it's time to step up. It's time to end all this nonsense.

"Here we are at the Ranch, sir," the driver says. "Just give me a call when you'd like a ride back."

"Thanks, son," I say and slip him a twenty.

The staff has been great. My family, not so much. I think about Krystle picking out her own wedding ring. I don't suppose that's a conventional way to do things, but it guarantees the woman likes her ring. I mean, she's the one who will be wearing it. I'm excited to see what she picks out. There can't be any bad choices at the Twin Palms, right? I hope. No, it's fine. Together, we are the future of Kingsley. I like it. With the right clothes and the right setting, Krystle does fit in. She's not the cheap and tawdry person Richard saw yesterday. No, she's changed. Literally. And she loves me. That's something I haven't felt since Rachel died. And I need it.

This place is nice, tucked away, private. I see a golf course and the walls of the canyon. It's very green and rustic, and hot and windswept like everywhere else. I step inside, and there's Walter. I haven't seen him in person for years, but he hasn't changed much. Florida must agree with him. He's a thinner, tanner, better-looking version of Richard.

"Look what the cat dragged in," Walter says, giving me a big hug. "I'm glad we're starting over, John. I always liked you, even though you framed me for stealing when you knew I was innocent. It's fine, now, though. I blame your father. He instigated everything to force me out of the company. I know that."

I take a deep breath. "I didn't have a choice. Dad . . . Well, he knew I'd do anything for him, especially back then," I say.

"I know, son, and I forgive you," Uncle Walter says.

"That means a lot. And I forgive you for making me pay you all that bribery money after you stole the file on my computer."

He bursts out laughing. "What a family we are! Come on in here. They have a great bar at this place."

I follow Walter down the hallway, and we take seats at the very end of the bar, away from any nosy vacationers.

"So the board meeting today was a bust," I say after we've ordered our beers. "Sibley was even there. Paige has given her a job at the company."

"That's ridiculous. She's never worked a day in her life," Walter says. "She's so ungrateful. After everything I did for her. I treated her like my own daughter. And then she just lied to my face. Won't return my calls. It's sad, really."

"She's the least of our worries, though," I tell him. "I'm going to need you on the board. Have you acquired enough shares?"

"Working on it, Johnny. Likely be in the next couple of weeks," he says.

"I don't know if I can wait that long," I say. "I'm disgusted just being in the same room with her, you know it?"

"Paige? Why? Consider her a placeholder. A pretty, benign, ineffective placeholder that you will remove soon. Take a breath. This is a journey, not a destination. You're going to give yourself a bad heart like Richard's," he warns me. He takes a big gulp of beer.

"You're right. Well, so far we have you—once you've bought enough shares—me, and Evan, who will vote for me as CEO," I say.

Walter raises his eyebrows. "You're going straight to the top?"

"It's time," I say. "And if anyone tries to stop me, I have some documents that will ruin Kingsley Global Enterprises. They're in a safe, but let's just say there is a direct tie between the company and a toxic chemical dump site near Catalina Island. The company will be ruined by litigation. Dad thinks I destroyed it, but I couldn't. My wife gave her life, so to speak, to find this shit."

"Dark," Walter says. "You'll blow it all up if you don't get what you want?"

"Yep," I say. "It's time for me to take charge of the company or for the whole thing to go down. I cannot be sidelined any longer. I am the oldest son; I am the loyal soldier. I am the only one who can lead this company. And I won't give him a choice, not any longer."

"Richard will be furious," he says.

"It doesn't matter anymore. He's irrelevant. Put him out of your mind," I say. "I have."

"OK, right. Will do. Son, how's life in general? I hope you've been able to move on after Rachel's accident," Walter says.

He's the first member of my family to care about me, about my life. I've made the right decision bringing him back into the fold. I know it now.

"Thanks for asking. It's been really tough. My mom helped me through, and my church. In fact, I met a great gal there, at church. You'll love her," I say. Will he? Who knows. "I'm going to propose to her tonight at the fancy dinner. I wish you could come."

"That would tip our hand, John. We need to keep our connection a secret until I've bought the shares. I'm flying back to Florida tonight. Once we have the shares, I'll return to Orange County. Then we pounce, so to speak," Walter says. "Want another round?"

I could stay here, talking to my uncle at this cozy bar tucked away in the canyon, far away from my siblings and their drama. Why not.

"Sure, sounds good," I say. "How's your life, Uncle Walter?"

"Much better since you called me. Great, in fact," he says. "I'm even thinking about moving back here. I miss it. Not the Santa Ana winds—not that, but they will pass. It's just so gorgeous here. Florida has its pluses, but not much can beat Southern California."

"Well, your old office waits for you," I say. He could be a good right-hand man—much better than Ted.

"Once we get Paige out, that leaves Ted, right?" he asks. "What's your plan for him?"

"Promise him the president title and then force him out over the land deal," I say. "I sent you all of that, right? It's a mess."

"He's an idiot. A handsome salesman with a gambling addiction and a woman problem," Walter says. "I'd get him out of the way as soon as possible."

"Agree. I'll likely need your help." I clink my new beer glass with his.

"It would be my pleasure," he says.

And just like that, we're a team.

30
SERENA

I come out of the boardroom and spot Paige alone in the hallway. There is more going on here than I know; I can feel it. I've tried calling and texting Richard, but he hasn't picked up. I'm going to go over to his suite, beg him to see me.

"Paige, I'm worried about Richard," I say. "It's not like him to not answer the phone when I call. Even when he's furious with me."

"I'm afraid he's mad at everyone and vice versa. Look, Serena, why don't you give him a little space? Maybe by this evening, he'll be sorted out," Paige says. "Let me go check on him. I was planning on it, anyway. It's official, as president and as his daughter-in-law. OK? I'll let him know you want to see him, too. Sound good?"

Paige is the best.

"Yes. Really good. Thank you. I really cannot thank you enough for welcoming me back into the family," I say. "I made such a huge mistake. I don't know what I'll do if Richard doesn't take me back. I'm serious. I love him and need him in our lives. I just don't know what's going to happen. I don't know what to say to make him forgive me."

"We all make mistakes," she says, her eyes misting over with kindness. "It's what we do to fix them that matters most. You're here. And you told me and Sibley the truth about what happened to Rachel. No one else did. You're helping to fix things."

"I hope so," I say. "But it's Richard and I that need fixing. I love that grumpy old man."

"I know you do. How's the baby?" she asks.

"Good. But I need a new nanny. I'll go work on that now. Sibley's friend Ty at the concierge desk gave me a card for a nanny service," I say. "I should get that all sorted so I can be one hundred percent focused on Richard and me."

"I didn't know Sibley had a new guy," Paige says. "Who is he?"

"He works here, and he's cute. Can tell he's falling for her." I smile. "Poor guy."

"Yes, most likely—poor guy," Paige agrees. "I need to go, but I'll call as soon as I have an update on Richard. You do know he loves you. We both saw the look in his eye when you showed up yesterday."

"I know."

Paige turns away and walks back into the boardroom, closing the door behind her.

I pull out the card to dial the number to the nanny service, but all I really want to do is talk to Richard.

I slip the nanny-service card back into my pocket. I'll have Tata make the call and set up interviews. She knows more than I do about what Sophia needs.

I decide I don't care what Paige says—I'm going to find Richard and talk him into giving me one more chance.

OC SCOOP

Hey, Kingsley fans! We don't have to tell you that the whole clan is tucked away at the Twin Palms, away from most of our prying eyes. But rest assured that our little birdies are always on the clock, and wow, did they deliver the juiciest worm! Turns out, John Kingsley, Richard's oldest son—whom we hear is also a son of a @^#%$—has a serious younger girlfriend who was spotted trying on ginormous engagement rings at the resort's jewelry store. Now, our tipster was pretending to be a customer but was hustled out of the store once Miss Krystle Carrington asked to try on some of the larger, blingier rings. The store was closed, a big security guard posted outside. We need you tipsters to tell us if John actually did put a ring on it . . . and how many carats and the cut, of course. Stay tuned. You'll know when we do. Have a great Saturday night. And stay safe. It's fire weather outside, but that's nothing compared to the hot gossip at the Twin Palms Resort, that's for sure.

31
PAIGE

Justin and I each carry a printer-paper box of items collected from the boardroom, placed carefully inside with gloved hands. Again, spy-novel time. We reach Richard's suite, and I try to breathe and stay calm. I've never been good with death; or funerals; or dead bodies, even when presented in the best light in open caskets. I shake my head to get my dad's dead face out of my mind.

"You OK?" Justin asks, looking at me with concern while knocking on the door. "Alex, it's me and Paige."

A chill races down my spine, and bile stings my throat. I can't be sick. I won't be. "I'm fine," I manage.

Alex opens the door and checks the hallway behind us before letting us in. "Come in," he says, and we step inside. He double-locks the door and adds a chain. He's built like a special ops guy you see on TV shows. Short, dark hair. Thin lips. Handsome in his own bulky, muscle-clad way.

I brave a sniff of the air. It smells normal. I take another breath.

"How's it going?" Justin asks. "We brought the things you asked for."

Alex takes the box from my hands. "It's going well. We have the body ready to transport to the funeral home. Everything is cleaned up. The bed has been made to look slept in."

He opens the box with gloved hands and pulls out the water glass and pitcher Ted used at the meeting, and the notepad and pen he used to scribble nonsense. John's coffee mug is inside, too. Justin's box has the agendas we passed out the first day, including the one Richard picked up and tossed in anger. We have his water glass and coffee mug as well.

Alex places the items on the coffee table, arranged as if a meeting has just taken place. A meeting between John, Ted, and Richard.

For all we know, maybe it did?

"Their prints are already in the room," Alex says. "They were here last night. Both of them. That's good for us—very good." After finishing setting up the meeting display on the coffee table, Alex takes photos from many angles. We watch him work in silence. He coats a brush with a white powder and wipes each of the glasses with it, moving in a circular pattern. Next, he unrolls clear tape, places it on Ted's water glass, rubs it over the fingerprint. He takes the tape to the corner, puts it on a piece of acetate. "Gotcha." He's referring to Ted and Ted's fingerprint. I have to smile.

"Of course they were here," Justin says. "One of them did it. I'm sure of it. And now we have the proof to frame either one. Where's the knife?"

"I have it tucked away. If we need to take the next step, we will," Alex says. "If they don't back down and agree to the story that he died in his sleep, the knife will reappear. It was wiped clean by the killer, but we can add whichever fingerprints we'd like to it, of course."

"That seems like a solid plan, but how will we know who did it?" I ask. I wrap my arms around myself.

"Murderers have a way of giving themselves up, in time," Alex says. "They slip, they reveal something."

"Makes sense, I suppose," I say. "And when one of the boys reveals himself as Richard's killer—"

"You'll have everything you need to prove it," Alex says.

I like this plan. I like knowing someone will be held accountable for Richard's death—or at the very least, using this against Ted and John if need be, to keep control of the company. I never thought I'd be talking about such things or dealing with a situation like this. It turns out, bad things happen when you're a Kingsley.

"Where is Richard?" I ask.

"He's in the bed," Alex tells me. "That's what we decided, right?"

"Yes." I swallow again.

Justin wraps his arm around me. Alex's eyes widen at the gesture, but he looks away.

"Paige, we're ready. You can text the family, tell them to gather here—at Richard's suite—immediately," Alex says.

"I need to see the body, please," I say. I need to be certain I can handle what's coming next.

"Sure, go ahead," Alex says. "I'll wait here."

I walk to the door of the bedroom of Richard's massive suite. The shades are drawn; it's dark and very still. I flip on the light and close my eyes. I feel Justin behind me.

"Paige, he's inside a body bag. You can open your eyes," he says.

I open my eyes. Justin is right. It's a black bag, the shape of a man, lying in bed. I exhale.

"OK, let's do this," I say. We walk back into the suite. I look toward the corner where Richard died, and there's no sign of any struggle. No blood. Nothing. "You have photos of the scene?"

"Of course, ma'am," Alex says.

"Send the text, Paige," Justin says.

I type: Please come to Richard's suite. Immediately. And press send.

There's a knock on the door.

"That was fast," Justin says.

"I'll get it." Alex walks over to the door.

"Richard, honey, it's me. Sisi!" Serena calls out from the other side.

Justin and I look at each other. This will be sad—horrible, actually. Alex lets her in.

"Who are you? Where's Richard?" she demands. And then she spots me and Justin.

"Paige, what's going on?" she asks.

"I'm so sorry to tell you this, but Richard is dead. He died last night," I say.

"No!" Serena screams and drops to the ground. She begins to wail—a deep, painful sound that breaks my heart. I bend down next to her, trying to comfort her. She begins to rock back and forth, still moaning. Alex moves over to us, and in one quick motion, he scoops her up and carries her to the couch, as if she were a small child. The wailing stops but the tears don't. "Oh, Richard," she says. "You can't leave me now. You're my everything. Richard."

I take a seat on the couch next to her and pat her hand. "It's sooner than we expected, I know. It's going to be OK—it will be. I'm here for you."

Justin says, "Do you want me to walk you to your room, Serena? The rest of the family will be here soon, and, well . . . it could get ugly."

"No," Serena says. "Where is he? Richard?"

"In the bedroom." I point in my father-in-law's direction. "Alex here is going to transport him to the funeral home, discreetly. We'll announce his death on our terms, once everything is in order."

Serena nods. I think she's in shock.

Alex answers a frantic knock on the door. He opens it to reveal Ted, Meredith, Sibley, and Evan.

"What is it, Paige?" Ted says, leading the others into the room.

"Richard is dead," I say, standing and crossing the room to face him. I'm taking charge. I cannot wait to watch him crumble in front of me.

"What? How?" he asks. "Dad can't be dead. He can't be. Tell me what happened."

I'm standing so close I can smell the booze on his breath. He must have been drinking all day. Desperate and demanding at the same time: that's my Ted. I think back to all the lies, all the things he's done to hurt me. "That all depends."

Sibley says, "He died peacefully in his sleep. Right, Paige?"

"That's an option," I say, staring at Ted. I do feel bad for Sibley. She sounds like a small child, but I cannot comfort her. Not yet. I stay laser focused on my enemy.

"What's that supposed to mean?" Ted asks. He looks like he wants to punch me. He certainly better not try, not with Justin and Alex in the room. He wouldn't. He's a coward at heart. I shake my head and step past him to address the room.

"Where's John?" I ask. I cannot wait to confront him, much like I'm doing with Ted. "Anybody seen him?"

Sibley walks over and sits next to Serena. They hold hands, both in tears. Sibley turns and says, "Ty drove John to the Ranch, a hotel down the street from here, back in the canyon. He's picking him up now."

"OK, thank you," I say. "Sibley, could you take Serena to your room? You both are in shock. I'll handle things, and we'll plan a memorial for Richard that will make him smile from heaven. You both will be in charge."

Sibley nods. "Come on, hooker. Let's get away from this depressing room. You can feel death in here."

Justin walks them to the door as I turn back to Ted and continue our standoff. I smile as he glares at me.

"I want a divorce," he says. "Richard can't make me try to get back together with you. Not anymore."

"You're so pathetic," I say. How did I ever fall for this man? "I'm already working on the divorce papers."

"Good," he says.

Meredith sighs. "What an inglorious ending to a storied life. Poor Richard. I guess this sets up quite a showdown, what with the will, the company . . . everything."

She looks at me with a deeply furrowed brow. But I keep smiling. I'm certain there won't be a showdown, not if my plan works. "It all depends, Meredith. It all depends."

32

JOHN

I'm just about to pound on the door of Dad's suite when it opens, and Meredith and Evan walk out past me.

"Where are you going?" I ask. "What's going on?"

"Paige asked for the room, for just immediate family," Meredith tells me.

"Sorry, man," Evan says and walks into the windstorm.

"Sorry for what?" I ask. A large guy appears in the doorway. Clearly someone's muscle. "Who are you?"

"Alex. Come in." He steps aside.

"What's going on, Ted?" I ask my brother. He's standing face-to-face with Paige in some sort of weird weaponless duel.

"Ask her," he says, pointing at his wife.

"Paige?" I ask.

"Richard is dead," she says, not looking at me. Still staring at Ted.

"Dad? What happened?" I ask. My heart starts pounding with fear.

"One of you should tell me what happened," Paige says. Her voice is deep, calm. Kind of threatening. No wonder Ted's glaring.

"I have no idea. How did he die? Was he killed?" I ask. This cannot be happening. Richard was feeling fine—I saw him. Oh my God.

"That could be one scenario," Alex says.

"Who the hell are you?" I ask. I need to take charge of this situation. I need all the facts. "Tell me what is going on, who that is. What has happened, Paige?"

"Alex is a fixer. He can fix this or not," Paige says.

Her smugness is about to make me explode with rage. "I'm the Kingsley fixer. I fix this family's things."

"Not this time, John. You see, both you and Ted have a bunch of fingerprints all over this suite. In fact, you seem to be the only ones who visited Richard before he died. And with your track record of murdering members of your own family, like your wife . . . well, of course you killed Richard, likely with Ted's help."

"How dare you!" I yell. "Rachel fell." Who told Paige the truth? It wasn't Richard, or Ted. No, it had to be Serena. Shit.

"No, she didn't fall. You shoved her overboard. We all know the truth now," Paige says.

If I could, I'd force that smile right off her face. But I can't. Not now. How I loathe this woman.

"John, focus. She's trying to frame us for Dad's murder. This guy is helping her," Ted says, pointing to Alex. "So is Justin."

Justin appears. "Hey, John."

This will stop. I will not be threatened by the likes of Paige, this so-called fixer, or her boy-toy assistant. "I need Justin and Alex out of here. This is a family matter, and I'm the Kingsley-family fixer. I'm also in charge now that Dad has expired. How did he die?" I ask again. I'm getting tired of these games.

"You're a good actor, John. So is Ted," Paige says. "Richard died of a stab wound to the neck."

"What?" Ted says.

"No," I say. I've regained my composure. I will assert myself again.

Alex steps forward. "Here is your choice, gentlemen: I will take the body to the funeral home and have them prepare a service fit for a king. I will say the cause of death was heart failure. No scandal."

"Or," Paige cuts in, "we will call the police, tell them he was murdered by one of you. And with both of your criminal histories—murder, theft, and who knows what else—you're going down."

"We have all the proof," Justin says.

"'We'? Since when are you part of anything? You are supposed to be spying on her for us," I say. It takes everything in me not to punch his pretty face. "This is all out of control. What the hell."

"It's under control," Paige says.

I stare at her, shaking my head. I cannot believe Paige has orchestrated all this, using my father's death to her advantage. How evil. And at this exact moment, I'm not sure how to stop her from framing me for his murder. "What do you want, Paige?"

"Complete control of Kingsley Global Enterprises. No more obstruction and scheming from you. Ted resigns. I cannot bear to work with him another moment."

"Feeling is mutual, dear," Ted says. "But I didn't kill Dad."

"Desperate men do desperate things, as you two know all too well," she says. "But no one will know. John will get away with another murder, and we'll bury the secret with Richard."

I need a minute to think. I walk to the sliding glass doors, pull one open, and step outside into the howling wind. At least I don't have to hear Paige's voice in my ear. I need to call Uncle Walter, ask for his advice. I cannot believe she's doing this to me, to my company.

"Hey, we don't have all day!" Alex yells at me. I notice a couple of people walking around the pool. They're staring at me—mistaking me for Richard himself, I'm sure. Everyone at the resort knows this is his suite. *Oh, Dad.*

I walk back inside. "Ted, we need to talk," I say.

"No, you aren't going to get your stories straight together. One or both of you did this; we all know it. So what is the decision?" Paige asks.

Ted and I lock eyes. I shrug. She wins, for now. "Sure, Dad died in his sleep of heart failure. Sounds good, rest his soul. And you're a bitch."

"Thanks for that, Johnny. Ted?" Paige says.

"I agree. On everything," Ted says. "Let's get out of here, John."

"Gladly," I say. "This isn't the end of anything, Paige. You'll see."

As I walk out of the suite, Ted behind me, I realize she's played us well. Dad was furious with both of us yesterday, and the reverse was true, too.

Outside, we walk by the pool, and the same two women are watching again. Only when we make it inside and step into the elevator alone do we speak.

"I didn't do it," Ted says.

"Nor did I," I say. Neither of us believe what we hear, I'm afraid. "I'm strangely not saddened by his death."

"It's almost like he had it coming," he says. "I don't feel anything, either. Well, except toward Paige. I'm not resigning."

"You have to," I say. "But I know the perfect place for you to work. Uncle Walter is in town. He wants to come back into the fold. You can work for him, his company."

"Interesting," Ted says. But he doesn't sound convinced. "What if I refuse to resign?"

"She'll go public; you know she's not bluffing," I say. I need to find a way to get the upper hand. Until I do, we have to play by her rules.

"I didn't kill him," he says again.

"That doesn't matter anymore. Don't you get it?" I say, exploding with the rage I've held in. "She's won this round. She'll make it look like you killed Dad, or I did. Or, likely, both of us did it. You need to keep quiet. Do you understand?"

"Sure, whatever. Just calm down." He raises both hands up in surrender. "You're not helping anything, looking like you're about to have a heart attack. Besides, don't take it out on me. It's my lovely wife who is screwing us over."

He's right. I take a deep breath, tell myself to calm down. I pat him on the back. "Sorry. You're right. I'm taking my anger out on the wrong person. Look, I know you'll love working with Uncle Walter. Sure, it's a change, but sometimes change does a man good. Do you want to get a drink? I'll invite him over and we can talk, make a plan."

"Why not," he says. Then he lets out a brief laugh. "At first I was going to say Richard is going to kill us for talking to his brother."

"We don't have to worry about that anymore." I refocus my rage on the real enemy. "Now we only need to worry about Paige."

33

TED

And just like that, I'm out. I can't feel anything inside. I'm empty. I'm pointless here. John is happy; Paige is happier. I need to talk to Meredith, tell her I'm resigning, but I can't tell her why. This is all awkward and awful.

I look at John. He motions to a table where we'll meet Uncle Walter. I shrug and take a seat. What else do I have to do? We sit at a table in the lobby, one with a view of the whole room. I'm surprised when, moments later, Paige and her lover boy, Justin, appear in the lobby, too, and walk over to a table where another woman sits. I don't know who she is or why they're meeting with her, but things look a little tense. *Interesting.*

"John, do you see Paige and Justin over there, at that table?" I ask. "Do you know the person they're with?"

He turns his head and looks where I've indicated. His mouth drops open. "It's Rachel's sister. I'm sure it is."

"Why would she be meeting with Paige? Do you talk to her?"

"No, not since Rachel died. Last time I saw her was at the funeral." He scratches his chin. "I'm going over there."

"No, don't," I say. "Let her be the one to talk to the sister. I mean, she won't tell her anything because she knows it will ruin the company. She looks a lot like Rachel. What's her name?"

"Rhonda," John says. "She's a piece of work. Always jealous of Rachel because she had a big career and, well . . . me. Ha!"

"You're beginning to sound more and more like Dad, you know," I say. I don't mean it as a compliment.

"John! There you are! I've been texting you!" It's his date, Krystle. She's so loud that Paige, Rhonda, and Justin look our way. Busted. I wave at Paige, just to mess with her, and take a big swig of my vodka martini. I cannot believe she set us up, that she's taken control. I sigh and focus on John and his date. This should be fun to watch, a distraction from the reality of my evil wife sitting across the room.

John stands and pulls out a chair for Krystle. "Hi, honey. It's been hectic. Sorry I haven't answered. My father died in his sleep last night. We just found out."

"Oh Lord. Bless his soul," Krystle says. She drops her head and puts her hands in the prayer position. "John, Ted, pray with me."

Really? "Here? Now?" I ask.

"Yes," she says. "Heavenly Father, please find room in Heaven for Richard Kingsley, who left this earthly world this morning. Please forgive his many sins, including how rude he was to me, his new future daughter-in-law."

I look at her across the table, and she winks at me. Holy shit. Is she flirting with me? I look away. That's the last thing I need. John's girlfriend will not get a crush on me. I will learn boundaries. I will not encourage any of it. Do I tell John? No. I'm sure it was just a harmless wink, an it's-going-to-be-OK-even-though-your-father-died wink. I take a deep breath.

"Help those who truly loved the man to find some sort of peace, including his sons right here. Because I know that even though he didn't show it in a healthy way, your daddy loved you both very much. Remember that," she says. "In God's name, we pray. Amen."

A tear works its way down my cheek before I can stop it. John's eyes are wet, too.

"Good, you need to let those emotions out. I cannot begin to imagine the depth of your sorrow. Your dad was such a force in your life. I know—mine died too young, too. But there's only one thing to do: cry when you need to. And I'll be here for you, John. And if you want to take your mind off of it, I have something special to show you, in private," she says. Her eyes are twinkling in the afternoon light.

"You can show us both," John says. His eyes keep darting between Krystle and the table where Rachel's sister sits. It must be rather haunting for him.

"OK, here goes," Krystle says. She rummages around in her purse for what feels like forever and then pulls out a jewelry box. She was serious about the engagement thing, it appears. She opens the lid. "Do you love it?"

The ring is enormous, an emerald-cut diamond that must be worth half a million dollars. She slips it onto her finger.

"John, what do you think?" she asks.

"It's pretty, honey. Just like you. Good job," he says. "I'm sorry I can't manage more enthusiasm, with Dad and all. But it's nice, it really is."

"Do you want to keep it? You can propose properly tonight, like we planned," she says and slips the ring back into the box, closing the lid. "If you're not up to it, I can keep it until you are."

"No, let's do it. Sure, good idea. We'll make something positive of this day," John says, and the ring box disappears inside his suit coat.

I sit and watch the *Krystle and John Show* as if they're actors on a television screen. I'm here, but I'm not. My mind races with the reality of Paige's threats, her ultimate power play. Here is John, ready to get married again while I cannot wait to get divorced. Paige is trying to ruin my life. She *has* ruined my life.

"Earth to Ted! Don't you want to say something to us?" Krystle says.

"Sure, of course. I'm sorry, I'm a bit distracted, with grief," I manage to say. "Let me be the first to congratulate you on your upcoming engagement."

Krystle giggles. "I know. It happened so fast. But we're so happy. Right, Johnny?"

John's staring at the other table again, ignoring her.

"I know it's hard to be sad about your daddy and happy about me all on the same day, but we'll get through it," Krystle says. "Say, I have a facial at the spa, but if you want me to stay here with you, help you with your grief, I can cancel it."

"No, honey, it's fine," John says. "Ted and I need to talk, spend some time working through the shock. Thanks, though, for offering."

"Of course. That's what love is all about," Krystle says. "OK, if you're sure, I need to run. Getting a manicure, too, so my social media posts will be perfection. It's all about engagement. See you later!"

John and I sit in silence for a couple of moments, letting the whirl-wind of Krystle die down. Paige is still talking to Rhonda. She is so conniving. She thinks she has everything under control. The one thing I know is that in this family, just when you think you're on top, you're going to take a big fall.

I cannot wait to watch her plummet. I'll be there to applaud her on the way down.

NEWS ALERT!

A fast-moving wind-driven wildfire has ignited in the Laguna Canyon Nature Preserve.

Residents in parts of Laguna Beach, California, were told to be ready to evacuate after an early-morning wildfire was spurred on by winds gusting over 50 mph.

The fire had burned about 145 acres of land as of late morning.

Initially, the fire spread quickly, but firefighters were able to slow its advance. More equipment, including air tankers, has been called in to help hold the flames at bay.

Mandatory evacuations have not been issued yet, but the entire city is under an evacuation warning, and residents there are being advised to be ready to leave.

34

KRYSTLE

I'm positively walking on air as I make my way to the facial appointment. Even Ted the jerk couldn't ruin my vibe, though he kind of tried. I was being nice to him, comforting him through his loss, and he was acting strange, like I want him. I don't. I'll need to make that perfectly clear. He also had such a weird expression on his face whenever he looked across the lobby to where Paige was sitting. But who cares about Ted. Not me. I will focus all my energy on John, and so far, the plan is working.

John seemed pleased with the ring. It's the most gorgeous, most expensive thing I've ever touched in my life. It's time to call Momma. She's going to be so proud of me. Finally.

"I picked out our ring!" I say as soon as she picks up.

"No, you did not," she says.

"I'm serious, Momma. I texted you a photo. It's worth half a million dollars," I say, dropping my voice as a couple of California-cool people strut past me, full athleisure regalia on display. Both women have defined biceps, and both have sparkly diamond rings smaller than mine. I want those kinds of arms—arms with visible muscle. I make a mental note to start working out. I already have the biggest ring. I win on that account.

I remember Momma is on the phone.

"Ooh, honey, I think I might faint," she says. "I am just so proud of you. Your daddy would be, too."

"I know. It hasn't been easy," I say. Although, this weekend has been fabulous. Time with John, shopping, ring-buying, and now a spa afternoon before the proposal. Pinch me.

"I know you've given a lot—well . . . everything, really—but it has paid off," she says. "When's the wedding? I'd assume right away?"

That's my mom. Keep pushing. "Yes, I'll try. We'll need to wait until after the funeral."

"Who died?"

"Oh, it's kind of hush-hush, it seems. But Richard Kingsley is dead. Died last night, I guess in his sleep." I look around. I'm not sure if I should be telling her this. "Hey, don't tip off the OC Scoop people, OK? The family is keeping it quiet. They'll announce it when the time is right, so don't go messing that up. Be respectful."

"I'll be as respectful as Richard Kingsley. How's that?" Mom says.

"Momma, come on. We're making progress here," I say. "Don't ruin things. I have to go. I have a couple spa treatments."

"Wow, you're really living high on the hog."

"I am. You wouldn't believe how much these treatments cost," I say. "They must be amazing. Facial, manicure, massage. I'm going to be glowing when he proposes tonight. You should see the dress I bought to wear. I do feel like Cinderella."

"Don't let an evil or jealous stepmother or other family member get in your way tonight, Krystle. You might not have them all on your side. Make sure you become John Kingsley's next wife, no matter what."

"I've got this, Momma." I open the door to the spa. "Gotta go. I'm in my happy place."

My two favorite salesladies grin and welcome me in like I'm an old friend. I know they see me, maybe like me, but they like my limitless room charge even more. Despite the original reason for going after John, I could get used to this lifestyle. I really could.

And maybe, with his father's death, John will become less aggressive, less angry. Heck, maybe he will allow himself to feel happy again. I know he feels guilty about Rachel's fall. But it wasn't his fault. He has survivor's guilt. And really, my mom's revenge isn't against John, either. All in all, maybe this can all work out and I can come to the spa here on a regular basis. John and I could buy a house here. There are people who own homes adjacent to the Twin Palms who have full access to the resort. Can you imagine? I'd be living the dream.

"I want to live here," I say to the ladies behind the desk.

"Everyone does," they say in unison.

The difference is, I have a way to make that particular dream come true, if I play my cards right. And so far, I'm winning every round.

"You're here for three services, right, Miss Carrington?" she asks. I almost forget to respond. That last name is completely made up. Anyone remember *Dynasty*? It was before my time, but my mom and her mom are huge fans. My real last name is Dugger. My brother, Joey Dugger, worked for the Kingsleys at one of their big housing developments in the inland empire. That's the jobsite where he died, falling from the sixth story. A shudder runs down my spine when I think of it. Anyway, I never liked our last name, and there were some newspaper articles about the fall, and the subsequent wrongful death lawsuit, and the fact the Kingsleys won. All bad news for the Duggers. So I dropped that last name when it came time to meet John.

"I am, ladies," I say with a grin. "Miss Carrington is ready to be pampered." *And she's also ready to get engaged.* Krystle Carrington Kingsley. If that isn't a great name, I don't know what is. My phone pings with a news alert from the OC Scoop.

My mom and her big mouth. I hope the family doesn't trace this back to me.

OC SCOOP

My dearest Kingsley fans, it is with the heaviest of hearts that we report we have received an uncon-firmed tip that Richard Kingsley died in his sleep last night. He was eighty years old. Call us, text us, email us if you have more information. So far, the Twin Palms Laguna Beach has not confirmed the story, and none of the Kingsley family members have returned our calls. If this is true, it will be the end of an era. More when we have it.

35

PAIGE

My suspicions were correct about the person threatening me. I had a hunch it was a family member, and I was right, I realized, as soon as I spotted Rachel's sister, Rhonda, waiting for me in the lobby. My blackmailer looks just like Rachel. Sitting with her now is like being with a ghost. She dresses conservatively in a suit just like Rachel, talks in long sentences with big words just like Rachel, stares at me just like Rachel did in that judging way of hers.

"Are you surprised, Paige? Or did you know it was me?" Rhonda says.

"I thought it was someone in the family, someone who loved Rachel. So no, I'm not that surprised," I say, careful to keep my composure. I'm not surprised, but I am angry. How dare she? "This is my assistant, Justin. He'll be discreet."

"I said come alone," Rhonda hisses.

"You don't call all the shots," I say. "And you do know I wasn't a witness to Rachel's death, don't you?"

"I don't know anything about that. How was I to know who saw what? I do know Richard would never even talk to me after it happened. I thought you'd be softer. I thought, you know, since she's married to one of them, too, she'd understand. She'd help me," Rhonda says, tucking her dark hair behind her ear like Rachel would do.

I soften a little. She did lose a sister. "I am sorry for what happened to Rachel. It was a tragic, horrible accident." I look across the lobby at John. He must be squirming. He must know who I'm seated with. And now he realizes I know what he did to his wife on that yacht. He must know I will ruin his life if I tell Rhonda what she wants to hear. I smile at John, and he looks away. Having the meeting here, in public, was security for me in case I was wrong about the letter writer and threatening for John if I was right. I was right.

"I'm thinking about calling the Coast Guard and getting them to reopen the investigation," she says.

"Based on what?" Justin asks.

"A hunch," Rhonda says.

"I don't think they would respond to hunches. I'm going to look into this for you. I'll question everyone who was there, you have my word," I say. "If I learn that anything other than what we were all told happened, I will be in touch."

"Thank you," she says. "I need answers. When the Coast Guard closed the investigation, well . . . I didn't know what to do. Where to turn. But I know there is more to the story. The Kingsleys always hide things, and they always come out on top. But this time, I want something in return. Answers, especially."

"Do you need anything else? Money perhaps?" I ask. "I don't know who received Rachel's death benefits."

Rhonda looks across the lobby. "He did. Like he needed that cash. Ridiculous. He never checked in on my mom after my sister died. He just vanished after the funeral. Poof. Like she was never part of his life. The bastard."

"I do know people grieve in different ways. But the money—you're right, he didn't need it. Let me see if I can get some of that to your family. Sound good?" I ask. I assume John will be happy to pay, considering the alternative. I'll suggest a large sum. A very large sum. I'm relieved by our conversation. Rhonda doesn't have more than a hunch that Rachel was murdered, and she doesn't seem to know anything about the chemical dumping by the Kingsley company that Rachel had discovered. All in all, she's just a sad person who misses her sister.

And hates John Kingsley.

We share that sentiment.

"Thank you for meeting with me. I'm sorry about all the anonymous notes and the threats. I was just trying to get someone's attention. *Your* attention," she says, standing up.

"You got it," I say. "I'm glad we've reached an understanding."

"Oh, and my condolences are in order, it seems," she says.

"For what?" I ask as we all stand up. Justin stares at Rhonda.

"Says here Richard Kingsley is dead." She holds up her phone.

"What are you reading?" Justin asks.

"The gossip site, OC Scoop. Tell me you don't read it? It's all about the Kingsleys," Rhonda says. "Hope he wasn't killed, too."

"No, he had congestive heart disease. He died peacefully in his sleep," I say, but my eyes dart over in John's direction. Not sure if Rhonda notices.

"OK, well, let me know what you find out about my sister. And thank you for being the only good Kingsley, as far as I can tell," she says.

"No more threats, Rhonda. Understand?" Justin asks.

"Girl Scouts' promise." She waves goodbye. As I watch her walk away, I see Alex leaning against the wall in the corner of the lobby. How does someone so large blend in so easily?

"What's Alex doing here?" I ask Justin.

"Watching over you. I asked him to. Hope you don't mind, but I don't trust any of them," he says. "They're all out to get you, your job. Even with Ted pretending he's going to go along with resigning, I'm still worried."

Justin and I get up and walk across the lobby, ignoring Ted and John drinking at the table nearby. They ignore us, too, although I'm sure John is dying to know what I said to Rachel's sister. That makes me wonder if

John carries the document Rachel uncovered about the company—or did he really destroy it, as Richard commanded? I may need Sibley and her breaking and entering talents. Then I remember the fixer.

"Does Alex know how to pick locks?" I ask as we wait for the elevator.

"Sure. But what's wrong now?" Justin asks.

"I may need him to break into John's room, search the safe," I say. I look at Justin. I've trusted him with everything else; I may as well tell him everything. I hope he is what he seems to be. I need to believe he is. I take a deep breath. "Before Rachel died, she announced she had proof of chemical dumping off the coast of Catalina Island by our company. Richard was furious. The past is the past and that sort of thing. The fact is, though, that if it came out, it would be years of litigation and, perhaps, personal liability for the family. Richard assured me John destroyed the document. But John being John . . ."

"I bet he has it," Justin says.

"All of this is highly confidential. You understand?"

"Don't you know by now you can trust me? I know you are accustomed to a man who was a cheat and a liar. You deserve better. I am trustworthy, Paige. And I really care about you, too," he tells me.

I hope I'm not making a big mistake, but I'm going to trust my heart. "I believe you. And I care about you, too."

We step outside into the never-ending wind. This time, though, I smell something. Like someone is using a wood-burning fireplace, but it's too hot for that, and most have been banned for air-quality reasons.

"Do you smell that?" I ask Justin, panicked.

"Smell what? Just the ocean breeze," he says. "Are we still hosting that dinner tonight?"

"Yes, it's paid for. We'll turn it into a remembrance for Richard. Our last event of this failed retreat, and then we can get out of here," I say. "I love the Twin Palms, but not with all of these people."

"Even me?" he asks. His finger touches my hand, and my entire body surges with electricity. I'm dizzy with desire.

"If it was just you and me, that would be a whole different weekend," I say. I take his hands in mine and lean in to whisper in his ear, "Want to come in? I don't feel like being alone."

"You're not. You have me," he says and follows me into the suite. He keeps the door open for a minute, and I see him nod to Alex, who is posted across the hall. The reality of all that has happened crashes back into my mind.

"He's already back from the funeral home?" I ask. "Can we bury him soon?"

"Alex has a physician he uses who signed the death certificate and registered the death. The funeral director has what he needs. Just awaiting word about the ceremony. Everything is buttoned up."

I hadn't thought of all that, the process behind death. I'll have Serena plan the funeral. Maybe that will give her closure of some sort. "So it's congestive heart failure. No autopsy?"

"Correct. We have all the evidence to use if Ted and John don't get in line."

"You guys are taking this seriously," I say. "I can't thank you enough. But why is Alex still here?"

"Somebody killed Richard, and that person is still walking around this resort," he says. "We're going to keep you safe for as long as it takes, Alex and I. My dad insists, and I agree."

"Why does your dad care about my safety?" I ask.

"Because I do. Like I said, he's a real estate and tech guy; he's made a fortune, but he's a self-made guy, so he doesn't have all of this generational dirty laundry to deal with like the Kingsleys have," Justin says. "And it's only me. I'm the only child, so there's none of this posturing for succession. It's mine if I want it."

"Why did he send you to work at Kingsley?" I ask. "Tell me the truth."

"As a spy, honestly. I can't believe Ted and John didn't run a deeper background check on me, but I guess they were in a hurry to watch you, and that was more important than finding out who I really was. Anyway, our companies competed in the past over deals," Justin says. "But now that there's been a leadership change, we want to work together. He likes where Kingsley is headed with you at the helm. I couldn't agree more, obviously. But enough about my dad . . ."

When he leans in for a kiss, I'm more than ready. The Kingsley men fade from my mind as my body takes over. I grab Justin's hands and pull him into the bedroom, all the pent-up sexual tension pulsing between us. Our eyes lock, our bodies inches apart. My heart races as I undress quickly, hungry for more.

36
SIBLEY

I had to go out and get some air. Serena is a disaster. She can't pull herself together. It's as if her last hope for a happy life just went *poof*. I told her we'd all take care of her, at least Paige and I, but I've decided she really loved my dad. It's breaking her heart that she wasn't there with him when he died.

"I could have called 911," she said over and over. "I could have saved him. If only he'd had dinner with me. What will I do without him?"

I don't know. I mean, he was my dad. And I'd just decided to pick him over Uncle Walter. So now I'm on Walter's shit list and Dad is dead. I have a knack for making bad choices; everyone would agree with that.

I make it through the dust and wind bowl and take the elevator to the lobby. I love the view up here, overlooking the pool—which I can't believe I haven't used because of this stupid windstorm—and the ocean beyond. The whitecaps are crazy, still.

Wait. What is Uncle Walter doing here? And is that Colson, my ex-boyfriend? I was over him before I stepped foot off the yacht; Uncle Walter knows that. What the heck. I blink. It's not a bad dream. They're still sitting there, at a table, with John and Ted.

I take a deep breath and walk over to the table. "Gentlemen. What's going on? Uncle Walter, why are you here? Colson, go away."

"Nice to see you, too, Sibs. Come on, sit down. Join us," Colson says. His bleached-blond hair and overall biker look could be cool, but now it just looks out of place.

"I don't think so," I say, hands on my hips. "What are you guys up to? Plotting Paige's overthrow, as usual? Doesn't it get old?"

"Now, look, young lady, I raised you. You don't talk to me like this, and your loyalty should be with me," Uncle Walter says. "I brought Colson along because he told me you two were friendly. My mistake, obviously."

"Obviously," I say and glare at Colson. Why would Colson lie to Uncle Walter? What is his endgame here? So annoying, but I'll ignore him until he leaves, which will be soon. Out of the corner of my eye, I see Ty. That makes me smile.

I turn my smile toward this pathetic group of double-crossing men and shake my head. "Well, I'll leave you to your scheming. But just so you know, Paige is president, and she's going to remain president. You are wasting your time here." Then I soften and kiss Uncle Walter on the cheek. "I do love you."

He smiles. "I know. You're just a little jumbled. I don't blame you. Richard had that effect on people."

I nod and wave and hurry over to flirt with Ty. I truly hope Colson is watching.

"I'm so sorry about your dad," Ty says. "I just heard the news."

"It's not supposed to be out yet, that he died," I say. "But thank you. It's tough."

"It was on that gossip site, so everybody knows," Ty says. "The management is freaking a bit because he died here, in bed."

"Yeah, that's bad for people wanting to stay in the best suite. I get it," I say. "Sort of like the ghost of Richard will always be at the Twin Palms. Although, there are probably tons of people who would pay extra to sleep in the suite where they know a famous billionaire died."

I notice people are staring at us and pointing. One woman aims her phone camera at me. I hold up my hand to cover my face.

"Let's go outside, over here," Ty says.

"Why are people staring at us?" I ask.

"It's not us; it's you. The OC Scoop site ran a photo of the family, so they're recognizing you," Ty says. "Come on. In here."

We duck into what appears to be an employee break room, just past the valet stand. Nobody else is inside. Ty shuts the door behind us and turns on overhead lights.

"I love this hideaway," he says. "Only a few of us have a key. And you can get out on the other side," he says, pointing to a door across the room. "That leads to the elevator. Fast escape."

"Thank you," I say. He is really cute. "Want to make out a little?"

He flushes. "I do but not on duty. I love my job. Can we meet up tonight? I'm off at six."

"Perfect. Can you be my dinner date? We're all having dinner at the Point, which will be miserable unless I have a fantastic dinner date," I say.

"Let me ask my boss. I'd love to be your date, although he might not let me do it. Maybe we can plan a date off-property, after your dinner?" he says. "For right now, let's get you out of here. Escape hatch."

He opens the door and peeks around. "All clear. I'll text you after I get the clearance from my boss. I'm going to be there, or we'll make plans for after. Sound good?"

"I'm planning on it," I say. And then I lean in and kiss him, and I watch his face flush as shivers run down my spine. I love this dance—the first kiss, the promise of more, teetering on the precipice of crossing the friendship line. I break our embrace reluctantly. "Thank you for everything."

He grins.

"Can't wait for tonight," he says. "See you later."

As he walks away, the electric charge of desire fades and a wave of dread rolls through me. I hope Colson doesn't decide to beat him up.

37
JOHN

This little lobby reunion between Uncle Walter and Ted seems to be going well. Things always seem to go more smoothly with Ted when alcohol is involved, I've noticed.

But I'm finished with small talk. It's likely we are only behaving this way because Sibley's former boyfriend and thug burglar Colson is sitting with us for some reason. I know Uncle Walter brought him along to mess with Sibley, but why are we stuck with him?

"Colson, shouldn't you be chatting with Sibley?" I ask. "I bet you can find her in her suite."

"It was pretty obvious she didn't want to talk to him," Uncle Walter says. "My mistake, son, bringing you along. Why don't you go have the front desk help book you a flight back home tomorrow morning? I'll cover it. Charge it to my card on file."

"First class again?" Colson asks with a lopsided grin.

"Sure. Why not," Uncle Walter says. "Go on. We need privacy."

"OK, well, great seeing you all. Have a good life, which you do but none of you fools seem to realize it. Always wanting more—that's the problem with you Kingsleys," he says.

I change my opinion. He's an observant thug. That's likely a dangerous combination. But at least he's gone. As I watch him walk away, I realize a group of women is staring at our table. The word has spread about Dad's death like an out-of-control wildfire. Next the news stories will turn to succession and the will. I need to figure out how to get a copy of his will before anyone else can. I make a note to find out the executor of his estate and get to him first. My thoughts are interrupted by my ridiculous brother.

"I want you both to know I didn't kill Dad," Ted says, slurring a bit. "It wasn't me, so I'm thinking it's you."

That was a guilty outburst, as far as I'm concerned. We weren't even talking about Dad's death.

"What? Don't look at me. You think I killed Richard? I loved him the most. I was his first son," I say.

"You have practice," Ted says.

He is poking the bear. I feel my anger ignite. "Shut up, Ted."

"I thought Richard died peacefully in his sleep. That's what all the news outlets are reporting," Uncle Walter says, looking back and forth between us. "What's going on?"

"Nothing. He's drunk, as usual," I say.

"They want me to resign, Uncle Walter. Then Paige and John will have a fight for control," he says. "Can I have a job? I'm sort of done with this shit anyway."

Uncle Walter looks at me. I quickly shake my head no, indicating Ted doesn't know about his stock purchases.

"Ted would be a great asset to *your* company, Walter, the one you were telling me about at the marina," I say. "He's great at sales and acquisitions. Easily transferable to your yacht sales business."

"That last land deal you did was a disaster, though," Walter says.

"Yes, so I've heard, over and over again," Ted says. "It's not my fault. Paige approved it."

"Uh-huh," Walter says, sounding just like Richard. "You want to move to Florida, son? Most of my companies are headquartered there."

"Sure. A change of scenery is just what I need. I'm sick of it here. Besides, Florida is beating California in every metric. I might as well join the migration," Ted says. He waves to the waiter for another round.

I cover my glass. "I've had enough to drink. I need to go get some things done. You two can work out the details. You should come to the dinner tonight, Walter. It's going to turn into a memorial of sorts for Dad, I bet."

"When is the family releasing an official statement?" Walter asks. "I can handle it, if you'd like. I am his only sibling."

"Paige would kill you," Ted says.

"Wow, she's really cut your balls off, son," Walter says, shaking his head. "You need to man up here, nephew."

"Yeah, well, Dad created her, and now he's dead. So we're stuck with her," Ted says. "Well, you all are. I'm done with her. With *this*."

"So you've said, Ted," I say. "But actions speak louder than words. Draft your resignation letter and send it to Paige. That's when you'll be out of it. I'll make sure you have a significant severance package. And then you're off to Florida. Send me a postcard."

"You're enjoying this too much, Johnny," Ted says.

Oh, I really am. I smile. He's been a thorn in my side since he was born. A constant point of comparison for my father, a comparison where I always came up short. But not anymore.

"See you both at the dinner tonight. It will be a great send-off for you, brother," I say.

"I don't know how you're going to get rid of Paige, unless you're planning to kill her, too," Ted says.

"Ted!" Uncle Walter says, looking around the lobby to see who may have overheard him.

"Don't be ridiculous," I say. "Unlike you, I play the long game, Teddy. You never had a chance against me."

As I turn and walk away, I feel more than Ted's stare. I look toward the other end of the lobby, by the fireplace, and I swear every one of the people sitting at those tables is watching me. Do they know about Richard? Do they presume I'm the new CEO?

They'd be correct.

38
TED

Uncle Walter is offering me a fresh start. Paige is forcing me out, of course, and so is John. Demanding I write a resignation letter on the day my father died. Correction: was *murdered*. By John. It's tough for me to let him win like this. I need to talk to Meredith. She'll know what to do.

"Hey, Walter, thanks for the offer. I'm really going to consider it," I say. "Do you have murder winds there?"

"What do you mean?" he asks.

"These Santa Anas. Some people call them murder winds. They make you do crazy things, like murder people," I say.

"No, son, we don't have Santa Anas," he says. "Is there something you want to tell me?"

"People also call them devil winds," I say. "Maybe they bring the devil with them? Stir up evil. I don't know."

"Why don't you go take a nap," Walter says. "Sober up, get your thoughts together. If there's anything you want to tell me in confidence, I'm here for you, son."

"I don't have anything to confess to," I say. He's irritating me now.

"Son, I know you've cheated on your wife regularly, you have a gambling addiction," he says.

"*Had.* I'm finished with that, with Vegas," I say.

"Well, let's just say you have a lot you could confess to," Walter says.

"Sure, I'm not a Boy Scout, but who is, in this family?" I ask. "Certainly not you. I have to go. Thanks for picking up the tab."

I walk away feeling as confused as I ever have in my life. And sad. I feel sad, I'll admit. I loved Richard even though he put us through the wringer. I loved him even when he yelled at me, I realize. He only wanted to make me a better man. He just had his own way of going about it.

I push the door and step outside. It smells like a bonfire outside. I think back to when I was a teenager, enjoying bonfires on the beach, drinking beer, making out with the prettiest girl at school. I was the big man on campus back then—through college, too. How did I end up knocking on the door of a sixty-something woman, desperate for her advice and attention?

Meredith opens the door. She's wearing jeans and a T-shirt. I didn't think she owned such things.

"Come in. How are you doing?" she asks.

Her kindness brings tears to my eyes. "I'm sad," I say. "He was a terrible father, but he was mine. I never thought he'd be gone. I just didn't. So I'm not doing so great. And I miss him already." And it's true.

"He had a way of getting into a person's head and never getting out," she says, taking my hand and leading me to the couch. "Just remember, he was proud of you, Ted."

He didn't sound proud. Richard's hurtful words to me Friday night are seared into my brain: *I don't need you, Teddy. I've never needed you. You need me. Without me, you'd just be another washed-up, aging pretty boy. In fact, you're doing a really good job playing that role so far this week-end. Bravo, spoiled loser. Maybe I should just cut you off, see how you'd fare in the real world.*

My dad called me a spoiled loser. I take a deep breath and swipe at the tears. I was furious at the time, but now all the furor has been replaced with a heavy weight of sadness.

"I don't know what to do," I say. "My uncle Walter offered me a job. In Florida. I'm sort of lonely, and everything is a mess. Maybe Florida will be a fresh start?"

"No. Why would you do that?" she asks. "Your place is here. At Kingsley."

"Paige is demanding my resignation," I say. "John agrees. I'm out."

"How can they expect you to just resign? You haven't done anything wrong—well, besides that idiotic land deal and that little embezzlement problem you had. But that was years ago," she says. She stands and begins pacing. "Are they threatening you with something? Did you do something I'm not aware of?"

"No." I'm not telling her about the murder thing. She'll think I did it, too. Nobody believes me. "Paige is mad I came to her room, drunk, last night. That's all. She's calling it harassment."

Meredith stops pacing and looks at me. "It is harassment. You need to get over her and move on. I have one idea." She winks at me.

"I'm moving on. For sure. Maybe to Florida. Come with?" I shrug. I wish I could ask Dad what to do. I think he'd probably tell me to stay and fight. How did I get into this position? I'm not a loser at heart—or am I? Maybe I am just as awful as Paige thinks I am and as horrible as my dad said I was. A fresh wave of tears floods my eyes.

"Hey, Ted, it's going to be OK. Look, I never took you for a quitter. Have you seen the will? That could, and probably will, change everything," she says. "I'm not sure when your father made his latest revisions to it. He did mess around with it a lot. Another game, I suppose. Which of the kids gets what, who gets screwed, that sort of thing. Oh, Richard."

"I didn't even think about the will. Can he dictate what happens to the company through his will?" I ask. Maybe there is one more chance for me. I wipe the tears from my face and manage a half smile. I need to think. I stand and walk to the windows and the view. "This could be my one last chance."

"Yes, of course. It could be," she says. "His shares have to go to someone."

"We need to get a copy of the will—the latest copy," I say. "He was going to promote me on Friday, until I messed up and didn't go to the meeting. Maybe I'm in charge in the will?"

"I'm assuming you can get a copy from the executor," Meredith says.

"I don't even know who that is," I say.

"It's me," she says with a smile.

As her words sink in, I rush to her side and give her a huge hug. "It's you. Of course it's you."

39
SERENA

The phone rings in my hotel room, but I ignore it. I'm sitting alone, in the dark, in mourning. My phone pings next to me with another text from Paige. I'm afraid if I don't answer her soon, she'll come over here. I don't want to see her. I don't want to see anyone. Except Richard.

My phone rings again. Fine. If this will make her stop bothering me, I'll answer.

"I'm worried about you. Sibley says you're inconsolable," Paige says.

"I am," I admit. "I'm lost. I came here to find Richard, find our love again. And now he's gone, forever."

"I know. And I'm so sorry—sorrier than you know. It was my idea for you to come, and I do know how much he loved you. I saw it in the boardroom," she tells me. "We need to be strong. For Richard. You are family. I need you to be in charge of the funeral. Can you do that? Honor him that way?"

"Yes," I say. "Of course. I am his wife."

"You are. Good. I'll text you the funeral director, Mr. Mortison's, contact information. Whatever you'd like to do to make it special, please do. I also thought the press release from the family should come from you," she says. "We've written something up for you."

"Thank you, Paige. That means a lot," I say.

"I think you loved him the most and the best. I really do. And I know that if he had lived, he would have taken you back. I know it."

"Me too. I saw the look of love in his eyes," I tell her. "Someone took him from me."

"No, it was his heart," Paige says. "I'm worried about you, Serena. You don't sound well."

"I'm not well. The love of my life is gone. Murdered. I don't believe you. He was fine; I saw him last night," I say. Richard wasn't ill aside from his congestive heart failure; he had years of life left to live. He was mad. At everyone. But he was not sick, his heart was not stopping. "His heart was broken, by me, but we were going to mend it. We were going to get back together. He was going to protect me and Sophia. Now we have no one. I wonder if Richard's murderer will kill me next."

"What? No. Why? Stop thinking these awful thoughts. Richard wasn't murdered. You're in shock. It's understandable," Paige says. "Maybe you should rest. I could see if there is a doctor on call here at the resort, maybe get you something to calm you down. Why don't you call the funeral director later."

Paige is covering for someone. She knows more about Richard's death than she is saying—much more. I'll ask the funeral director for details.

"I'll call now. See you tonight," I say and hang up. I walk to the front door of my room, making sure it's locked, bolted, and the chain is still on. It is. Next, I check all the doors and windows, making sure they are locked, too. They are coming for me next; I know it. I need Richard. I drop back onto the bed. I've pulled the curtains, and it's as dark as a tomb in the room.

I pull out my phone, find the funeral director's number in the text, and call him.

"Hello, Mr. Mortison. This is Richard Kingsley's wife," I say.

"I am so sorry for your loss," Mortison says. He has a deep, soft voice, just like you'd expect for a man who works with the dead. "Are you calling about the funeral service?"

190

"I am. The family has put me in charge of the planning," I say. "When can we meet?"

"I'm available tomorrow afternoon. Would you like to come here, see the available rooms for the funeral service?" he asks.

"Yes, I would. And I'd like to say goodbye, too. I'm assuming open casket is an option?" I say.

He clears his throat. "I'm sorry, Mrs. Kingsley. Your husband has been cremated."

"No . . . Who said to do that?" I ask. I've dreamed of kissing Richard one last time, but he's only ashes now. In my dark bedroom, I imagine he is beside me on the bed. I reach for his hand, and it's only a pile of sand.

Through the phone, I hear him rustling through paperwork. "It was at the direction of the president of his company, Paige Kingsley, on behalf of the grown children of Richard Kingsley: John, Ted, and Sibley. Everything is in order. I am sorry if you were surprised."

Why didn't Paige tell me that? I thought I was in charge of everything. Oh my gosh. Poor Richard. Something is going on here. Something is being hidden from me. I know it. Every Kingsley action is calculated, so I wonder what her motive is. Richard would never want to be cremated. He'd want us staring at his face during an open-casket ceremony, his ego fed one last time.

I wonder, though, if I'll ever find out. Paige is up to something. I guess she is becoming just like the others. I think about John, his blind rage. If he was capable of killing his wife, why couldn't he kill his father? And Ted. He's out of control. I can't believe I ever found him attractive. Now he looks manic, lost, and mostly drunk. Could he be the one who killed Richard? Maybe. He seems desperate to me.

And what about Paige? I can tell he upset her Friday. I hope he isn't trying to move her out.

I try to imagine Paige killing someone. But it's ridiculous. I picture her two daughters, their lovely life together. She wouldn't risk all that. No, I can't imagine her killing a bug.

The answer is with the sons. I just don't know why Paige is covering for them. But I intend to find out. I walk to the sliding glass door and pull open the curtains. The bright sunset hurts my eyes, but I can't hide away any longer. I need to plan a funeral.

"All of your children were threatened by you, darling. You had so many enemies," I say to the ghost of the man I love. "Who did this to you, my darling? Why did you have to leave me and Sophia?"

He doesn't answer; he simply smiles.

"Don't worry, darling. I will find out what happened and get the revenge you deserve."

"Mrs. Kingsley? I can barely hear you? Did you say something to me? Are you still on the line?" Mortison asks. I've left the phone on the bed on speaker, so his voice is even more hushed.

"I was just speaking with . . . Well, yes, tomorrow afternoon works. I'll be at your funeral home around two o'clock," I say from across the room. I remember my manners. "Thank you."

"You're welcome. And again, my sincere condolences," Mortison says before hanging up.

It's not his fault Richard is a pile of ash. But I will find out who did this, who killed Richard. And then, I will kill them.

Because unlike Paige, I am a killer at heart. I grew up with nothing and had everything with Richard. Someone took that away, just when I was getting it all back. For me. And Sophia. Now we're adrift without Richard, without his money, without his protection. I am unhinged, it's true. I don't need sedatives, though; I need revenge. Someone will pay for this. I will uncover the truth.

40

KRYSTLE

When John walks through the door, I greet him with a big hug. I am fresh from relaxation nirvana at the spa, pampered and perfect. I'm dressed in a long pink silk slip dress that the boutique owner promised fit me like a glove. A sexy glove with curves, that is.

"Welcome home, handsome," I say. I hope I'm taking his breath away.

"You look gorgeous, honey," he says, stepping back and taking me in. "Wow!"

"Thank you! Do you need to freshen up before, you know, asking me to marry you?" I ask. I'm trying to suggest that it would be nice of him to take a shower, get all that male business energy washed off him. I can smell it, like something rotten in the back of your refrigerator.

"Um, yes, sure. I'll just go hop in the shower, put on a suit and tie. Sound good?" he asks. Like it was his idea.

"Sure, sounds fab. I'll have champagne waiting."

It's strange to think about the day your life changes forever. Today is that day for me. Do all people getting engaged feel that way? I mean, despite the reasons I got into this in the first place, I've grown fond of John, and I've fallen in love with the lifestyle. I happened to swing by the house for sale next door. It's gorgeous from the outside, with a swimming pool and everything. It's only $22 million. It would make a great wedding gift. I place the glossy brochure I picked up at the front desk on the coffee table next to the bucket of ice chilling our champagne.

I decide to take a selfie and send it to my mom. After all, I'm here because of her. I capture my sexy dress, the champagne, and the brochure, as well as enough of the suite to be able to tell just how big and amazing it is. I text it to my mom.

I text: Thanks for pushing me, Momma. I am just about to get the proposal of a lifetime.

She texts: Wow. Is that dress too sexy for a good Christian woman? ☺ Take another photo and send it to me as soon as he gives you the ring! I'm so excited!

I text: Will do.

I hear the shower turn off in the other room. In just a matter of minutes, I'm going to be engaged. I'll be able to take care of my mom for life. And as for me, I'm going to be a Kingsley. Pinch me.

John walks into the room, wearing a dark suit, navy tie, and a frown. *Uh-oh.*

"Don't you look handsome," I say, hoping my enthusiasm is catching. "Champagne?"

"No, well . . . You know, I'm not sure if this is the right time for us to get engaged. I mean, my dad died here last night," he says.

All this waffling is driving me crazy. I dig down deep inside to find some compassion. OK, found some.

"John, your dad is in a better place, free from suffering. He would love to see you happy, engaged, and in love," I say. "You know that. I say push out that bad energy with some loving juju of our own. Come on, you know you want to."

"I don't know. I mean, we're on a business retreat. The optics . . ."

Someone has gotten into his head. *Better not be Ted.* "Who told you not to marry me? Tell me."

"No one. It's not that," he says.

"You've been with your brother all afternoon." Now I'm sounding a little huffy.

"I know. He's a mess, but he didn't say anything about you." He sits on the couch, knee bouncing up and down. "I just need to think. Walter isn't moving fast enough."

"Who?" I ask. Speaking of moving, let's put a ring on it already. I touch his bouncing knee with my hand, my left ring finger noticeably bare.

"Nothing," he says. He's lost in thought.

"What are you trying to do? Maybe I can help."

"No, you can't. That would be impossible," he says.

Rude.

"You want to take the company away from Paige. Either become the CEO so she reports to you or take the president title," I say. Now I have his attention. I really don't know why he thinks I'm such an idiot.

"Yes, that's exactly it," he says.

"You told me Richard picked Paige seven months ago because she had a good family, that she and Ted and the girls looked like the all-American family. Right?"

"Among other reasons, yes."

"Well, you need a wife and a family," I say. "I can make both of those things happen for you."

He looks at me then. Really looks at me. I smile.

"Richard isn't here anymore to judge me or my family. I don't need window dressing; I just need what's rightfully mine," he says. "And I'm going to get it. By the end of this weekend."

I can't help it; tears fill my eyes. I turn away from him and face the ocean view. He's not going to propose. He doesn't care about me. Not really. All he cares about is the stupid company. I pinch the inside of my wrist to stop the tears. I hear my mom's voice: *Remember, Krystle, you don't care about him, either. You just want the money. You want what is due to the Duggers.*

I turn back to John. "A little window dressing might soften people's opinion of you. Just saying." I force a smile. "I already picked out the ring. You might as well give it to me."

He reaches into the breast pocket of his suit. He pulls out the box, opens the top, and stands up. "Krystle Carrington, will you be my window dressing?" he says. He hands me the ring, and I slide it on.

Not quite the romantic proposal I dreamed about, but nonetheless, I prevailed. "Yes," I say. I'm never taking this thing off. Not ever.

"OK, then. That's that," he says.

Ridiculous. "Honey, give me a kiss at least?"

"Sure," he says, then plants one on my cheek. "Champagne? Oh, and what's this?" He's pointing at the glossy real estate flyer I left out for just this reason.

"Yes, champagne, please. Oh, and that's our dream home," I say, although I'm not sure window dressing gets to pick dream homes. Probably not. "Wouldn't it be fun to just live at the resort full-time?"

"You do know my dad died here," he says. He's acting like I'm an idiot again.

"Yes, John, rest his soul. You could stay close to his spirit here," I say. I'm grasping at straws, but I don't have a choice. He's driving me crazy. I take a breath and remember the money. The blood money. For my daddy. For my brother. For me and the life I want to live.

He picks up the brochure, flips it over. "Less than I thought," he says.

I am going to be so rich. It's ridiculous. Twenty-two million is less than he thought it would be?

"I don't have to live here at the Twin Palms; we can find something else," I say. I'm flexible.

"I have a nice place in Irvine," he says.

"I don't want to live in the house you and your wife lived in. That's bad karma," I say. "Besides, we need to be by the ocean. The beauty here—well, I've never seen anything like it. It's heaven on earth, even in the winds."

"OK, well, I've spent enough time talking about all this. If you want to find a new home for us, that's fine. Probably would be good to have a change of scenery. I've sort of kept the house a shrine to my dead wife."

I know. I've been there. "Yes. Let me handle everything. And all the wedding plans. I'm thinking next month, right there on that lush green lawn, ocean sparkling behind us. We can have the reception at that restaurant on the point. Sound good? All you need to do is show up to the ceremony, wearing your best CEO attire," I say.

With that, he finally smiles and pops the champagne. "Sure, yes. That sounds good."

Easy peasy, sort of. I need to get Momma involved in the wedding planning. As soon as possible. I've put a hold on the date a month from now, secured it with a big fat deposit and something that may have seemed like a bribe. Of course this place was booked up for years, but as I'm discovering, money talks. Very loudly. Despite their propensity for accepting bribes, I like the staff here. I know they'll help me make the wedding ceremony and reception classy and elegant—expensive, obviously, but I'm worth it.

"I'll send a calendar invite for our wedding date, just so you have it blocked," I say. "You don't need a honeymoon, right? I'm sure you're too busy for that."

"I am. Hey, I need to go talk to someone before the dinner, if you don't mind," he asks.

I pout. "At least drink a little champagne with me before you run off?"

He clinks my glass with his. "Cheers. To wedded bliss."

I smile. "And window dressing to be proud of."

And then, with a chuckle, he's out the door. Happy engagement to me. I snap a selfie with the huge diamond ring sparkling in the forefront of the shot.

I text: He put a ring on it.

Mom texts: What an idiot. Congratulations!

41

JOHN

I need to talk to Paige. I need to make sure we have an understanding. I round the corner of the hotel's hallway and run into Rhonda. Literally.

"Excuse me," I say before realizing it's her.

"There's no excuse for you," she says. "How dare you?"

"Look, Rhonda, I don't know why you're here, and I don't know what you want, but if Paige invited you, then you're her problem, not mine," I say. I start to walk down the hallway.

"I know you did something to Rachel. Otherwise, you wouldn't be acting so nervous. You would've stayed in touch with Mom. But you didn't. I'm going to get to the bottom of it, with Paige's help. She promised," Rhonda says.

Oh, I just bet she did. "Look, why don't I give your family, including your mom, some money."

"That's funny. I wrote to you, you know. Asking if you could give my mom the accidental death–benefits payout because you didn't need it. She did. You know Rachel supported Mom all these years," she says.

"I don't remember that letter." I'm lying.

"You're lying," she says. "I know all about you, John Kingsley. Remember, I'm her sister. I know things."

She's bluffing, or she wouldn't be meeting with Paige. She'd be calling the cops.

"So your mom needs money. Fine. I'll pay. Whatever Rachel gave her a month, I'll match it for the rest of her life," I say. Some people might call this blood money. I don't. "And you? Do you need money?"

Rhonda considers me. It's hard to look at her because she looks just like Rachel, God rest her soul.

"Everybody needs money, John. Except you people who have too much of it," she says. "I want a lump sum. I want to be finished with you forever."

The feeling is mutual. "I'll talk to my attorney, draft up an agreement for both you and your mom. And then this will all be over, right?"

"Send me the money and the agreement, and then it will be over," she says. "Don't forget, Johnny. Or I'm going to call the Coast Guard and have them reopen the investigation. And while they're doing that, they could poke around on the sea floor for some toxic chemical drums."

We lock eyes. Rachel told her sister what she had discovered. I can't believe it. Well, she could try to get an investigation going, but I have the only proof. I need to destroy that document as soon as I take control of the company.

"Threats aren't becoming on you, Rhonda," I say. "Excuse me. You'll hear from my attorney by Monday afternoon."

"See you tonight at dinner, Johnny. Save me a seat next to you. Oh, wait, never mind. Paige already took care of that. It was supposed to be a surprise, but now you know."

Paige seated me next to my dead wife's sister tonight. How lovely. It's time for us to have that chat. I burst through the door to the outdoor walking path, and I'm as riled up as the winds. Stepping outside feels and smells like stepping into a hot fireplace. I wonder if there are fires nearby. It smells like it. I'm sure the resort is watching things. I reach the door to the main building and pull it open.

My sister is standing there. Sibley seems to be the only one out and about in this weather. Of course it's just the two of us. This little walk is turning into a nightmare.

"Johnny. Where are you going? What's the rush?" she asks, hands on hips. "You look nice. Are you excited for the dinner tonight? Should be interesting. I'm going to get all dressed up myself. Can't wait."

"Right. See you there," I say, trying to walk past her and get inside.

"Johnny," she says.

Here it comes: the Sibley Slam.

"Your hair is a mess. Remember how you used hairspray on the yacht? You should travel with it," she says.

"Whatever, Sibley. I don't have time for your silly games. You're irrelevant, always have been."

"I'm not irrelevant, Johnny. Why did you bring Uncle Walter here? Are you trying to do a stock run? I tried that once; it didn't work out so well," she says. "You're not being original at all."

I really cannot stand this brat.

"It's none of your business what I'm doing, now that I'm going to be in charge. You should watch your tongue," I say. "Just because Dad supported your ridiculous lifestyle doesn't mean I will."

"You aren't in charge. Serena told Paige and me what you did to Rachel. We can't have a murderer in charge of Kingsley, now, can we?" She smiles.

I want to strangle her, but that wouldn't help my reputation. "You don't know what you're talking about. You weren't there. Serena has it wrong. She hates me, so she's spreading lies like she spreads her legs. All the time."

"Wow, that's dark, Johnny," Sibley says. "I really don't like your energy."

"I don't like yours, either," I say. "Now, get out of my way."

"Or what?" she asks. "Are you going to hurt me, too?"

Defiant as always.

"You aren't worth the effort, sis," I say, stepping around her. I yank the door open and hurry down the hallway. I reach the elevator and push the button hard.

I watch as she holds open the door to the outside inferno, smiling like a person who thinks she's winning. She's not.

I step inside the elevator, thankful the door slides closed, half expecting her to race down the hallway and into the elevator. She's a menace.

I really wish she'd just disappear. No one would miss her. And sometimes, I realize with a smile, wishes come true with a little help. Too dark? Too bad.

42
PAIGE

I'm almost ready for the dinner tonight. It should be lovely and elegant, despite the company I must tolerate. But I remind myself I'm the leader here, and I need to set the right tone. We should be remembering Richard, joining together in our shared grief. It should be a decorous and solemn but lovely evening.

Are Kingsleys able to be decorous? I don't know.

I look in the mirror and smile. I look good. I realize it's because I'm glowing. I haven't had sex since the last time Ted and I slept together. And that was perfunctory, at best. With Justin, it was everything I'd always heard making love could be. I long for him to hold me again.

He left to get ready for dinner and to meet his dad up in the lobby. The three of us will talk before Justin and I head to the restaurant. If his dad and I see eye to eye—if he's not a jerk like Richard Kingsley—I will welcome his help. I need to trust myself. I've become a savvy judge of character over these past few years. I've been forced to, in this position. Trust but verify. I've researched Justin's dad and his business, although I didn't admit that to Justin. I liked what I read, what I learned. So tonight, if we reach an agreement, I'll solidify my position and leave no room for John or Ted to try to take the company from me. I pull on my dress, long and silver. It shimmers in the last glow of the sunset.

Someone knocks on my door. I walk over and check who it is. John. I'm relieved to know Alex is watching me, protecting me. At least, I *hope* Alex is still watching. With Justin's dad's imminent arrival, maybe he's with them.

"What do you want, John? I'm getting dressed for dinner," I say.

"We need to talk, Paige. We need to settle some things now that Dad is dead."

"You mean, now that you killed your dad, John," I say. I open the door but leave the chain in place. "I know what you're capable of. I don't feel comfortable talking to you alone."

"Don't be so melodramatic. I didn't hurt my dad," he says. "Look, Ted is going to resign. I got him a job with Uncle Walter. We just need to figure out *us*."

"There's nothing to figure out with us," I say. "I'm moving to CEO. You need to find another position, optimally with Uncle Walter's company. I hear Florida has much lower taxes. Krystle will love it there. Your money will go even further."

"You've got things all wrong. You're going down in a no-confidence vote. I have Evan, Ted, and Meredith on my side. Dad was going to oust you; that's clear from the minutes of that short board retreat you hosted. What a joke. That land deal you approved will be your demise," he says. "Enjoy your last night in charge of Kingsley."

I slam the door in his face. I am so sick of these guys threatening me. I remember to take a deep breath. Women who step into their power always rile up insecure men. So they lash out, but that doesn't mean they keep us down. That just makes us fight harder, smarter.

At least, that's what the podcast I've been listening to says. And it makes sense. All the animosity from Richard started when I began being honored at women-in-business events, celebrated by the media, and when I started to feel powerful myself. Instead of being proud he'd made the right decision, he started scheming about how to bring me down.

Ted can't stand to see me in charge and happy. It's driving him crazy. I hope John's telling the truth, that Ted moves to Florida. And that he'll take John with him. Sure, Emily and Amy would miss the thought of Ted being nearby. But they're living their own lives, happily immersed in college. And the fact is, he was never there for them, anyway. I was, and I still am.

I think about Krystle, John's girlfriend. He doesn't know who she is, but I do. Should I have warned him about her? Maybe, if he was ever the least bit supportive of me. But he's not. He's a COO who is out to get me with a burning, singular focus.

Why should I stop a woman from burning him a little? I shouldn't. That goes for Krystle, and Rhonda and her mom.

My mind turns to Richard, to this family he created. To the monsters he created. Power, money, and family do not mix well when there's a maniacal narcissist like Richard in the kitchen. To think, I wanted to make him proud. I let him back into the girls' lives and portrayed him as a sweet, doting grandfather. That changed, too, of course, once he felt threatened by my power. No more Sunday dinners with the girls, no more anything for the girls. It's like they had become as useless to him as their mom. Even so, both girls were appropriately distraught when I called with the news of Richard's death. He was their grandfather, after all. I'm glad I reached them before the news broke.

It's a shame, it really is. All of it. But in some ways, I suppose, it was all inevitable.

My telephone rings. It's our PR chief. I'm assuming it's another media call. "Yes, Charlotte?"

"I have the *New York Times* on the line. They'd like a comment from you," she says.

"Put them through," I say.

It's ironic, really, that I will spend the next ten minutes singing Richard's praises. Highlighting his commitment to family, to the company, and to the community. I'll speak about him lovingly as a daughter-in-law.

You certainly can't believe everything you read, Richard always said. He had an extreme mistrust of reporters and the media.

But regarding this interview, he was completely right. Most everything I'll say about him is a lie—so if you happen to read it, don't believe it.

I finish with the reporter and realize it's time to meet Justin and his dad at the lobby bar. I cannot believe how excited I am to see Justin again. I feel like a teenager. I grab my purse, and as I'm reaching for the door, there's a knock. I check the peephole. It's Alex.

"Here to escort you, Mrs. Kingsley," he says. This is the kind of caring I could get used to.

"Thank you." I step outside. The fire smell is stronger now. The winds must be whipping up an inferno. I try not to go there, to remember running for our lives. "How far away is the fire, do you know?"

"Several miles deep in the canyon, but it's growing," he says. "Don't worry. I'll keep an eye on the news. I'm watching out for you. Seems like you've got a few enemies lurking around here."

"All family members," I say. Although, who knows? There could be others. We are a high-profile wealthy family. "Do you think my daughters need security? They are away at college."

Alex pulls open the door to the main building, and I step inside. "You know, Mrs. Kingsley, I always tell my clients better safe than sorry. So yes. They could be at risk."

I've never thought about this until now, until what happened to Richard. Until our family, and our photos, were front-page news around the world.

"Do you know someone I could hire? They are attending two different schools," I say as we ride in the elevator to the lobby. "Now I'm really worried."

"Don't be. I'll have a person on each girl by the end of the evening," he assures me. "We'll assess the risks, monitor the dark web. We'll let you know if anything else is needed."

"Thank you again," I say as we step off the elevator. "I can't imagine what I'd do without you, and I just met you today."

"Happy to be of service." He nods toward the lobby. "They're seated in the corner, right over there."

I turn to where Alex nodded and instantly, Justin and I make eye contact. His grin is as big as mine. Before I reach the table, he's wrapped me in a hug, and we kiss, quickly.

"I can't stand being apart, even if it's to meet my dad," he says.

"I know. Me too," I say.

Justin's dad stands up as we approach the table. "Paige, you're lovelier in person than even in your media hits," he says. "And that's tough to do."

"Thank you, Mr. Reyes," I say. "It's so nice to meet you."

"Call me Tom, please," he says and pulls out a chair.

A gentleman, just like his son.

"I must say, the electricity between you two is something else," Tom says. "I'm sure the whole office can feel it, even though Justin assures me no one knows."

"I hope they don't. But at this point, I don't really care," I say.

"Me either," Justin says and squeezes my hand.

As I settle into my seat, I turn my focus to business. "I've done some research, Mr. Reyes—I mean, Tom—on you and your company. I'm impressed. I'm especially in awe of your seemingly spotless reputation in business and in the community. I am, unfortunately, accustomed to quite the opposite with Richard Kingsley and this company."

"Well, yes, Richard inherited his company. I had the opportunity to build mine from scratch, the way I wanted to—no baggage, no secrets in the closet," Tom says. "I am sorry about your father-in-law's passing, though. He was a worthy adversary."

"He was something, that's for sure," I say. "And as you know, there are a billion issues connected with his death, so my apologies, but I'd like to discuss your idea. Justin told me it's a great idea and mutually beneficial, but that's all."

"I appreciate the directness, Paige," Tom says. "My proposal is that my company comes in on the land deal that's giving you so much heart-ache. We'll take the property off your hands for what you paid for it, minus ten percent. We need the state to approve several other ventures of ours. If they do, we'll offer to donate the land to create a park for the surrounding community to enjoy forever. Win-win."

"Thank you. This is a very generous offer." I know he doesn't need to do this deal. He's doing it to bail me out; he's doing it for Justin. And maybe he's doing it because he truly is a nice guy. Refreshing, if true. I smile. "You must really love your son."

"I do. And I sense I'm not alone." Tom smiles at Justin.

"OK, enough already," Justin says, but he's clearly enjoying himself.

"Do we have a deal, Paige?" Tom asks. "Of course, your team will review the terms, but I know they will find them to be favorable."

"Yes, we have a deal." We shake hands across the table.

"Good. The only other condition is that Justin is going to need to quit, come back to my company. No sleeping with the boss and all. Besides, I'm looking to retire in a few years. Maybe you guys could do a merger," Tom suggests.

Maybe that is what is driving his magnanimity. He's setting me and Kingsley up as a takeover candidate, cloaked in merger terms. Maybe Tom is more like Richard than I realized. "Actually, Justin and I will be able to keep business and personal life completely separate, especially with his resignation. Right, Justin?" I say. The one thing about new lovers is, we only have eyes for each other. That trumps even his father's wishes—for now, at least.

"Whatever you say," Justin says. "We need to get to dinner . . . I guess my last one as your assistant."

That makes me a little uneasy, the thought of him leaving the company. Who will I have on my side day to day? Hopefully, Sibley and Serena, if they're both still willing to be part of the management team. And the girls will be back this summer as interns. I'll be fine. I smile at Justin as he takes my hand.

"Your last night as my assistant but your first night as my boyfriend," I say as we walk toward the elevators and the inevitable chaos of the last night of the family business retreat.

43

SIBLEY

I check myself out in the mirror. I look OK, I decide. I'm wearing a long sheath dress I found at the boutique here. The saleslady said it was made for me. It's blue and brings out my eyes, so I bought it. I'm ready for the family dinner tonight, no matter what happens. There will be fireworks, guaranteed.

There's a knock on my door. I'm stupidly nervous, wondering what Ty will think of my outfit, wondering if Ty will survive my family.

"Hey," I say, opening the door.

It's Colson.

"Go away. My date will be here any minute," I say. "I mean it."

"Your valet-parker guy? Come on, you deserve better," he says, taking a step toward me.

"I'm serious, Colson. Get away from me. I'll call Uncle Walter, tell him what you're doing. He'll cut you off. Whatever he has you doing, it'll end. Poof." I hold up my phone, Uncle Walter's contact on display.

"You used to need me, Sibs. What's happened?" Colson asks, looking more sad than menacing.

"I'm a businesswoman now. I'm part of Kingsley Global Enterprises, working for Paige," I say. "Go back to the swamp you crawled out of."

I see a figure hurrying our way down the hallway. I smile at Ty as he approaches. He looks like he's ready to tackle Colson.

"Sibley?" Ty says. "Is everything OK?"

He looks so handsome in his dark suit. And he's holding a bouquet of roses. For me.

"Colson's just leaving," I say.

"You're making a big mistake, Sib," Colson says, turning to Ty. "Aren't you supposed to be parking cars?"

"No, I got the evening off," Ty says. "Have a good night, sir."

I grab Ty's wrist and pull him inside my room, slamming the door closed.

"Don't be so nice, especially not to him," I say, pulling him in for a deep kiss.

"You look gorgeous. That dress really brings out your blue eyes," he says. "These are for you."

I've never liked a kind guy before. Always the bad guys, guys like Colson. I'm not sure I can handle this.

"Thanks. I think," I say.

"What's wrong? You OK?" he asks.

"Yes, it's just I'm not used to a guy like you."

"That's something we can fix. I'll grow on you like a friendly barnacle," he says and starts laughing. "I don't know why I said *barnacle*."

And that's when I start laughing, too, so hard tears are streaming from my eyes. I can't remember the last time I laughed. The last time someone brought me flowers. The last time I felt pretty, and wanted, for me. First Paige, and now Ty; it's almost too much love. Maybe Dad dying before I could see him was meant to be. I came here to reunite with him, but I know that never would have lasted. We're family, but we were strangers. Estranged. But this trip was worth it. I realize I have people who really do care about me. Paige, Serena, and maybe there is even something here with Ty. Sometimes family is who you make it. I take a deep breath.

"OK, now I'm going to need to redo my makeup," I tell him. "Give me a minute."

After I get myself together—and after we suck face a little more—we head to the dinner. "I'm not sure what to expect. It should be a good meal."

"The best in Laguna Beach, maybe all Southern California. The chef is famous. I've had some leftovers when I've worked dinners here before," Ty says.

He's so cute. "Great. I know the food will be good, but my family won't be. Just try not to take anything personally."

"You mean like valet-parking digs?" he asks.

"Yes, and worse. Who knows?" I say. We make our way to the stand-alone building—perched on the cliff above the white-capped, wind-whipped ocean—and step inside. Candles glow on every table; crystal sparkles. A sign reads KINGSLEY CORPORATE RETREAT FINAL DINNER.

That's funny. We didn't do any of the activities Paige planned to bring us all together. As usual, when the Kingsleys are together, trouble abounds. I spot Serena in the corner, talking to one of the waitstaff.

I wave. I tell myself not to call her *hooker* tonight. She's in a very fragile state. Her face looks weird, puffy, like she's been crying all day. She's wearing all black—conservative, high neck, long sleeves. I don't really recognize her without cleavage popping out all over.

"Come meet Serena," I say to Ty. "She's the opposite of serene tonight, though. She looks like she could kill someone."

"Why?"

"Not sure. Hope it's not me," I say. "Hey, Serena, how are you? Meet Ty."

"Hi, Ty," Serena says in a monotone.

I was right. She's off. Really off.

"Can I help with something?" I ask. "I know you're upset about Richard."

"They're all lying about him. I know it," Serena says.

"OK," I say. I don't want to be the one to disagree with her.

"You'll see," she says. And then she looks past us outside, toward the ocean. "He sent someone. Of course he did. I should have prepared for it."

OK, she's really lost it. There's no one outside. Just the wind, and the palms, and the water.

"Serena, ma'am, can I get you a glass of water?" Ty asks.

Serena's attention turns back to us. "No, thank you. But do me a favor. Both of you. If anything strange starts to happen tonight, run and don't look back. Excuse me."

As she walks away, I say, "Welcome to our wacky family dinner. Oh, and be prepared to run at a moment's notice." I shrug. What else is there to say?

"Oh, crap." Ty pulls out his phone. He answers. "Yes, sure. I understand. Be right there."

"What is it?" I ask. I already know he's not going to be my date any longer.

"I'm so sorry. My boss needs me. Apparently, the fire is growing and moving closer to Laguna Beach, and everybody is on alert in case of an evacuation order. Can I have a rain check?" He leans over and kisses me on the lips.

"Yes," I answer. "Turns out, I really like you, and I'd love a rain check."

"Great," he says. "And let me know if you need me to get you out of this dinner. It could be a personal evacuation. Just say the word."

I smile. "I'll be fine. Can I text you when I'm out of here? Maybe come over?"

"I'll be waiting," Ty says before slipping out of the room and into the dark, windy night.

It takes everything in me not to follow him. I'd rather be anywhere but here tonight, but I know Paige needs support. So I'll stay.

Just one more night with all these losers. My dad's face pops into my head, and tears fill my eyes. Despite how horrible he was, I'm going to miss him. Every day, for the rest of my life. And as for my despicable brothers, tonight I'm going to help make sure Paige keeps her position. The worst thing for a Kingsley man is for a Kingsley woman—or two—to outshine him.

44
TED

It took all afternoon and a brief, but hopefully fulfilling, sexual encounter, but I've finally convinced Meredith to read Dad's will tonight at the dinner. I mean, it is what everyone is waiting for. She will not agree to let me have a first look, though, even when I promised to make her orgasm twice.

She laughed and said no, even then.

I'm headed to her room to walk with her to the Point restaurant. I'm excited. Because one of two things will happen: I'll discover Dad really did like me the best and he put me in as CEO upon his demise or—and frankly, more likely—he didn't. In that case, I'm moving to Florida fast so Paige can't frame me for murder.

I guess she could still do that no matter where I go. But out of sight, out of mind, I think that's what she wants. If I give her what she wants, she'll leave me alone. I think. I hope. I've never considered my former wife to be vindictive or malicious. But then again, I didn't give her much thought. I took her for granted, and worse. Does she want revenge? Isn't being president of Kingsley—my dream job, which she took from me—enough?

It must be enough. Besides, I'm the father of her children. That should count for something. I think of the girls, glad they're off to college and don't know what's happened this weekend. Did Paige tell them about their grandfather? Or did they just read about it in the news? I guess I should call them. I will tomorrow.

I tap on Meredith's door. "I'm here. You ready?"

She pulls the door open with a smile. "Always, Teddy, but we don't have time to mess around before dinner."

"You look lovely," I say. And she does. She's wearing a long red dress and a wrap around her shoulders. Definitely not sexy, but neither is Paige. Serena, on the other hand . . . I shake her out of my head. What a big mistake.

"Thank you. You look handsome. We should go." She steps out.

"You have the will, don't you?" I ask.

"Of course," she says, patting her purse. It's red, too. I fight the urge to grab the purse and run somewhere to read the will. But it wouldn't change anything. It will be what it will be.

"Are you sure you can't give me a tiny hint about what's in the will? Have any of my siblings contacted you about it?" I ask while we walk through the hellscape. The air is thick with smoke tonight. Fires are close. I remember when we had to evacuate our home, Paige and I each grabbing one of our daughters from the bed where they slept and running for the garage, with only the clothes on our backs. I'd always made fun of people who had go bags stashed, valuables and important documents ready to grab. As we drove through the smoke and ash, I thought we'd lose everything. And I kicked myself for being so nonchalant. But our house was saved by the brave firefighters. This smell reminds me of that dark night.

I guess in the end, Paige and I did lose everything anyway.

"I already told you no, a million times. It will be read in public for the first time, with all of you present. And no one has asked to see it yet—except for you, greedy bastard," she says. "I'm kidding. It's fine. I'd be the same way if I were in your shoes."

"Nice to hear. So do I take over, or do I slink away to the Florida swamps?" I ask.

She shakes her head. "Nice try."

We reach the Point and see most of the family is already gathered inside. From outside, in the darkness, you can see them all, as if they're standing on a well-lit stage, but they wouldn't be able to see you. Interesting.

I hold the door open for my elderly date and escort her inside.

"Ted, Meredith, nice of you to join us," John says. "Hear you two have been busy together."

"We've been busy, too!" Krystle shouts, shoving her hand in my face. "We're engaged!"

"Oh, wow," I say. Really. Rachel was a corporate lawyer, one of the best in Orange County. Krystle is a waitress, I think. I thought John was just humoring her when he was talking about the ring and proposing. What's John doing? Does he know? Well, I guess I shouldn't talk. I have no idea what I'm doing, either. I've come a bit undone—for a number of reasons, truth be told.

"Congratulations to both of you," Meredith says. An appropriate response. "When are you tying the knot?"

"In three weeks. Right here, on that beautiful lawn overlooking the ocean. Hopefully no wind," Krystle says. "You'll all be invited."

No, we won't.

"Well, we've got an exciting announcement, too. Don't we, Mer?" I say.

"Don't tell me *you two* are engaged," John says.

"No," I say, a bit too sharp. "Meredith is going to read Dad's last will and testament tonight. Won't that be fun?"

Krystle gasps. "I don't think that's appropriate."

I don't think you *are appropriate,* I almost say.

Paige appears, the jerk Justin on her arm. "What's not appropriate?"

"Having sex with your assistant, for one," I say.

"He quit," Paige says. "As of tonight, he's not my assistant. He's my boyfriend. Not that it's your business."

Krystle points at me. "Ted has a copy of Richard's will, and he's going to read it tonight."

"No, you're not," Paige says. "This isn't the place or time. This is a dinner of remembrance. A somber tribute to an amazing man. And a fitting way to wrap up our corporate retreat."

I smile. "This wasn't a retreat. He wasn't amazing; he was an ass with a lot of cash. We'll all remember him, all right. We'll all remember if he screwed us in the end or not. Am I right?"

"Teddy, if they don't all want to hear it tonight, we can read it after dinner, before bed," Meredith says.

Serena has appeared as if out of the shadows. She's wearing a very un-Serena dress: black and conservative and sack like. She looks like a ghost of herself, pale and without her signature red lips. She points at me.

"Are you sleeping with Meredith now?" she asks, shaking her head. "You really don't have any sort of boundaries, do you?"

"Leave me alone, Serena. I didn't do anything to you," I say. "Where's the bar?"

"A waiter will get your drink order . . . not that you need another," Serena says. "And it's not true that you didn't do anything to me. You ruined my relationship with Richard. And before I could fix it, you killed him."

"Serena, stop it," Meredith says. "You don't look well. Maybe you should go to your room."

Serena glares at Meredith before turning and walking back into the shadows. She's lost her mind, I realize.

"Why does she think you killed Richard?" Meredith asks.

"Ask Paige," I say, glaring at her and Justin. "She's threatening to frame me for murdering Dad, which I didn't do. She thinks she's so clever."

Meredith shakes her head. "This family is ridiculous. Richard died of natural causes. His heart failed, end of story. That is the story, correct, Paige? You've spent all day on press interviews confirming it."

"I have," Paige says. "Anyway, let's all go get a cocktail and find our seats. They're about ready to serve the first course."

Evan arrives at the restaurant and heads immediately to John's side. They are a team. And he's got Uncle Walter on his side, too. I see them all in the little John fan club circle with Krystle. Paige has the support of Sibley and Serena, but they don't have any real power, even if Paige has hired them at the company. I have Meredith, and whatever Dad gives me in the will.

"Mer, you need to read the will," I say. "Ignore what Paige says. Together, with John's posse over there, we have the votes. And we have a quorum."

"Let me go talk to Evan, make sure they'll side with us. We should have the no-confidence vote, too, if the will doesn't make the succession plan clear," Meredith says. "He did seem like he was leaning your way in the end, even though the land deal was your fault."

"She approved it. She'll take the fall for it." Did I know the deal was bad? Not really, but I didn't do the due diligence I should have. I feel my temper flaring. Paige will not get the better of me. She will go down in flames with that stupid land deal. I'm glad I forced it on her. I stare at my wife. "No, Mer, I don't feel bad about it. Look at her over there, flaunting her relationship with her assistant. It's gross."

"Calm down, Teddy." Meredith takes a step back. I may have raised my voice a bit. I remember to keep myself under control. "You're talking too loud."

"I know. Sorry. I'm just over all of this."

"Go get a drink, and I'll talk to Evan."

I watch her walk across the room to where John holds court. She and Evan step away from the group, and I observe them as they banter. Meredith looks over and gives me a thumbs-up.

I don't know what Dad left each of us, and I don't know if he screwed us all in the end. But tonight, we will find out.

OC SCOOP

We can now exclusively report that not only will John propose to his girlfriend, Krystle, tonight with that dinosaur-egg ring she picked out, but in addition, all the Kingsleys will gather for a lavish last meal, even as the canyons around them burn with an out-of-control wildfire. I guess when you're that rich, you don't worry about anything, including Mother Nature. Meanwhile, over here in regular reporter land, we've got our go bags packed, ready to flee when the evacuation order is issued. It won't be long, people. So keep the tips coming for as long as you're safe, and then evacuate when told to. And please, stay out of the way of the first responders. The world lost a titan this weekend, right here in Laguna Beach. We don't need to compound the tragedies.

45
JOHN

We all do as we are told and take our seats at a long table set up in front of huge glass windows looking out to the sea. The people with their backs to the ocean aren't missing a view. It's dark, very dark, outside. The howling winds rattle the windows when a particularly big gust comes along, adding to the eerie setting.

Paige placed herself at the head of the table, with her assistant-now-boyfriend to her right. Krystle and I are across the table from each other. She's seated between Sibley and Ted—a sibling sandwich, poor girl. I'm seated between Serena and Evan; at least I can turn to the right side of the table to find conversation. Serena isn't talking to anyone, isn't eating the appetizer, which was good. Some sort of caviar. Delicious. Krystle wrinkles her nose at the dish, but I told her to try it. Her taste buds are like a little kid's. Uncle Walter sits at the foot of the table, with Evan and Meredith on either side.

I thought Paige invited Rhonda tonight, just to mess with me. I suppose she thinks she didn't need the extra pressure. She thinks she has me right where she wants me. But she's wrong. I'll pay off Rachel's family, and they'll go away. Money buys silence, as we all know. As for Paige, we have her right where we want her. She just doesn't know it yet.

I tap my fork on the water glass. "Let's all raise a glass to Dad, to Richard, to a great man with even greater ambition and business sense, who created a company that's the envy of the world. Sure, he was challenging at times, but he loved us in his own way, and I'll miss him forever." I wait for the room to quiet before I continue. "What a grand way to end this miserable weekend. Thanks again, Paige, for a colossal waste of money and time. The Kingsley Corporate Retreat was one for the history books." I shake my head dramatically as my end of the table chuckles. "So, before the next course arrives, I wanted to call us to order on the little business Dad was working on before he tragically died: removing you as president of the company due to our lack of confidence in your leadership."

"This is not the place or time," Paige says. "Uncle Walter isn't on the board, and neither is Krystle. Serena and Sibley are employees."

"They won't vote. Problem solved," I say. "All board members in favor of removing Paige as president of the company due to lack of leadership and her approval of the inland land deal, say aye."

"I have a buyer for the land," Paige says, standing. "But the deal only goes through if I'm president."

"You're bluffing," I say.

"I'm not," she says. "The Reyes Company is executing the purchase agreement as we speak. Do you want me to kill the deal?"

I cannot believe the luck this bitch has. How did she manage to woo the biggest competitor we have and convince them to help us out? It doesn't make any sense. The Reyes Company would more likely celebrate our demise than save us at the last minute. "What's the catch? It sounds too good to be true." My voice shakes with anger as I speak. "You're probably bluffing. That's it, isn't it?"

Paige turns to Justin. "I am not bluffing, and I had a little help with an introduction to Tom Reyes. Turns out, he's been watching our company from the inside. He's been impressed by me and the direction of Kingsley."

"How would Tom Reyes possibly be watching our company from the inside?" I lean forward with hot rage. This is good. She's done something to let the competition inside our business. I'll get her for this one.

"Actually, John, you and Ted hired his son to be my assistant," Paige says. "Oh, and to spy on me. Funny, isn't it?"

"What? You are a corporate spy?" I say, pointing at Justin and standing in rage. We vetted him as much as the other candidates; I remember. But we were in a hurry to put someone in place, and he ticked all the boxes. This is unbelievable. I cannot believe that little jerk pulled this off. "Your résumé says your last name is Robinson. You double-crossing son of a bitch."

"My last name is legally Robinson. My dad is a billionaire, so he's into security, for obvious reasons. There are a lot of bad actors around. He and my mom decided I'd use her maiden name. For safety reasons, so I can fly under the radar everywhere, like I did here," Justin says.

I really cannot believe this. I'm still not letting her win. I'm not.

Paige chuckles at the end of the table and says, "For someone who spent so many years as Richard's go-to fixer, you really don't seem to have done your homework. And for the record, I'm a good leader, John. Sit down. The salads are ready to be served."

To say I'm furious is an understatement. I drop into my chair. "I'm going to need to review that purchase agreement."

"Naturally, but you'll find everything in order. I've found the Reyes men to be true to their word, unlike the Kingsley men," Paige says with a smile and sits down.

I look at Meredith across the table. The will is the only answer, unless I want to tank the whole company with the proof of toxic dumping in our past. But I can't do it. I love the company too much. That particular truth can never be revealed—not if we want anything left of our legacy.

"Read the will," I say to Meredith.

"Now? At dinner?" Serena says. "How crass. I really cannot believe this."

"They don't have any class, just a lot of money. You should realize that by now, hooker," Sibley says. "Go ahead. Get it over with before the main course. You guys are such losers. I hope he cut you out."

"You're the one who should be worried about that, little sis," Ted says. He's slurring his words again.

Meredith stands and pulls out a notebook. She begins to read. It's all a lot of formal stuff that I'm tuning out. I look around the table, and everyone seems to be tense. It's almost like Richard's back in the room with us, ready to reveal the next way he'll pit us against each other. A visitor from hell.

"*And now, for my wishes, I am leaving equal shares of Kingsley Global Enterprises to each of my children: John, Ted, and Sibley; and to Paige, my daughter-in-law.'*"

Oh my God. He's given Paige shares equal to mine? This is outrageous.

"Yes!" Sibley says. "He didn't cut me out! See? He did love me." She and Paige share a smile.

Meredith continues. "*My brother, Walter, will not receive any of my company shares, nor shall he have any role in my business, ever. You all are likely wondering who will become CEO upon my demise. The answer is, if I am the CEO when I die, if I haven't chosen any of you to take my place, why would I do it now, from the afterlife. Ha. So, for continuity, whoever I've allowed to be president at the time of my demise will remain in that position for a year from this date. We need continuity with me gone, don't you agree? Hopefully, you do. If one of my sons has been named president, well, good for you. I always hoped one of you would lead the company. If it's still Paige, well, good for her. She hung on. And despite my constant undermining, she has done a good job. At the end of this grace year, you will get a team of outside consultants to evaluate how the company is doing and if the president should be replaced.*

"*I hope you all have a happy life and don't fight with each other too much. In the end, all you have is family. They can hurt you the most and love you the best. I did love you, kids, in my own way.' And that's it,*"

Meredith says. "Congratulations, Paige. You have another year at the helm of Kingsley."

"Thank you, Meredith," Paige says. "Please, everyone, enjoy your salads."

"Enjoy your salads." Ted mimics Paige. "You're so annoying. You know, Uncle Walter, moving to Florida sounds like a good idea."

"It's nice there," Walter says. "I can't believe the bastard didn't leave anything to his only brother."

I can. Richard hated Walter with a passion. And now I'm stuck with Paige for another year? I'll build a case; I'll wait patiently. Ted will be out of the way in Florida. I'll be the one to succeed her. I take a deep breath. It's fine. I look across the table at Krystle. We'll get married; have a long, expensive honeymoon and maybe a kid on the way; and the year will be up. Maybe I'll buy her that house next door to the resort.

A year is no time—not really. Not in the whole scheme of things. I stare down the table at Paige. It's annoying and frustrating. And I feel genuine hatred toward her: her smugness, her practiced perfection. And now she has considerable shares of stock. From Dad. Who was going to fire her if he had lived.

"Johnny, hello over there. How are you doing?" Krystle asks, breaking my concentration. "Look how my ring sparkles in the candlelight! Isn't it gorgeous?"

"It's a rock," Sibley says. "Is your hand tired from holding it up?"

"No, it's not bad. It kind of floats in the air because it's so beautiful," Krystle says.

"Leave her alone, Sib. I'm serious," I say.

"Oh, Johnny, I'm harmless. You know that." Sibley takes a sip of red wine and laughs. "But you're not harmless, are you? Does your fiancée know what you did?"

"Shut up," I say. "You don't want to go there; I promise you that."

Serena turns and stares at me. "We all know the truth, John. You should tell her. She's going to be part of the family. This sick, warped family."

"What is it, Johnny? You can tell me anything," Krystle says.

She's so innocent and pure. So simple and sweet compared to Sibley and Serena, and awful Paige.

"Nothing, Krystle honey," I say. "We'll talk later. They're trying to rile me up, but it's not going to work, because I have you now to calm me down."

Sibley leans forward with a smile. "Oh, that's so sweet, Johnny. You're a changed man with Krystle Carrington on your arm, right?"

"I'd like to think I help him, make him happy," Krystle says, eyes sparkling.

"Well, he needs the help," Sibley says. "Truth is, he killed his first wife. Who knows what he'll do to you. Congratulations on your engagement, though. Cheers!"

NEWS ALERT!

The canyon fire has exploded in size and now threatens the town of Laguna Beach. Citizens should be prepared to leave if an evacuation order is issued for their homes. Prepare now. And stay tuned to this emergency channel for more updates.

46

SERENA

The revenge I sought for Richard's death has arrived, although none of the Kingsleys know it yet. I close my eyes, accepting what I've drawn here, realizing my fate. I open them. It was not my imagination. He is here.

The man stands outside close to the window, not trying to hide his presence from me. We are basically staring at each other. The others haven't noticed him; I think because they wouldn't imagine he exists. But I know. I was married to Roman long enough to know about the criminal ties he has. I was married to him long enough to know he would want revenge over baby Sophia. Yes, he is the father, but I decided I made a big mistake. So I had a lab fake the paternity test and used that at trial to get sole custody of my girl. He doesn't like that I outmaneuvered him, and he doesn't like that I wouldn't spend all my divorce settlement from Richard to help his rotten family out of debt. He is a small-minded thug, so of course he sent someone else to do his dirty work.

I learned the hard way that at heart, Roman is a con man and a coward.

I don't care anymore. I'm numb. I came back full of love for Richard, ready to take care of him in his illness, ready to be by his side again. My protector, the man who made my life grand. He meant everything to me, to my future. And now he's gone. And someone will pay, and then I will go, too. I cannot imagine a life without him. Not anymore.

Of course, I will need someone to care for Sophia. In my will, I have named Paige. I am glad to see that she is happy with Justin. A baby is a lot of work, but I would imagine it's more fun with a partner. I look over at the lovebirds and smile.

"Are you doing OK, Serena?" Justin asks. "Can I get you anything?"

"No, thank you. I just have a broken heart, and I don't think anything—or anyone—can fix it. Not ever," I say.

"You'll feel better with time," Paige says. "I know what a shock Richard's death is. I'm still processing it, myself. But you're strong, and you have beautiful baby Sophia to take care of. And you have us. We're your family, and we will always be here for you."

Good. That's what I was hoping for, for my daughter.

Paige stands again. "As the main course arrives, I hope you've all enjoyed the meal so far, as much as possible with all the infighting. I, for one, am proud Richard had the foresight to give me another year to be in charge of Kingsley Global Enterprises. I have so many plans, and it will be great to not always have to watch my back, John, Ted. So cheers to that!"

"A year goes by pretty fast, Paige. I wouldn't stop watching your back," John says.

He's so terrible. I really think he's the worst of the bunch. I can't believe the woman seated across the table actually loves him. She's pretty and sweet, and he's ugly and angry all the time. Maybe she's marrying him for the money. That's got to be it. Look at the two of them. Good, she'll drain his bank account before he realizes what's happening. I smile at her.

"That's a very pretty, very expensive ring," I say. "Good job."

"Thank you." She grins.

I turn my attention to the man outside. I wonder if I met him when I lived in Italy. I wonder where he will shoot me: in the head or the heart? And I wonder when. On my walk back to my room from dinner? I can't go see Sophia, not with him following me. I hope wherever he shoots me, he shoots to kill. I don't want a long, agonizing death. But who does. I hope Richard didn't suffer.

I still can't believe he died alone.

My phone pings. It's an alert from the Laguna Beach government warning system. We are to be prepared to evacuate. The wildfire has doubled in size.

I see everyone checking their phones around the table.

"What are we supposed to do about the fires?" Sibley asks. "I mean, should we go somewhere now?"

"No," Justin says. "The authorities will tell us if we need to go. And I'm sure the Twin Palms is on it. Also, Alex is here."

Paige nods. "Thank goodness."

Ted says, "So for now, we eat, drink, and be merry and pretend like Dad didn't screw his sons in the will."

"Exactly," Meredith says, then leans in to whisper to Ted.

He's drunk and will likely embarrass himself as usual. I look at him and cannot believe I thought he was attractive. I thought he was a catch when actually he's a spoiled little boy. Crazy thinking. Richard was the catch. Richard was the strong one, the handsome one.

Richard is gone. I feel another round of tears begin. I can't stop them, just like no one can stop the Santa Ana winds and the fires. So many dangers when you live in Southern California, but the beauty of it all is irresistible. It keeps us all here, living through the tortures, because most days, it's paradise. Much more so than Italy could ever be, at least for me—at least for me with that horrible man I married.

I watch as the killer paces back and forth, a shape more than a person, outside in the winds. For a minute, I imagine he has decided to leave. But he won't. Not until he's done what he came for.

I look down at the fancy meal a server places in front of me. Both Justin and John have started to eat, but I can only stare at the meat, the blood seeping onto the plate.

"Bon appétit, everyone," Paige says. "We're having filet mignon, medium rare, in honor of Richard. It was his favorite."

I wipe the tears away with my napkin. The sliding glass door directly in front of me opens. Wind whips through the room as he steps inside. He's holding a gun. I think I hear Paige scream, or maybe it's Krystle? I don't know.

"All of you waiters, get out, go to the kitchen. Stay in the kitchen until I tell you otherwise. Do not call anyone, or you'll die," the man from outside orders. They don't need another minute as I watch them all exit the room, running into the kitchen.

My heart thuds in my chest as I realize these are my final moments.

"Nobody at the table move. Hands where I can see them. All phones on the table. Now!" the man barks. His English is awkward. It's his second language, of course, to Italian. He's pointing a gun at me.

"Where's Alex?" Paige whispers.

"Shut up, now!" the man from outside yells. Then he stares at me with dark, cold eyes. "Which one is it? Kiss him. Now!"

I realize he thinks one of these guys is Richard.

"He's dead. Richard is dead," I say, tears falling again. "Just shoot me."

"No, he's not. You're lying. Look, Roman will let you keep Sophia, but only if I assure him the baby's father is dead. I cannot leave without killing him. So hurry up and show me. Which one is he? Kiss him now," the man says. He's stepped closer to the table, just behind Krystle. I need to decide which of the awful, terrible brothers to pick. Do I pick Ted, the chronic adulterer, the liar, and gambler, who always got his way because of his looks? Or do I pick John, the murderer? Which one of them do I choose when both deserve to die? I know at least one of them killed Richard. I look across the table at Ted, then focus on John. It's a surreal choice, but for my baby, I will do it.

I have no other option.

I watched John kill Rachel that night on the ship. I take a deep breath as the room seems to tilt. I kiss John on the cheek, leaving red lipstick marks.

John looks at me with hate in his eyes. He turns to the assassin.

"I'm with her," he says, pointing to Krystle. "This is my stepmom. She's gone crazy. I'm engaged to her."

Krystle sobs and shakes. "He is," she says. "We just planned our wedding."

The man from outside aims his gun and shoots John in the chest. The sound is subtle, a pop. Blood flows from John's chest as he falls forward onto the table, as if he's taking a nap. I touch my cheek to wipe blood spatter away. Blood is everywhere, flowing toward me like lava.

"Everybody, stay down!" a man's voice says from behind me. I'm startled, and I think I hear myself screaming, but maybe I'm not. Everything is in slow motion. In front of me, Roman's hired assassin is shot and falls to the ground beside the table. Again, blood flows from his body, seeping out from under him as I stare.

I'm rocking back and forth now in the chair and making a foreign sound, low like a moan. It's chaos, everyone running away. But I stay seated.

I have nowhere to go. My phone vibrates with a text from Tata: The fires are coming. We need to leave with the baby.

"Everyone, calm down. My name is Alex. I work for Paige. You're all safe now," Alex says. Then he is beside me, checking John's neck for a pulse. He won't find one; I already know that. We watch as he moves around the table to where the assassin lies. He picks up the gun before touching his neck, too. Also dead.

"John!" Krystle screams.

"Someone take her out of here," Alex says. "You, Evan. Help her get to her room. We are going to need to evacuate."

"Yes, OK," Evan says, pulling Krystle from the table, away from the carnage. Sibley decides to help, too. I watch them as if I'm at a movie theater. Everyone is moving in slow motion; nothing seems real.

"Paige, Justin, I need you two to wait for me. Everyone else should be moving to their rooms, packing essentials, and evacuating," Alex says. "You, too, ma'am."

Is he talking to me? He is.

"She's in shock," Justin says. "Serena, can I help you to your room? It's over. You're safe."

Not true. Roman can always send more men.

"She can come with us," Alex says. "The rest of you, move!"

Ted finally stands. I wonder if he knows how close I was to giving him the kiss of death. I stare at him, and he stares back. Meredith slides her arm into his. Uncle Walter is already heading out the door.

"Let's go, Ted. There's time for this later," she says.

"I guess with John gone, I should stick around?" he says. He's looking at Paige now. "I'll be the natural heir, the only surviving son. Of course it will be me."

"Dream on," Paige says.

"Get moving. All of you. Now," Alex says. "Let's go, ma'am."

I feel strong arms lift me to standing. I don't know if I can walk. My legs buckle, but Alex catches me.

We make it outside, and the air is thick with smoke and flying ash. The fires are closer than I imagined.

And finally, I wake up. This isn't a nightmare. This is all happening. "I have a baby at the hotel," I say to Alex.

"We'll go get her, and we'll all leave together," he says. "Justin and Paige, meet us in the lobby in ten minutes. Mr. Reyes has sent a van. It's waiting for us. We'll join you there."

We make it inside and hurry to Tata's room, pounding on the door.

"The fire's coming," she says, opening the door, Sophia in her arms.

"Yes, let's go," Alex says. "Can you walk, ma'am?"

"Yes, I'm fine," I say. Alex takes the baby from Tata's arms, and the three of us hurry down the hallway. "No elevator."

We hurry up three flights of stairs. Smoke fills the hotel, and at every turn, I expect to see flames. We reach the lobby and see firefighters everywhere. I cannot imagine running into danger when everyone else is running away.

I need to summon a little bit of that bravery for myself and my daughter. Alex leads us to the front door of the hotel.

"Over here," he says. He pulls open the door of a sleek black van, and we climb inside. He hands me Sophia before closing the door again. Alex climbs into the front passenger seat.

"We're waiting for two more," he tells the driver. "I'm going to go look for Justin and Paige. Stay here and wait for us unless you can't."

"Understood," the driver says. "If the fire comes before you're back, we go."

47
KRYSTLE

Well, that was a disaster. That's all I can think as I grab a few of my new clothes from the closet and change out of my fancy dress. I know I'm in shock. I realize John is dead. I stare at the gigantic engagement ring on my finger.

At least I've got something to show for all this trouble. Sure, it sounded easy. Cozy up to a man whose first wife died tragically, make him love you, marry him, and be rich. Now that John's dead, it's not going to be the same. I'll never have enough money to make my mom feel whole from Joey's death, but at least I can give her something. She'll always be able to pay the rent. And the ring's value could never replace my dad, who died of a broken heart. But for me, Cecilia Dugger, the ring and these clothes . . . well, it's enough. If the resort doesn't burn down, I'll have plenty to show from my relationship with John when I come back and pack all this up.

I look at John's side of the closet, reach down, and pick up a shirt he wore yesterday, and I smell him like he's here with me. Tears roll down my cheeks. I was getting used to him, to his life. I think I was looking forward to being his wife. I turn back to my side of the closet. I need to save these gowns. I grab a shopping bag from the floor and start stuffing in the finery. Soft silks, beautiful colors.

"Krystle, we have to go. Now," Sibley says, appearing at the closet door. "I'm in charge of getting you out of here. Come on! Leave everything. It's all replaceable."

Except for John, of course. "You're right. I've just never had things like what John got for me," I say, hurrying out into the hellscape behind Sibley.

She turns and yells over the wind, "Play your cards right, and Paige will take care of you. You know that, right? You were almost part of the family. We take care of our own."

I wonder if that's true, especially if they were to find out who I really am.

"I'm not quite who I seem to be. My name is Cecilia," I yell back.

"Nobody is, and I already knew that. Takes a con to know one," Sibley yells. "Come on. Hurry!"

Sibley pulls the door open, and we race inside, down the hall, and up the stairs to the lobby. It's hard to breathe. Fire alarms are blaring; the air is thick with smoke. But we made it. I'm shaking with fear, and images of John being shot race through my mind. The blood, the look on his face.

"Sibley!" A hotel staffer is running toward us, darting through the chaos of the lobby. "You need to get out of here. Do you two have a ride?"

"No, I don't think so," Sibley says.

"The shelters are full. You can't go there, anyway. Stay here. I'll figure something out," he says and kisses her fast on the lips.

John is dead. He'll never kiss me again, never admire me, never call me his window dressing.

Sibley wraps her arm around my waist. I touch my cheek. I didn't even know I was still crying.

48
PAIGE

I'm rattled, of course, but I'm trying to breathe even with the thick smoke filling my hotel room. I know to only pack what's most important. I look around the room one last time, see all the binders I had prepared for Sunday's part of the retreat. What a joke. We didn't accomplish any of the team-building exercises I had planned. Not one. Ironically, this retreat has become the event that likely will drive us all further apart.

But, on the plus side, I accomplished a lot, it turns out. I hear a knock on the door. It's Justin, I'm sure.

I open the door without looking. It's Ted.

"I just want you to know you better watch out for me. I'm coming for you," he says. "I'm going to Florida with Uncle Walter tomorrow. To get away from all this. But I'm not gone. You're not taking what's mine. Do you understand me?"

"If you try to interfere with me or the company again, I will frame you for killing Richard," I say. Ash and smoke and howling winds make for a surreal scene—a perfect setting for a villain like Ted. He's forced to yell to make himself heard over the wind.

"You just admitted that you know I didn't kill him, didn't you?" he says. "We both know it was John. Once a killer, always a killer."

"Doesn't matter anymore, does it?" I ask. "You're the only problem I have left. And don't think for a minute I'm bluffing. I'll do it, Ted. Trust me. I have all the evidence I need."

"No, you won't," he says.

"Yes, she will," Alex says, stepping around Ted. "Let's go."

I nod, sling my day bag over my shoulder, and push past Ted, happy to have Alex by my side. "Where's Justin?"

"I assume still in his room," Alex says, hurrying his pace. "Have you heard from him?"

"No," I say, my heart filling with dread as my lungs fill with smoke.

We reach Justin's room, and Alex bangs on the door. "Justin! Come on!"

I see something in my peripheral vision—something or someone lying on the ground outside, just beyond the hallway door.

"Alex!" I scream. "Out there!"

As we run down the hall and push outside, all I can imagine is Justin has been shot in the chest, like John. We reach where he's fallen in a lavender bush. Alex checks his vitals. Justin groans.

"Someone jumped me from behind," he says. "I think it was Ted."

I'm sure it was Ted. Of course it was Ted.

"We should go," Alex says, pulling Justin off the ground. "You're bleeding on your head there, but not too much."

I lean forward and kiss him. "I'm sorry."

"Let's release the photos, the evidence. Let's bust the bastard," he says as we follow Alex through the smoke.

"Couldn't happen to a better guy," I agree. Even as I say that, I worry about the effect it would have on my daughters if their father went to jail for killing their grandfather. It would be a tough public stain on the family, but they are strong. And I'd be there to help them cope if it comes to that.

"Let's focus on getting out of here first," Alex says. "But yes, just say when, and he'll go down."

"What about the guy you shot? What happens to him—and to you?" I ask as we make our way inside the main building.

"He's been taken care of, as has John's body," Alex says. "You can tell whatever story you'd like about what happened tonight, and my team will back you up. So will the resort staff. But you'll need a story. I'm assuming you have a team you trust?"

"The Kingsleys are keeping your funeral director friend busy. And yes, you're right. I will manage this carefully. I have a team I trust," I say. I need a story. There cannot be a media piece about a shoot-out during our corporate retreat. No, that wouldn't be good. I'm going to challenge our crisis PR team to tackle the fact that two Kingsleys who attended this corporate retreat are now dead or murdered. I'm not sure what the spin on this can be, but we'll need one.

"We'll need to take the stairs. Follow me," Alex says, helping Justin.

As we make our way up, I think about Krystle, wonder if she's doing all right. Sibley is with her, so I know they'll make it away from the fire. And I worry about Justin, and his head injury.

"Almost there," Alex says to Justin. "You OK?"

Justin looks like he's going to be sick. White, sweaty.

"I'm fine," he says. But he's not.

"It's a concussion. We'll get him help right away," Alex says, and I nod. We finally make it to the lobby, and I'm stunned by the number of fire trucks and police cars outside the resort. It's all hands on deck, it appears. From the corner of my eye, I spot Krystle and Sibley, huddled together.

"Alex, we need to bring two more with us," I say, then hurry over to them.

"Paige, thank goodness. We don't have anywhere to go, and they said the shelters are getting full—and, well, she's distraught and in shock over John. I just want to get out of here," Sibley says. "Ty went to try to find a ride for us, but he hasn't come back."

"He'll be fine. I know the resort is looking after their staff. Text him that you'll send an address for him to meet you when he can. You two come with me." I slide my arms through theirs and march them out the front door, where I saw Alex heading with Justin.

"Paige, over here!" Alex calls. He pulls open the door of a van, and we jump inside. He climbs into the passenger seat, and we're off. I don't know where we're going. It doesn't matter. We're safe.

Serena is resting with the baby snuggled on her chest. Her nanny looks petrified. Sibley and Krystle sit side by side, silent. Police car and fire engine lights flash through the windows. It's surreal and terrifying.

"It's going to be OK now," I whisper to them all, and to myself.

Beside me, Justin leans against the window of the van. I put my hand on his knee. He'll be fine, too, I'm sure. He is strong and good. He will be just fine.

I take a moment to breathe. I used to be good, too. And naive. I used to believe Richard when he told me I was doing a good job, and I never believed him when he said I wasn't. I learned a lot from him these past couple of years. On the *Splendid Seas*, I learned how to charm him, how to become what he wanted me to be. I believed him when he said Rachel fell overboard. I believed him when he said I was the perfect choice to run the company.

And I believed him when he told me he was going to take me down, to humiliate me and ruin my reputation. I believed him when he said he'd leave the girls with nothing unless I stepped aside. He tried to crush me, confuse me, gaslight me, and, ultimately, push me out of everything.

And that's why, when he started choking, I didn't do anything to help. I didn't go to his hotel room to kill him, no . . . But when he began hurling himself at me, threatening me, I grabbed the steak knife to defend myself.

Was I afraid of him at that point? Yes, probably. I'd seen his recklessness, his disregard for other people.

And I saw the hate in his eyes when I refused to render the Heimlich maneuver. And that look of pure hate, that's what made me drive the knife into his neck. He'd pushed me too far. He'd threatened me and the girls. He was considering promoting Ted or John or both. I snapped. I became as ruthless as Richard.

Maybe that makes me finally and officially a Kingsley. I'll do anything to win, and to keep power.

The difference is, the male Kingsleys don't realize that about me yet.

I need to create the story about what happened tonight, much like Richard did the night Rachel died. John had a heart attack, poor man, and died at dinner. Seems like the easiest, most reasonable tale. He was overweight, and was eating steak, and he had recently proposed to a much younger, physically demanding woman. And his beloved father had just died. Heartbreaking stuff. Everyone will agree to the story of John's death, or else. Alex will handle the NDAs with the resort staff, and a hefty payoff. It's all just part of fixing a problem, he explained. And with a resort team so well trained in discretion, the story should hold.

I look out the window of the van and see a wall of flames shooting high in the air on the top of the ridge. I hope the firefighters can contain it like they did the last time we ran for our lives. I thought we'd lose everything. This time, I don't even know where I'm running to.

"Where are we going, Alex?" I ask. I don't really care, as long as it's with Justin. But I should check in with my girls. I'm sure they've heard about the mandatory evacuations in Laguna Beach. I'll also need to call my girls and tell them their uncle John died.

"Mr. Reyes has a home in Monarch Bay. You will be safe there," he says. "A doctor will meet us, check out Justin and the baby, just to be safe. Your daughters have been informed of the plan."

"Wow, thank you," I say. I can't wait to hug both of them, and I know I will soon. As for Ted, this is the end, one way or another. And this time, it's not the husband; it's the wife. A nice plot twist, if I do say so myself.

And then it hits me.

Justin's family may be wealthier and more connected than the Kingsleys. Who would have imagined that to be possible? And then I realize that if they have more of everything, they likely have more skeletons in the closet, too, despite Tom's pure image and his son's assurances their company and family is nothing like the Kingsleys. Will the Reyes family have more dysfunction and entitlement? Could that be possible? I glance at Justin as he rests.

Well, I know what I'm getting myself into this time.

And no matter what happens, at least now I know how to win.

ACKNOWLEDGMENTS

To my publishing team at Thomas & Mercer, thank you. Thank you for believing in Richard Kingsley and the gang, enough to provide them with two books. Your vision for my stories and belief in me is simply the best and keeps this author's creative juices flowing. I'd especially like to thank Gracie Doyle, Megha Parekh, Charlotte Herscher, and Sarah Shaw. This book, and each of the four novels I've had the chance to work with you on, are better because of you.

To my agents, Annelise Robey and Meg Ruley, and the rest of the team at the Jane Rotrosen Agency: Thank you for guiding my career and always pushing me to take my writing to the next level. You've also forced me to learn how to outline, lightly, and I'll be forever grateful. Thank you, too, to Ellen Goldsmith Vein, Ross Siegel, and the team at the Gotham Group for their efforts on behalf of my film/TV rights.

To Margo Lipschultz, editor and friend, who helped wrangle the Kingsleys early on, and for acquiring *Best Day Ever*. You made my dreams come true. To the team at BookSparks, including Crystal Patriarche, Taylor Brightwell, Maggie Ruf, and Grace Fell, thank you for your expert publicity guidance. To Heather Sadlemire and Sara Hellmuth of On Top of That Marketing for helping me wrangle—or try to—social media. And speaking of social media . . .

If you haven't yet, check out the Killer Author Club, a show created by Kimberly Belle, Heather Gudenkauf, and me. We have a great time featuring fellow authors and discussing killing, of the fictional kind. Join us at www.killerauthorclub.com.

Thank you, always, to our country's brave first responders. I must admit, it was rather surreal to write about Laguna Beach and a wind-driven wildfire because there was a horrible fire here on October 27, 1993. Tragically, that fire destroyed many homes and acres of land. Unfortunately, we experienced this terror on February 10, 2022, during the Emerald Fire that threatened our home and the entire community. Writing is a way to work things through, at least for me, and writing about the fire in this story helped a bit. I'll always remember waking up at three thirty that morning, unable to breathe due to my asthma. I thought our home was on fire. I checked the whole house and found nothing amiss. I decided to try to go back to sleep, but ten minutes later, I knew something was wrong. I went to the front of the house and stepped outside. The hills above our home were burning, orange flames shooting to the sky, threatening the houses a few blocks from us. And, as they warn you, if one home goes in a densely populated community like ours, many more will.

As we rushed to gather our dogs and the essentials, the first responders started driving into the community. As we ran to the car and into the dense smoke, ash swirling like snow, more fire trucks started arriving. As we pulled out of our community and onto Pacific Coast Highway, support was arriving from the air, including water-dropping helicopters and Calfire Air tankers, and from the ground. Dozens of fire engines staffed by brave men and women drove into the fire as we fled for safety. When we stopped on PCH and looked back at our community, all we could see was a growing wall of flames. I thought there would be nothing left of our home. And that would have been the case if these heroes hadn't arrived, fought the fire, and won. They have our gratitude and thanks every day. And while the burn scar surrounding our community has grown again, the memory of their heroics that morning will stay with me for the rest of my life.

I should say this was my second fire encounter. My family home burned down when I was in high school, the fire starting in the early-morning hours as we all slept. We made it out as our home collapsed in flames around us, but my cat did not. One of the firemen had me slip into a firefighter's suit and go back in to try to call my cat, Snicki. Needless to say, in the dense smoke and falling embers, the cat did not respond to my calls. But I'll never forget that kindness. Happy ending: the next day, when we went to see what remained of our home, Snicki appeared—covered in soot but alive.

Thanks, most importantly, to my husband, Harley, who encourages me daily and inspires me always. Despite the twists and turns of life—and maybe because of them—I am so proud to call you my husband and partner. And to my kids, Trace, and his new wife, Annika; and to Avery and her new husband, Paul; and to Shea and Dylan: I feel so lucky to be your mom (and mother-in-law). And to Tucker, my beloved dog, happy thirteenth birthday. Thank you for keeping me company every day as I write. Seeing your little face watching me work helps keep the muse flowing, and our walks together, although slower now, are my favorite part of the day. Our mini Bernedoodle would be disappointed if she didn't get a shout-out, too. So, Cali, thanks for making me laugh every day.

And to you, the reader: Thank you for taking a chance on my novel. You are the reason I have the honor of living the career of my dreams. Truly, since third grade, I wanted to write novels. I hope you enjoyed this story.

ABOUT THE AUTHOR

Photo © 2023 Candice Dartez

Kaira Rouda is a *USA Today*, Amazon Charts, and internationally best-selling, multiple award–winning author of contemporary fiction that explores what goes on beneath the surface of seemingly perfect lives. Her domestic suspense novels include *Best Day Ever*, *The Favorite Daughter*, *All the Difference*, *The Next Wife*, *Somebody's Home*, *The Widow*, and *Beneath the Surface*, the first book in the Kingsleys series.

She lives in Southern California with her family and is at work on her next novel. She is a founding member of the Killer Author Club, supporting other suspense and mystery authors. For more, please visit her website, www.KairaRouda.com.

Instagram: @kairarouda
Facebook: @kairaroudabooks
TikTok: @kairaroudabooks
Pinterest: @kairarouda